"Stories can enlarge our capacity for empathy. In her brave and compelling novel, *All That Fills Us*, Autumn Lytle grants us the privilege of inhabiting the mind and heart of a young woman battling an eating disorder. Nothing is concealed here; the fears, shame, self-hatred, and obsessive thoughts that plague and assault Mel Ellis provide opportunities for us to explore our own shadows in the light of God's grace and compassion. Mel's journey toward revelation and hope is an invitation for us to see ourselves as God sees us and to discover—or rediscover—why our stories matter."

Sharon Garlough Brown, author of *Shades of Light* and the Sensible Shoes series

"You don't have to have poor body image or an eating disorder to be fed by the charmingly disarming debut novel *All That Fills Us*. I did not want this story to end. With humor and compassion, intricate insights, and singular descriptions, Autumn Lytle has captured the pain of encroaching mental illness. She's also taken us on a journey with words to breach wounds and remind us of the grace of unexpected community. May there be many more healing stories from this truly gifted author."

Jane Kirkpatrick, bestselling author of *The Healing of Natalie Curtis*

"Brimming with beauty and perfectly paced, this poignant novel connected with me in ways I didn't think a story about a girl with an eating disorder could. I was stunned to see so much of myself in the character of Mel—striving to achieve, consistently hard on herself, and hoping that her efforts might amount to something meaningful in the end. Autumn

Lytle's moving debut is one of those books that will linger in the hearts and minds of those who read it."

Erin Bartels, award-winning author of *All That We Carried*

"Autumn Lytle's *All That Fills Us* takes the reader on a journey they will not expect—both as they accompany the main character's physical adventure and her emotional pilgrimage. But it's a story that will truly make the reader believe they know and may have embraced—or perhaps are—the main character. They'll also want to play all the supporting cast member roles (or most of them) and will emerge from the reading experience wholly altered. Rich imagery, emotive language, and relationship tangles that snarl and resolve under the hand of a gifted writer."

Cynthia Ruchti, author of *Miles from Where We Started*, *Afraid of the Light*, and *Facing the Dawn*

ALL THAT FILLS US

All That Fills Us

A Novel

Autumn Lytle

Revell
a division of Baker Publishing Group
Grand Rapids, Michigan

Published by Revell
a division of Baker Publishing Group
PO Box 6287, Grand Rapids, MI 49516-6287
www.revellbooks.com

Printed in the United States of America

Library of Congress Cataloging-in-Publication Data
Names: Lytle, Autumn, author.
Title: All that fills us : a novel / Autumn Lytle.
Description: Grand Rapids, MI : Revell, a division of Baker Publishing Group, [2022]
Identifiers: LCCN 2021045652 | ISBN 9780800740160 (paperback) | ISBN 9780800741570 (casebound) | ISBN 9781493436330 (ebook)
Subjects: LCSH: Pilgrims and pilgrimages—Fiction. | Anorexia—Fiction. | Self-realization in women—Fiction. | LCGFT: Christian fiction. | Novels.
Classification: LCC PS3612.Y79 A77 2022 | DDC 813/.6—dc23
LC record available at https://lccn.loc.gov/2021045652

This book is a work of fiction. Names, characters, places, and incidents are the product of the author's imagination or are used fictitiously. Any resemblance to actual events, locales, or persons, living or dead, is coincidental.

Baker Publishing Group publications use paper produced from sustainable forestry practices and post-consumer waste whenever possible.

22 23 24 25 26 27 28 7 6 5 4 3 2 1

For those who welcome the constant ache of hunger
like an old friend, yet still long to be filled.

PROLOGUE

SOMETIME IN JUNE
SOMEWHERE IN NORTH DAKOTA

I think there was a time in my life when I used to be dry and warm, but I can't remember it. Have you ever wondered what's worse than walking through North Dakota? It's walking through North Dakota during a weeklong rainstorm. Oh, and remove shelters of any kind, along with the illusion of replacing your soaked socks with a pair of dry ones. Trudging through the same mile I swear I've been walking for hours, I curse the ugly, swollen gray sky. I curse the lakes that used to be my hiking boots. I curse this ridiculous state that can somehow see a week of driving rain and still be brown and scorched-looking everywhere. I curse this stupid hike, and most of all, my stupid self for ever coming up with this stupid plan.

At least at this point there's a bit of tree cover. I left the endless plains a few miles back for a brief stroll through the forest, where the rain let up enough for me to see more than two inches in front of my face. But my lackluster optimism fades when either a few minutes or several decades later, I come across a massive beast of a tree that would have struck wonder into my heart if it had been vertical instead of lying very horizontally and stubbornly in my way. Beyond the mocking tree giant, I can make out what could only be described as a wall of stones that some disturbed trailblazer had once decided would be fun to make people climb up. Even from this distance, I can see that the stones have razor-sharp edges and slick surfaces and are my only way forward. Wasn't all of North Dakota supposed to be flat? And dry? And boring, easy terrain? Maybe I'm not even in North Dakota at this point. Honestly, it wouldn't surprise me.

I look down and around me at the brown earth, the brown shrubs, the brown spindly trees. I take a moment to consider that this probably isn't the nicest place to give up, lie down, and die. I look ahead again. The tree is still there. So are the rocks. It is going to be a hideous mess getting through this. But after a week pruning in the rain, I am a hideous mess to match.

With an animalistic cry, I try to throw my backpack over the fallen tree. Nine attempts later, it actually makes it all the way to the other side. Then, sighing with all the weariness I can muster, I lower myself onto the soggy, slimy earth and wiggle my way underneath the tree. I emerge on the other side more mud than human but feeling accomplished for the first time in days. Taking a brief intermission from patting myself on the back, I glance around for my pack, then search more feverishly when it doesn't appear. Eventually I see it. Staring, I almost hope this is some sort of joke. I should look around for a hidden camera and brace myself for some obnoxious TV show host to jump out of the bushes and yell "Gotcha!"

Nothing happens. Except it keeps raining, of course. And mud is now slithering down my back. And somehow into my pants. And my backpack remains halfway down a mud-slicked, comically steep ravine nestled in a grove of what I am one hundred and ten percent sure is poison ivy.

Literally between a rock and a hard place, I am left with no choice but to begin the slow, possibly deadly slide down the ravine. I get on my hands and knees and leave any remaining dignity I had at the top of the ravine. For a distraction, I start listing all the things I hate.

Myself, obviously. This hike. This rain. This godforsaken state.

I grab on to a muddy root as my boots struggle to find traction. My limp hair is in my face—a squirrel's nest of knots and tangles. My arms are covered in scratches, mud, and blood. My clothes are so drenched and torn, I'm practically immodest at this point. But there's a hint of a grin on my face. Because if I die here, at least my obituary won't accuse me of never doing anything memorable.

1

EARLY MAY

The worst part of regaining consciousness was the slow and unavoidable realization that the life I was waking up to was hardly worth the effort.

It didn't help the situation to realize I was back in the hospital, gown and all. I would never know exactly what happened in the time I was unconscious, but I could guarantee it was awkward, embarrassing, and involved being naked in front of medical personnel. I tried to pretend to sleep, but it was pointless. The blissful ignorance of the unconscious was long gone.

I could have postponed whatever was coming next by faking sleep for a few more hours, but a lack of patience had always found a comfortable place on my list of flaws, so I braced myself and opened my eyes.

My grandma glanced up from her magazine with a look just shy of a glare. I couldn't blame her. If I wasn't even happy to be awake, how could I expect anyone else to be?

"Nice of you to join us," she said before returning to her magazine.

"What'd I miss?"

"Nothing that paints you in a good light, I can assure you."

I could have guessed that. "Well, that's a shame. Who was my knight in shining armor this time?"

"A group of young men walking by the parking lot of your work. There you were, passed out for the whole world to see." She lowered her magazine just slightly. "Do you realize how lucky you are that they were the kind of men who call 911 when they find a young woman passed out in a parking lot instead of a group of rapists and murderers? Now you're here. You hit your head on the way down, but you'll be fine. Oh, and we have another ambulance bill added to our tab. I'm sure your parents will be thrilled."

I thought this over for a moment. A small part of me worried how strange it was for me to feel nothing about this new information. Normal people felt embarrassment after this sort of thing, right? There was, of course, the ever-present shadow of guilt for dragging innocent bystanders and my grandma deeper into my mess. But these days, that wasn't anything new.

Sometimes that gnawing guilt could be drowned out with a poor attempt at comedy. I turned to my grandma. "Were any of the guys cute? Any of them leave me their number?" When she put down her *Better Homes and Gardens* and shot me what was now certainly a full-on glare, it was clear my attempt at lightening the mood was in vain.

"Is this all a joke to you? You know, I was supposed to spend the day packing. That cruise I've been planning all year? They set sail tomorrow, as I've told you at least a dozen times over these past few months. But instead of my much-needed day of packing, I find myself here. Again." Her voice sank to a harsh whisper, as if she was worried about someone overhearing. "Do you think it's easy or enjoyable for me to make the three-hour drive out here every couple of weeks just to sit and stare at you wasting away until the doctor tells me the exact same thing I've heard a dozen times?"

She touched a finger to her temple like a migraine was inevitable after this conversation. "And this isn't something I can keep from my friends, you know. They ask about you with pity in their eyes every time we get together for lunch. I can barely stand to be around them anymore because of it."

She paused to bring a hand dramatically to her heart, and I bit back a comment dripping with sarcasm about the agonizing pain I feel daily over upsetting Ladies Lunch at the country club.

"And your mother," she continued. "Your mother hardly calls me anymore because she can't stand to hear what a mess you've become. I can't even have a normal conversation with my own daughter. We used to be so close, and now . . . Can you get out of your own head long enough to imagine how that feels for me? Don't you ever stop to think about others before you act?"

I never asked you to be here, I thought. But I managed an almost-sincere "I'm sorry" instead.

Because I *was* sorry. I had more apologies stored up than I knew what to do with. Here's the thing about screwing up over and over though: The sorries stop holding any meaning. It's like saying "you too" when the person at the movie ticket counter tells you to enjoy the show. The words are automatic and nonsensical. Both my grandma and I knew how inadequate that apology was.

She sighed and shook her head an almost indecipherable amount, taking care not to ruffle her hairdo, and returned to her article about, I could only assume, throwing an effortlessly intimate garden party. Even in her frustration, she was poised and graceful. My mom and sister inherited her slender frame and her delicate features. All my life, Grandma had seemed to be on a different fifties-era fad diet. I'd witnessed the grapefruit diet, the SlimFast diet, the cabbage soup diet, and my personal favorite, the baby food diet. Not that they ever made any difference to her naturally small waist. The only thing those diets ever shrank was her already dangerously short temper.

No matter how unpleasant we found each other, I couldn't deny we shared a core motivation. Over time, our images had become everything to us. My grandma showed this by spewing elegance and grace in every waking moment. I showed it by exercising for six hours a day and starving myself. Besides doctors and other medical professionals, who's to say whose methods are better?

While I began my day with 2,571 jumping jacks, 751 situps, and a 15-mile run, she began hers by measuring her waist, thighs, ankles, and arms and writing said measurements down in a notebook before slipping into a crisp pantsuit or perfectly starched dress. The similarities were funny if I didn't think about them too hard. Or at all.

She was wearing one of those dresses today. Blue with pale pink flowers. Its cheerfulness should have sharply contrasted with the current environment, but there was a sterility about it that fit right in. Her fingers flipped the page, flashing her always perfectly manicured nails. Never much for conversation, we continued to sit in silence.

Eventually she sighed and pulled a twenty out of her bag and grabbed her coat. "I was up driving most of the night. If I'm ever going to make it back, I'm going to need my Starbucks." She brushed invisible wrinkles from her dress like a nervous tic as she took a moment to compose herself. "If the doctor comes in when I'm gone, do not give him any of your sass. I swear, if I hear you were on anything less than your best behavior—"

"There will be hell to pay. Got it, Grandma. Thanks for the warning."

Her look of fury was softened with just a hint of lingering pity. I dropped my gaze to my hands, noticing a few new scrapes that I assumed came from my latest unconscious adventure. I could deal with Grandma's wrath, but not her sympathy. I felt her gaze linger on the pitiful sight that was somehow still her granddaughter for a few seconds longer before swishing out the door. The click of her heels echoed long after she disappeared from view.

I glanced over at her bag as her half-hidden cell phone lit up with a notification. It brought with it a memory that made me cringe involuntarily. Two hospital visits ago—or was it three?—I had reentered the land of the living to the familiar sound of my grandma's voice, except it held a note of desperation that made me jolt right awake. She was taking a phone call in the bathroom, unaware that the walls separating us were about as thin as the hospital gowns.

"Elizabeth, it's time. You need to come home." There was an urgent insistence in my grandma's voice. If I didn't know better, it sounded as if she were pleading. My heart began to race. I was legitimately scared now. My grandma wasn't the pleading type.

A short silence followed. Then my grandma's voice returned. Still pleading. Still scary. "For goodness' sake, she's your daughter. She needs you now more than ever. Things are bad. They are getting out of control, Elizabeth. I can't be what she needs right now. I'm trying, but I'm not making a lick of difference. You can't possibly be the only missionaries over there. Let someone else take over for a bit. No one else can be what she needs. No one else can be that girl's mother."

I tried my hardest to pretend I didn't know who they were talking about. When that failed, I tried even harder to bury it all—the searing pain and crushing guilt—before it immobilized me completely. When my grandma hung up a few moments later and the choked, muffled sobs started, I did the kindest thing I could think of. I closed my eyes and pretended to be fast asleep.

2

Sometimes it was nice to have a brain that could no longer land on a single thought for more than a few moments. I let the normal waves of guilt and shame wash over me, but nothing stuck. Whatever brain cells I hadn't yet starved immediately zeroed in on whether or not I had gained any weight while unconscious. I hadn't eaten but I also hadn't exercised, one of the many recipes for instant obesity in my book. Like I always said, who needs guilt when you have an eating disorder to keep you company?

I ran a few fingers up and down my ribs, counting each one as I went. I tapped my hip bones with my fists, making sure they were still sharp as razor blades and not swallowed up by fat, and was greeted by a satisfactory dull ache. I peeked into my hospital gown, trying hard to avoid staring in revulsion at my flabby stomach in the process.

A relatively fresh bruise bloomed over my right hip. I poked it gently, watching the color fade from blue to purple.

A light knock on the doorframe caused me to stop turtling in my gown. I stuck my head out to see Dr. Clifford.

"Melanie," he said as way of greeting. He raised an eyebrow. "Is this a bad time?"

"Well, hey," I said as he closed the door behind him. "No, just checking to make sure everything's still there. You can never be too sure when you wake up in a place like this." I placed my hands over my heart. "Which is, of course, a lovely establishment."

"Mm-hmm. Yes, you seem to truly enjoy it here. What is this, your third visit in two months?"

"I figured you might start to miss me if I stayed away too long."

Dr. Clifford crossed the room to the sink, completely unfazed by my comments by this point in our patient-doctor relationship. I noticed his new pair of Asics running shoes and thought it was probably a bad sign that I knew my doctor typically wore Nikes but had been thinking of switching brands due to a stubborn IT band injury. I hoped it hadn't kept him from the River Bank Run last week. He had been really looking forward to that. He often shared his running stories with me, knowing I let my guard down when we talked about safe things like road races and the best moisture-wicking socks. He never failed to follow up every story with the moral: *So, if you still want to be running at my age, you're going to have to make healthy changes to your exercise and eating routines starting now.*

"As much as I cherish your sarcasm and look forward to you ignoring my advice," he said, "I was hoping we wouldn't be seeing each other for a while." He dried his hands and turned to face me, one bushy gray caterpillar eyebrow raised. "Instead, your visits have become more and more frequent."

"But how could I stay away when I still needed to hear

how your new running shoes are working out? I've been on the edge of my seat for weeks!"

Dr. Clifford's face settled into his best concerned medical professional expression. "Melanie, this is serious. I'm assuming you saw the bruise? You're lucky you only hit your hip badly and the concussion you sustained was a minor one. What if you had been driving when this happened? Or where I know for a fact you spend most of your time, running on a treadmill? Your habits have become so worrisome, you've begun to put your life in danger on a daily basis. We don't want that."

He pulled the chair where my grandma had been sitting close to the bed and sat down so we were at eye level. Obviously, this wasn't his first time delivering unwanted news. I wondered how many other disappointed doctors and ashamed family members had sat in that very spot.

"I know you want to handle your recovery on your own, but so far there hasn't *been* any recovery. I think it's time we discuss getting some help. Maybe staying with us for a while. Your grandmother seems to think that would be best as well."

I raised an eyebrow.

"Okay, I see the grandma's opinion is not helping my case. Should have thought that one through."

"Now there's a sentence you don't want to hear your doctor say."

"Melanie . . ."

I sighed. "Listen, you've been a really, really great doctor. I appreciate everything you've done for me, seriously. But I'm okay. I'm not great, I'll admit that, but okay has suited me fine my whole life. I don't need help. I can handle this on my own. I just need some time."

"That's what I'm worried about." Dr. Clifford scooted the chair closer to the edge of the bed. There was a pang of unprofessional worry in his tone that made the knot of guilt in my chest tighten. He once told me that I reminded him of his granddaughter. Was he making that connection again? "If you keep heading down this path, I don't think you'll have much time left. I know you see it differently, but getting help is not a weakness. There is strength in admitting you have a problem and taking the necessary steps to overcome it."

My anger flared, dissolving the constricting guilt. "What is that, some doctor proverb? Listen, I know I have a problem. I *am* taking the steps, just in my own way."

He shook his head. "Melanie, I told you last time you were here if we didn't see progress soon, we were going to give our methods a try. You agreed to that, remember? Since then, you haven't shown up to any of your doctor or counseling appointments, and you've lost an additional three pounds. Three pounds you can't afford to lose at this point. I can't in good faith release you today. You have to understand that. Once your grandma gets back, we'll discuss our options moving forward, okay?"

I stared at him, hoping my look of flesh-melting anger and betrayal masked the panic roaring through me.

"I'll let you think this over." He patted the crumpled hospital sheet on my bed. "We're on your side, Melanie. All we want is for you to get better, and we're going to do what it takes to get you there."

He stood, glanced down at his shoes, then back up at me with a weak smile. "The Asics are working out great, by the way. My IT band feels better already. Thanks for the suggestion."

I tried to force a smile in return, but I knew it was useless. I nodded dully instead. “I’m glad I could be of some help.”

He reached over and gave my shoulder a gentle squeeze. “You’re going to be fine, Melanie. You’re taking a big step today. You’re on the road to recovery now, and we’ll be here to help you every step of the way. Remember, just like in running, the greatest accomplishment isn’t that you finished but that you had the courage to start.”

With that he left the room, his new shoes squeaking slightly on the linoleum floor.

I didn’t need the monitor to know I was close to panicking. I took a few shaky breaths to try and bring my heart rate back down.

Why had I ever agreed to give Dr. Clifford’s methods a try? I remember only wanting to get out of here. I would have agreed to anything to make that happen. And I’d been okay for a while, I really had. Then things happened, a whole bunch of little things, and I hit a roadblock or two. He should be able to understand that. I was on my way. I was getting there. People have setbacks. That doesn’t mean they need to be admitted.

I would explain all that to Dr. Clifford when he got back. He was a reasonable man. Sure, he used way too many running metaphors and thought that cotton was an acceptable fabric for workout gear, but that didn’t completely inhibit one from hearing rationality. I needed just one more chance. He had to give me one more chance.

I sighed and stared up at the ceiling, trying to piece together a way out of this. But all I could think about was how many calories they might have snuck into my system while I was out and how many miles I would have to run to burn off the imaginary number. There would be no running in rehab. No gym, no nutrition labels, nothing to do but sit around all day trying to talk away my problems while getting fat in the meantime.

Dr. Clifford had assured me multiple times that this wasn't the most accurate description of rehab, like that was supposed to change my mind. Besides, I had seen enough movies and heard enough stories to know that rehab is for people who have dark backstories or tragic pasts or epic falls from glory. Not for people like me who, I'd be the first to admit, were plenty messed up but didn't have any deep dark secret reason to blame it on. No one but me got myself into this mess. No one but me should have to try to get me out. I wasn't not the rehab type, and not because I thought I was too good for it, but because I was certain I wasn't good enough. I could already picture the therapists after they heard my story. Every single one of them would stop doodling on their notepad and look up at me with raised eyebrows.

"That's it?" they'd say.

"What do you mean?" I'd reply.

"That's your whole story?"

"Yeah, is something wrong?"

Then they would give a little laugh. Not to be mean—more out of surprise than anything.

"No, that's the thing—*nothing* is wrong with your story." They'd place their notepad on the table and politely fold their hands. "You've had a perfectly average, perfectly untragic and unspectacular existence. It really makes no sense, this 'eating disorder' of yours. Honestly, it's probably just a cry for attention."

Then they'd write me a prescription for a placebo drug

and tell me to suck it up and live my average life like every other functioning adult on the planet.

Dr. Clifford had also assured me that was an inaccurate play-by-play of a therapy session, like I was just supposed to believe him because he had a medical degree and had apparently saved numerous lives.

A part of me realized how ridiculous I was being, but that part was overpowered by my irrational half a long time ago. Those twisted scenarios had become the core truths of my existence. I believed every word of them while knowing they held no real weight in reality. All that to say, it was a lot of fun being me lately.

Eventually I heard the sharp taps of my grandma's heels approaching and she reentered the room, coffee in hand. She sat down without looking up from her phone, set the coffee on the side table, and focused her concentration on tapping away a message that was clearly more important than any crisis I was currently facing.

She looked up at me for a fraction of a second, I guess to let me know she acknowledged my presence.

"Did Dr. Clifford talk to you yet?" she asked, still typing.

"Yeah, he did."

"And?"

"Oh, we just chatted about running, like usual. He bought himself a new pair of shoes. Asics this time, not Nike. It was a big change, but we both think it's for the best."

She finally gave me her full attention along with one of the best glares I'd seen from her in a long time. Truly terrifying.

"Try again," she said, her words coated in ice.

I sighed. "He may have reminded me of a little agreement

we made last time I was here. But you and I both know I only honor blood oath agreements, so this isn't happening."

She set her phone on the side table. "Oh, it's happening. Long overdue, I might add, but it *is* happening."

"What happened to the idea of my body, my rules?" I weakly demanded as a Hail Mary.

She gave a short laugh. "That went out the window when you decided to starve yourself like a common sorority girl." She shook her head, and the curls didn't move an inch. "I take that back. Like everything else in your life, you had to make this your own. You couldn't just starve yourself to fit into a dress or something. You had to develop a full-on eating disorder and an exercise obsession to go along with it. Never giving less than your best to anything, that's the Melanie way."

Well, at least my grandma thought I was special. Although, she used to think I was special in ways that actually counted. I think she really believed at some point that I would make something of myself. Whenever I would visit her during college, she would toast me and whatever project I had finished telling her about. "To Melanie and her communications final!" or "To Melanie and her internship search!" It made me feel so regal and important, and I think I was the kind of granddaughter who made her feel that way too. And now . . . There was nothing to toast to anymore.

She stared at me hard. I knew she was willing herself not to soften before I showed some sort of remorse. Eventually, she gave up with a frustrated sigh and threw her hands up in surrender.

"I can't do this anymore, Melanie. If you won't get help

for yourself, do it for me or your poor mother. Do it for everyone left in your life that you've let down."

I stared at the wall in front of me, trying to push down my conflicting feelings of panic and shame. My throat burned, and my eyes stung from holding back the flood of tears I knew I would never let my grandma see. I was so tired of this.

"Fine," I said in surrender.

Her perfect eyebrows shot up. "Fine?"

"Yeah, fine. I'll go." I rubbed my eyes with the heels of my hands. "But I need to tie up a few loose ends at home first."

She continued to study me, nodding slowly as if not to startle me into changing my mind. "Dr. Clifford told me he'd like to admit you right away, but I'm sure we can arrange something. I would do it for you, but—"

"But you have a cruise to get to."

She finally broke her stare. "Right." She checked her phone absentmindedly and gently patted down her hair. She cleared her throat awkwardly. It was like she didn't know what to do with herself when there was nothing left to lecture me about.

"Well, I should get going, then. Hopefully I'll avoid traffic on the way back. I'll call tomorrow before we set sail to make sure you're all settled, and I'll talk to Dr. Clifford on my way out." She looked up at me once again. Under the lingering shock, I saw it was her turn to look guilty. "I'm very proud of you, Melanie."

I sighed. To my disappointment, it actually sounded genuine. It would be so much easier to hate her if she had kept that stupid wall up around her instead of choosing now of all times to show me her raw emotions. I loosened my resentment a bit. I couldn't keep pretending she owed me anything, that she was abandoning me. She was the only one who was willing to help, after all. I was in no position to discredit that help just because it was given reluctantly. I offered her a half smile, hoping it did what it could to absolve her of guilt.

It seemed to work well enough. I noticed her visibly relax, tension falling from her thin shoulders. She leaned down and gave me a polite peck on my forehead.

"Like I said, I'll try to call tomorrow before I leave, although I heard reception can be a little iffy on the ship. But I will stop in and check up on you as soon as I get back from the cruise, I promise. This is a good thing, dear. Everyone just wants you to get better, and at this point, I am certain this is your best option."

I didn't answer, keeping her words at a distance. I didn't have the energy to waste on feeling more than the bare minimum. All I wanted was for her to leave.

She walked toward the door then turned back on her heel before leaving the room. She opened her mouth to speak, but the words seemed to be stuck. I felt myself tense in preparation for a strained and forced sentiment. Fortunately, she also seemed to realize that wasn't really our thing.

We watched each other warily for a long moment, each of us hurt one too many times by the other to let our guard down. I couldn't help but think back to years ago when weekend sleepovers at Grandma's house were my favorite thing in the world. When we would build forts with her absurdly large collection of throw pillows and have Sunday Sundaes. When the biggest issue between us was whether to watch *Grease* or *The Sound of Music*. There were more recent moments too. That summer she rented the beach house on Lake Michigan to keep me from drowning in loneliness after my family left to do mission work overseas. When she presented me with a bouquet of roses at my college graduation and her eyes shone with tears of genuine pride. When Alex left and she pulled me into a fierce hug, assuring me I was strong and loved, and me believing her, at least a little bit. I wondered how a person goes about getting something like that back.

And then, back in that wretched hospital room, I wondered what I would say into the silence if I was a better granddaughter. Phrases like "Thank you" or "You being here means everything to me" or even "I'm sorry I'm doing this to you" stuck in the back of my throat. But instead of any unspoken truths from either of us, my grandma gave me her own half smile.

"Good luck," she said. And with that, she was gone.

3

It was early afternoon when I used my standard combination of shoves and kicks to unstick the door to my apartment, though apartment was a generous word for it. When the door finally opened and I stumbled around in the dimness long enough to find the light switch, I swear I saw something scurry across the floor out of the corner of my eye.

The room was equally as dark and depressing as when I left it twenty-four hours before. I struggled to shut the door then shuffled over to the five inches of counter space. It was one of the best spots to lean heavily on my elbows, cover my eyes, and moan dramatically. This must be how normal twenty-four-year-olds felt after a night of drinking and partying—a little sick, with a pounding headache and a vague feeling that I made one too many decisions I would come to regret.

This was bad. Why couldn't people just leave me alone? I wasn't hurting anyone, so I didn't see why anything had to change. An image of my grandma's tired face flashed through my mind, and the bruise on my hip seemed to pulse in reply. Okay, so maybe I was hurting a person or two, but there had to be a better way to go about fixing this than rehab.

Dr. Clifford had made me promise I would return by the end of the day, giving me a look that suggested he would not hesitate to hunt me down if he had to.

But doctors were busy people. Hunting down patients probably wasn't one of their top priorities. I couldn't hide out here forever. They had my address, after all. So I was once again faced with the same conclusion I had come to on the walk home—I had nowhere else to go.

I took in my surroundings, maybe in hopes of finding the answer written on the yellowing walls. All I saw was my futon (college Mel thought having a futon would be a better "expression of her personality" than a bed; postcollege Mel couldn't afford a bed), a beat-up couch I had proudly dragged down the sidewalk after spending five dollars on it at a garage sale last summer, my bookshelf, a dresser, a desk buried in unopened mail, and, of course, my treadmill.

Should it have been a warning sign that my treadmill had become my best friend? The hours we spent together drowned out the noise from the upstairs neighbors. While they laughed with the billions of friends they seemed to invite over every night, my treadmill and I laughed at nineties sitcoms and other mindless comedies while logging mile after mile. A few months ago, the treadmill suddenly would only work in jerky bursts. I was so desperate to keep exercising I even considered running outside or joining a gym, but that would mean I would have been on display for all to see and judge. In those endless forty-eight hours until a repairman could stop by, I had never felt so alone.

I put my head back in my hands. That sounded like the

type of thing I would laugh about someday but in the meantime never admit to anyone.

All of a sudden, cold sweat pricked the back of my neck. My skin felt itchy, and panic lingered in the back of my consciousness. I immediately dropped to the ground.

After exactly four sets of 13 pushups, 321 jumping jacks, 337 crunches, and 21 times going up and down the 23 steps in the apartment building stairwell—my neighbors weren't the only ones who could be annoying—the panic subsided. The cold sweat on my neck was replaced with the comforting sweat earned through hard work.

However, I was no closer to figuring out what I was going to do. The only thing that had made itself clear was that they probably weren't going to let me follow that routine in rehab.

For right now though, I could focus. I could only ever focus anymore in the rare golden moment when I was immediately postworkout and past the point of hunger. A sliver of time before I began obsessing about the next workout and after I stopped obsessing over what I last ate.

I figured step one was to call work and figure out if I would have to quit or if I was already fired. I was supposed to work an eight-hour shift today, and not showing up this morning wasn't my first strike. I fished my phone out of my bag. It was nearly dead, but the conversation wouldn't take long.

After two rings, I heard the voice of my supervisor. It was so artificially sweet it made my teeth ache.

"Thank you for calling Wendy's on Michigan Street. How may I help you?"

"Lizzie, it's me, Mel."

"Oh, Mel." She instantly dropped her "customer voice." Now she just sounded annoyed. "Yeah, your shift started two hours ago. Luckily Amy was able to come in and cover for you. You realize this is completely unacceptable, right? Please tell me you realize that."

"I do."

"Really? Because it seems to be a concept you can't quite grasp." I heard her sigh. I tended to cause that reaction in people. "Look, I know you're a good kid, but you and I both know you haven't been yourself for a while now. That's probably because you're going through something, and I'm sorry about that. But we can't all suffer because of it. I'm sorry, Mel, but you're going to have to find someplace else to work. I've already talked to Joe about it, and he agrees—"

"It's fine, Lizzie. You're being completely reasonable. Any good supervisor would do the same. Sorry I let you down."

She sighed again. "And I'm sorry I can't help you more. But I can't afford to get involved in this kind of stuff, you know? Listen, if the old Mel ever comes back, give me a call. I'd be happy to bring you back on board."

I nodded stupidly. "Thanks for being so good to me these past couple of years."

"Take care of yourself, honey."

I had almost hung up when I heard her say, "Mel?"

I brought the phone back to my ear. "Yes?"

"Make sure to return your uniform before next Friday so we can refund you."

"Oh, okay. Will do."

"All right, honey, bye."

She hung up.

I stared at the phone for a long beat. I might have thrown it across the room if I wasn't so exhausted all of a sudden. Instead, I plugged it in and sank to the floor.

It wasn't enough just to be fired, I also had to be humiliated in the process. I had joked for the past year or so that I would be fired any day from my minimum-wage fast-food job because I had to let the world know how little I cared about it, how beneath me it was. But now it was real. And I realized the only thing it proved was that I wasn't even good enough for the fast-food industry.

I wished she had just fired me because I missed a shift and left it at that, not gone on about how I wasn't the same anymore. I didn't want her stupid observations, her wasted sympathy. No one was supposed to notice my unraveling, not even me. Especially not a twenty-two-year-old shift supervisor at Wendy's who had the nerve to call me honey.

Through vision blurred with tears, I looked down to see the medical bracelet still on my wrist. This must be the rock bottom people were always going on about.

"What am I going to do?" I whispered. But there was no one else to answer the question. Not even my treadmill could solve this problem.

I brutally wiped the few tears that had escaped with the heel of my hand. I didn't have the right or the time to wallow in self-pity right now.

When I forced the tears back enough for my vision to clear, my view from the floor made me notice a box tucked in the far back corner under my desk. I must have put it there when I moved in a little over a year ago and forgotten all about it.

I crawled under the desk and gingerly slid the box out. It was lighter than I expected, which immediately made me realize what it was. I wrenched it open, and a wave of dust and melancholy washed over me.

Every photo, ticket stub, drawing, and letter my broken yet still hopelessly sentimental heart couldn't bear to throw away during the move. I had dragged them with me as a security blanket, and although I couldn't bring myself to look at them, I had desperately needed to know they were close.

I laid the pieces out in a neat semicircle in front of me. Photos of Alex and me at the park, at a party, in each other's arms on the shore of Lake Michigan. A photo I snapped of him during a backpacking trip in the Upper Peninsula. He was relacing his boots after a midhike swim in the lake. The setting sun splashed puddles of gold around him. The trees surrounded him in velvety green. He looked like he belonged there, such a natural part of the setting. Exactly like how he had been such a natural part of me.

"Look at this," I had said to him later that night around our campfire. I passed him the camera. "Look at how beautiful you are."

He studied it dutifully. We were side by side on the splintery picnic bench, his arm was slung across my shoulders, his warmth sinking in through my flannel shirt. "I don't mean to brag," he said, holding out the camera like it was a priceless work of art, "but I think this photo proves I have a shot at pursuing my lifelong dream of becoming a hiking boot model."

"That's the exact reason I decided to date you—your potential as a hiking boot model." I took the camera from him, zooming in on his sunlit face. "I can't wait to print this. I know the perfect place for it on my corkboard."

"There is zero chance you have room for another photo on that corkboard."

"Where there's a will, there's a way."

"Who even prints out photos anymore?"

"Me and others who still have the gift of appreciating art in its tactile form."

"So, you and a bunch of baby boomers who don't know how to use Google Photos?"

I had shrugged. "I suppose that's one way to put it."

In my quiet, dark apartment, I kept staring at the photo. Kept holding it in my hands and close to my heart. Eventually I added it to the semicircle.

He wasn't the only one I had tried to let go of but couldn't forget. I pulled out photos of my parents, of me and my sister, Claire, taken way back when we were still young enough to pull off pigtails, a few faded letters written in my mom's neat script, and finally, a postcard.

I held the postcard carefully. It had soft edges and a thick crease in the middle from being tucked away in my dad's wallet for a decade or two. But the image was still clear enough—the rim of the Grand Canyon under a sky painted with a sunrise. My dad spent a summer in the canyon after he barely graduated college.

"In those four years, I made more bad decisions than in all the rest of my years combined." He would begin the same story every time I asked to see the postcard. When I was younger, I loved looking at the colors painted in the sky and the fiery hues of the rim. It was like something belonging to a world beyond my reach. When I got older, I loved hearing the story as much as I loved looking at the postcard.

"I was out of time, luck, and money when I graduated. No job, no place to live. Just me and my VW bus and a drug habit I was broke enough to want to kick. So I threw the ten items I owned into the back of the bus and headed out to the Grand Canyon. I had always wanted to go, so I figured it was better to die out there than on the streets of Detroit."

He sold what few possessions he had left to pay for gas and drove for thirty hours straight to the Grand Canyon, right on time for the sunrise.

"It was my own personal pilgrimage," he would say, always growing reverent at this point in the story. "As soon as I saw the canyon, I knew I had found God."

He spent the summer working for the park maintenance crew and used every bit of free time exploring the canyon. On a hike near the end of summer, Dad met a man from Michigan who told him he wanted to start a homeless shelter in Grand Rapids. It took only another mile of hiking to convince the two of them they were meant to go into business together.

"My pilgrimage saved my life. It brought me to the God big enough to save me from myself." He would usually laugh then. "And all that time, He was just waiting for me to get up, dust myself off, and go to the Grand Canyon."

I smiled at the memory and ran a finger across the worn edge of the postcard. The smile faded as I remembered how bitterly I had received the card when it arrived in the mail a few weeks after they left for Uganda. I peered into the box, even though I knew the only things that remained. Photos, postcards, and paintings of an iconic snow-capped mountain surrounded by wildflowers.

While my dad had the Grand Canyon, I had my mountain—Mount Rainier.

I felt that same longing I so acutely experienced the first time I saw a picture of the mountain. It was in a book on national parks I had found at the library, and I was so overwhelmed by the photo I almost forgot to check it out before running all the way home and showing my dad.

"That," said an out of breath, eight-year-old Mel, pointing to the mountain in the book. "That's gonna be my pilgrimage one day. Like you and the Grand Canyon."

My father had nodded solemnly. "It called to you, didn't it?"

I nodded back just as solemnly.

"You know who it was who was calling?"

"God," I said. Like that was the most obvious thing in the world.

"Yup. It'd probably be in your best interest to answer that call one day, wouldn't you say so?"

"Yes, sir. I'm going as soon as I can."

He chuckled. "Do a little growing up first. When it's time for your pilgrimage, you'll know."

"How will I know?"

He shrugged, then thought about it for a moment. "When you feel lost and you need something big and bright to light your way back, when you need something more than food and drink to fill you up, that's when you'll know."

Sitting on the floor in my very small, lonely world, surrounded by images of everything I had let slip through my fingers, I knew it was time.

4

The one patch of sunlight that reached my basement apartment had moved from the kitchen to the living room by the time I had created my route. It was more of a rough outline, but it was the best I could do with a half-formed idea, a fast-approaching deadline, and no one around to be the voice of reason. Crude or not, I knew it was a good place to start. Experts in the field of Hiking across the US for No Apparent Reason had stressed over and over that it was pointless to try to plan everything, although they probably imagined their readers spending more than two hours on the initial planning.

Around me, several highlighters and dozens of maps I had collected over the years littered the floor. My dad was the reason I'd collected thrift store maps like a hoarder my entire life. He firmly believed apps like MapQuest and Google Maps took away a quintessential part of the American road trip, so I was always his copilot, navigating the roads of America with a paper map while my mother and sister slept in the back seat. I wondered who copiloted their road trips now but figured missionaries' schedules were too full of saving the world to bother with family time.

My trip would be a little more complicated than my father's had been. I didn't exactly have a car anymore. I would have liked to say I sold it six months back because I cared about the environment, but it was more along the lines of I couldn't afford to keep it any longer thanks to an increasing mound of medical bills my insurance didn't come close to covering.

So I would set off on foot. Plenty of people had done it and blogged about it as proof.

I would have also liked to say that the thought of how many calories I would burn a day walking from Grand Rapids to the West Coast didn't cross my mind, but I've never been a very convincing liar.

Walking over 2,000 miles along interstates didn't seem like the best idea. The internet-ordained experts suggested sticking to trails as much as possible was the best way to go, so that was my plan too.

I knew all about thru-hike trails cutting across the United States. After reading *Wild* a few years back, I became obsessed with the Pacific Crest Trail. I was distraught to find out that every other white girl in America had the exact same reaction, so I abandoned the thought of one day hiking the PCT for something more original. I kept lists of US thru-hike trails that stretched anywhere from 100 to 6,800 miles, and it looked like I was about to finally get the chance to embark on a few of them. I used to imagine the circumstances where I would conquer America's lesser-known thru-hikes. Details such as setting out with a well-thought-out plan and people celebrating my efforts instead of seeing them as a cry for help were always a given in my hiking daydreams, but anorexic beggars couldn't be choosers.

I studied the creased atlas of the United States I had selected for my final mapping. There was no clear path from point A to B, no neatly marked trail to follow all the way to Washington. But I liked it better that way. I would piece together different trails to make something entirely my own, something that no one else could claim.

From Grand Rapids I would make my way down to Chicago by following the lakeshore. After Chicago, I would work my way up to the North Country Trail into the heart of North Dakota. From there, I planned to follow the Lewis and Clark Historic Trail all the way to Washington. I could figure out the rest from there. How hard could it possibly be to find a mountain?

I had a haphazard Google Maps search to thank for figuring out approximately what I was signing up for in mileage terms.

From Grand Rapids to Mount Rainier National Park: 2,182.8 miles. Considering I'd be covering rough terrain and carrying a pack, I figured I would cover a mile in about twenty minutes. If I walked for eight hours a day, I would cover about twenty-four miles each day (burning approximately 3,500 calories doing so, but who's counting). Throw in a handful of rest days I might have to take (not that I would ever take a rest day, of course) or things going wrong, and that put me around one hundred days. About three and a half months. It was early May now, so Washington could expect my arrival sometime in September. With a Sharpie, I added the dates and mileage to the top of my map. My penmanship was all peaks and valleys, the telltale sign of an overly excited person, or possibly a psychopath.

I scooted back and studied the map and the numbers again. It wasn't like I had anything better planned for those three and a half months. Better to burn calories out there than in here.

I shook my head, disgusted with myself. *No, Mel, this is not a three-month-long weight loss trek. This is your pilgrimage. Your last chance to become something worth anything.*

With my route more or less set, I turned my attention to packing. My nervous energy manifested itself by causing me to sprint from one side of the room to the other, pulling out clothes from the dresser and the hamper. I dug out the giant North Face hiking backpack I used on a couple of overnight backpacking trips with Alex during college and began sorting through my belongings. Unsurprisingly, it didn't take long.

From the piles of clothes, I selected a down jacket that could be rolled into a small drawstring bag, a raincoat that could also fold up to an impossible size, two T-shirts, one pair of running shorts, a sports bra, a few pairs of socks, and a handful of underwear. The socks had a few holes and the jackets had been gifts from at least ten years back, but they would do just fine. I changed into my favorite pair of hiking pants that refused to stay on my hips without a belt anymore, a T-shirt from a road race years before that had gone soft with age, hiking socks and well-worn boots, a hat, my Garmin watch, and of course, an oversized sweatshirt.

I was able to fit in my sleeping bag and tarp with relative ease. With my phone at a hundred percent, I packed my charger and watch charger with futile hope, along with a pair of headphones. I also threw in a pack of baby wipes, a toothbrush, toothpaste, and deodorant in case I had any dignity left out there I'd like to try and save. I hesitated before leaving the bathroom. I tried to convince myself that I didn't need it, but I could already feel the cold sweat begin to prick the back of my neck again. I grabbed the bathroom scale and took it over to the bed and laid it next to the things I intended to pack. I stared at it. This stare down always happened right before I stepped up to let it read my fate, which was, at minimum, a thrice-daily occurrence. The scale had been a high school graduation gift from my mom. My cheeks still flushed with embarrassment whenever I thought about it.

"Not that you need it now, Melanie," my mother had assured me while the rest of the attendees of the small graduation party looked on with pity. "But you know what they say about the freshman fifteen."

And I did take it with me when I left for college. That was when I would only step on it once a week to make sure that terrifying freshman fifteen hadn't found me. Because as hard as I tried not to care, I craved my mother's approval more than anything.

The scale would fit in the backpack, it would be lumpy and uncomfortable and add dead weight to my already heavy pack, but it would fit. I breathed slowly, counting to ten. Nothing about what I was doing was rational but packing a bathroom scale to take with me on a cross-country hike was a whole new level of irrational. I ran a finger up and down my rib cage. Counting my ribs was usually a reliable method of calming myself down, which I needed to do while I tried to talk myself out of this insanity.

I started a mental list as well, aptly titled Why Taking a Scale on a Thru-Hike Is Unreasonable.

1. There would probably be days when I wouldn't have a completely flat surface to put the scale on, meaning its reading would be inaccurate. And wouldn't I rather not know my weight than know my inaccurate weight?
2. I'd be burning calories all day and eating as sparingly as possible. This was the best chance I'd ever have to get down to my lowest weight, so there was no need for a scale because there was no way I'd be gaining weight.
3. Muscle weighs more than fat. I'd be doing a lot of hiking and probably strengthening my leg muscles and back and arm muscles from carrying my pack, therefore replacing my fat with muscle. So even though I would probably *look* skinnier, the scale might not say I'd lost weight because I would have replaced the fat with muscle. And since I wouldn't have a mirror, I wouldn't want an inaccurate portrayal of my overall level of fitness.

I nodded to myself, convinced. I ran my thumb over my ribs one more time before putting the scale back in the bathroom. I shut the door behind me, unsure I would be able to resist taking it with me if I saw it again.

I turned my attention to the bookshelf. I knew it was stupid to take a book, but not nearly as stupid as taking a bathroom scale. *Lives of the Saints* and *Wild Food: A Complete Guide for Foragers* went into my bag. I could see the latter proving to be quite useful. Finally, I turned to the kitchen.

Armed with my foraging book, I figured I wouldn't need much, which was good since there wasn't much to choose from. I shoved the remaining bag of rice cakes in my bag along with four apples, a half-finished bag of baby carrots, and a box of Clif Bars. I located my water bottle in my work bag, filled it up, and added it to the pack.

I planned to stop by the ATM on the way out, but I also emptied my emergency fund that was haphazardly stored in an old cigar box. Not exactly the fortune that a bachelor's degree foretold. My plan to eat next to nothing should help keep expenditures down though.

I paused before walking past the still-open box of memories on the ground. I bent down and picked up the watercolor of Mount Rainier Claire had done for me so long ago. It was my favorite of my collection, and not only because my sister painted it. She was truly, and frustratingly, talented. I folded up the picture and tucked it in my pocket with my dad's postcard.

I put my hands on my hips and looked around. Not much worth saving. Not much worth coming back for. Although I lacked more than a semblance of any plan, I had a feeling I would not be returning to the basement apartment. On my phone, I typed up a somewhat cryptic email to my landlord telling him I had to go and anything left in the apartment was his to sell or include in the next rental. I understood enough about the lives of landlords to know this wasn't exactly a kind offer, more of a huge inconvenience, actually. But now that my mind had been made up, I had no other options. I added it to my long list of things to apologize for, and I scheduled the email to send the next day. On notebook paper, I scribbled out a brief letter to my grandma.

Grandma,

You know how Dad always talks about his pilgrimage? Well, I've set off on one of my own. I'll be heading to Mount Rainier on foot. Don't worry, I have a map. I know this may sound like an act of desperation, and I guess that's exactly what it is, but I'm doing this for (mostly) noble reasons.

Thanks for everything,
Mel

P. S. Probably best not to mention this to Mom.

I managed to find a stamp and an envelope and resolved to drop it off at the post office on the way out. My grandma didn't need to know about this until after her cruise. It was possible that good old Dr. Clifford would give her a ring when I failed to show up, but I would just have to pray hard for extra spotty cell reception and my grandma taking her "vacation and business don't mix" rule to a new level.

I said goodbye to my treadmill with a little more emotion than socially acceptable and took one last look around the apartment. I intentionally did not look at the box, its contents still neatly arranged on the floor. I even made it all the way to the door, but I couldn't turn the handle.

I sighed in defeat and returned to gather up the photos of Alex and me and his last letter, still in the envelope.

I tucked them safely away in a pocket of my swollen backpack, struggled to my feet under its weight, and walked out the door. Everything significant and necessary I now carried, leaving every other burden to, hopefully, fall away.

As travel mugs and tacky T-shirts say, adventure was calling. I felt a roar of excitement when I thought of how much weight I'd lose walking 2,182.8 miles across the country.

I nearly screamed at myself. I wasn't so far gone that I wasn't still acutely aware of how messed up my thoughts could get. This was a pilgrimage, a *pilgrimage*, not a weight loss journey. I said that over and over under my breath as I walked down the hall, up the stairs, and out into the sunshine. I kept saying it, hoping it would soon become truth.

5

I walked down the Fountain Street hill into the heart of the city I once loved.

I rolled my eyes at myself. I was being dramatic. I still loved this city. I always would. Even though I was certain it stopped loving me a while ago. Maybe that was my problem. I couldn't stop loving things that had stopped loving me.

Again, with the drama. If only my problem was that poetic. No, my problem was more like I'd always be convinced I was fat no matter how many miles I ran and how few calories I consumed. And since being fat was literally the worst thing I could imagine, I was doomed to always be in my own personal, self-created hell.

That was far more accurate.

Being fat wasn't always my greatest fear. There was a time not too long ago when going up a clothing size wasn't the stuff of nightmares. I used to have fears that actually made sense. Like disappointing my parents, or me and my sister drifting apart when she got older and finally realized how much cooler she was than me. Then when both those things happened, I went to college and adopted more mature, adult fears like never living up to my potential, never finding a job where I could use my degree, or being left behind by the love of my life. After that round of worst fears came true, I guess my brain decided it needed to choose ones that were a little less predictable.

I was tempted to flip off the hospital as I strolled by, but then remembered I was a coward who hated drawing attention to herself. So instead I crossed the street and flipped up the hood of my sweatshirt. Sorry to let you down once again, Dr. Clifford.

I passed the library, the building that helped raise me. My mom saw it as free babysitting in the summers. That meant less time at home and less of a chance of me messing up and my mom assigning Bible verses to memorize as punishment. In the library, I could find a quiet corner to hide away in and lose myself in other people's mistakes and shortcomings instead of my own. I had to hide away only once Claire became too overscheduled with summer camps and after-school activities to join me. Before that, the two of us ran the place. Looking at it now, I could almost see the younger, happier, still just as impatient version of me dragging Claire up the steps so we could get the best seats for story time.

"Find me the best book in the whole library, Melanie!" she would whisper-yell as soon as we walked in.

"Give me your three magic words, and I'll find you the best one," I'd whisper-yell back, which almost always earned me a reproachful glare from the woman at the information desk. My whisper-yells were mostly yells.

After a moment, Claire would answer. It was one of the few times her words ever tripped over themselves, that's how excited our stupid little game made her. I adored her for it.

She would list three words that she wanted her book to be about, and I would run around the library like a madwoman, much to her delight, trying to find the closest match. It took me only a few rounds of that game to realize it was a gateway into understanding what was brewing behind my sister's carefully composed demeanor. There were days where her words were "Gray, sad, rainy." And others like "Hero, alone, adventure." Sometimes she'd try to come up with the most nonsensical combination ("Mouse! French Fry! Castle!"), because she needed to laugh and let go of the burden of the perfect one for as long as it took me to scour the library. That's how I saw it, anyway.

My gaze shifted back to the sidewalk. It had been longer than I realized since the last time I ventured downtown. I used to run down here nearly every day until I could no longer deal with trying to discern what every stranger I passed thought about my weight.

This first leg of my walk was going to unearth a swell of memories, I realized suddenly. The ones I wanted to forget, the ones I wished I remembered better, and all the happiness and bitterness that came with them. I hoped I would feel it all.

Hunger had a tendency to wash out everything else. Emotions of any kind reached my heart, muted of color and depth. Nothing excited me anymore, nothing moved me. And that wasn't normal. I used to be the type who was moved to tears by Pixar shorts and who burst into exuberant song if my favorite cereal was on sale at the grocery store. But now, though my life was in shambles, I couldn't even find the energy to work up a healthy amount of anger or heartbreak or shame or *anything*. The constant numbness was interrupted only by waves of hunger—the only signal my brain listened to anymore.

Maybe I was turning into my mom. She didn't have time to waste on frivolous things like how something made her *feel*. As far as I knew, she had only two emotions: contentment and righteous anger. Anything in between was pointless. Things were either right or wrong, done or incomplete, a success or a disappointment.

As for me, I felt *everything*. My mother called me moody during my teenage years, believing her work-in-progress daughter was just going through a phase. But the phase never ended.

It was probably not hard to guess that I fell into my mother's "disappointment" category. I still rested comfortably in that category, but for different reasons.

I caught a hint of freshly ground coffee on the breeze and soon enough, The Bitter End appeared. The brick building hadn't changed at all and probably never would. There was something about the ever-luminous neon OPEN 24 HOURS sign and the rickety outdoor seating that breathed a sense of permanence. I wasn't a coffee drinker, but Alex's bloodstream had to be caffeinated at all times. I'm not quite sure how he ever managed to sleep. Because of it, The Bitter End had quickly become our favorite haunt when we both moved downtown junior year.

Through the coffee shop's large windows, I caught a glimpse of a vacant table near the back. Our table. Suddenly it felt like I was watching a rerun of my life play out at that scuffed-up table and those two empty chairs. Even the sky seemed to darken, mimicking the long nights we spent intaking study materials and hot beverages.

"What time is it?" I would yawn and stretch dramatically, more for his attention than anything else.

"Better not to know," he'd always say, head of dark hair

still bent over his notes. "Knowing will only depress you, especially considering you've accomplished next to nothing other than distract me for the past five hours. You haven't even touched your public relations notes, have you?"

I'd take a sip of tea, pondering. "I'm guessing it's 2:37. How close am I?"

"Not close to finishing that essay due in two days, I'll tell you that much."

"Am I within ten minutes? I have a gift for guessing time accurately, you know."

A sigh from him. The exasperation in it was all for show. "As impressive as that is, I'm not sure that's going to be what secures you your GPA."

"It's got to be 2:38 now. Come on, just check! I know you want to."

He would check. He always checked. "3:23."

"Ah, so close. Hey, check out this video I found. It involves a squirrel and an entire pizza."

It might have taken a few more attempts, but he would always let out another sigh, close his laptop, and scoot his chair over to my side of the table. He was great at pretending that he hated when I distracted him, except for the fact that he always invited me back to the coffee shop.

Watching the table now, that old familiar mix of nostalgia and melancholy stirred inside me. I welcomed it back like an old friend. It had been longer than I thought since I'd felt something substantial other than hunger. I would say I hadn't felt like myself because of it, but in truth I hadn't felt like anything at all.

And maybe that was why I decided to stop a mile into my pilgrimage to buy a cup of coffee I wouldn't drink.

6

"One Americano, please," I said to the barista. Alex always ordered at least four of those things over the course of a study session. I was a little surprised to see they hadn't renamed it an "Alex."

The barista gave me the polite barista-to-patron smile, then did a double take that would have made me sprint to the door if my reflexes weren't those of a sloth.

"Mel? Is that you?"

Recognition flickered in her eyes, and all my ideas for different characters I could present myself as vanished. Was there a polite way to tell a perfect stranger that I not only had no idea who she was but also preferred she pretended the same for me?

"It's Kat," she said. When that still didn't help, she generously added, "From interpersonal communications?"

Finally, the light bulb switched on. Well, more like flickered. I dimly recalled this waif-thin girl from class. I'm pretty sure we bonded over exchanging *Seinfeld* quotes. I tried to take a moment to collect my memories into some neat package, but all my brain kept insisting was that I answer the question, *Is she thinner than me?*

"Hey, Kat!" I said, hoping to fake it till I made it. "Of course. *Seinfeld*, right?"

She laughed. "Right. You know, you were the only reason that class was even remotely bearable. Dr. Burns was just awful, wasn't she?"

"The worst," I replied, finding it fascinating that there was once a time when I made things more bearable instead of unbearable. "Kind of ironic that someone so severely lacking in interpersonal communication skills taught a whole class on it."

Kat laughed again. "Maybe she was hoping we would teach her."

I smiled, warming to her. However, those warm fuzzies vanished the instant she gestured toward the case displaying small mountains of sugary, butter-laced pastries.

"Pick out whatever you want. It's on the house," Kat said insistingly. "It's because of you that I worked up the courage to apply for that internship at Steelcase. Remember what you told me about not having anything to lose? And now they're offering me a full-time position starting in the fall. It was all because of that nudge you gave me that I even showed up to the interview in the first place. The least I can do is throw in a free pastry."

Was that really me? Someone capable of looking outside themselves long enough to help another human being? The way Kat gazed at me now reminded me so much of Claire that I couldn't find it in my heart to refuse. I could always pull the old throw-it-away-when-no-one's-looking trick.

A few minutes later, a coffee and a pastry were laid out in front of me, and a giant backpack sat across from me in place of Alex. I stared blankly at the table, wondering why in the world I had thought it would be a good idea to spend three of the few dollars I had to stare at a coffee that made me feel as bitter as it probably tasted.

In the end, Alex's life had expanded far beyond the tiny coffee shop, while mine shrank so small that even a trip down the road felt like a herculean feat. I mustered up the energy to come here a few times on my own, but it wasn't the same without him to annoy.

I glanced at the grease-stained bag holding my reward pastry for being a good person and vigorously rubbed my fingers on my pants, desperate to remove any trace of grease that might have started to seep into my skin. I looked back up at my backpack almost self-consciously, almost expecting Alex to be there instead, giving me that incredulous look of his and saying in his very matter-of-fact voice, "Mel, you're acting insane. That's not even how that works. Which you would know if you spent more time studying for biology than pulling up videos of squirrels."

Instead, it was Kat's voice that cut through my insanity.

"Are you okay, Mel?" She was standing over me now, a look of real concern on her face.

She really was so much like Claire. She had the same big eyes, same gentle kindness. And it seemed like success followed her the same way it did my sister. "You look . . . Do you want to talk? My break just started."

Without giving me a chance to say no in a firm yet gentle voice, Kat pulled up a chair and leaned her elbows on the table. Instead of comparing the boniness of our elbows, I tried to focus on the fact that I really appreciated her not moving backpack Alex.

"Is something going on?" Kat gestured to my pack. "Are you going somewhere?"

I leaned back in my chair and decided to pretend like it was the sister I ached to talk to on a near minute-by-minute basis sitting next to me instead of this overly concerned almost-stranger. "I'm going on a pilgrimage, actually. To Mount Rainier."

She quirked an eyebrow. "A pilgrimage?"

"Yup."

"Isn't Mount Rainier in Washington State?"

"It is."

Kat studied my backpack, then glanced down at my hiking boots. "You're not . . . walking all the way to Washington, are you?"

"I am! Wow," I said, genuinely impressed. "Forget Steelcase. You should go straight into the CIA with those deduction skills."

Kat nodded slowly. At this point, Claire's forehead would crease, and she'd begin nervously pulling on a stray lock of hair.

"Do you think that's the best idea, Mel?" Kat said in a voice I had a feeling she usually reserved for very young children. I opened my mouth to tell her politely to mind her own business, but she beat me to it with a shake of her head. "I'm sorry, that's obviously not any of my business. That's really exciting! I'm really excited for you! How exciting!"

"If you say it one more time, I'll believe you."

Kat leaned forward, her voice dropping to a whisper. "Listen, I know we don't know each other all that well, but I just want to make sure you're okay. And that you know what you're getting into. Me and my boyfriend thru-hike up north all the time, and it can be challenging. I can't imagine doing it for that long a distance all by myself. Are you sure you're going to be okay?"

Of course I wasn't sure I was going to be okay. I wasn't even okay to begin with. But Kat obviously needed to hear that I would be, so I leaned forward as well, folding my hands in front of me in a professional manner.

"I'll be totally fine," I assured her. "I have tons of hiking experience too. Been planning this route for months." Lies. All lies.

She slumped back and crossed her arms, clearly unconvinced. "I haven't met anyone who has hiked a route even remotely similar to yours. Most people I know hike the Appalachian Trail or the PCT. Something a little more well-known and, well, an actual marked trail."

I shrugged in a way I hoped came across as good-natured instead of flippant. "Maybe I'll be the first. And anyway," I added with a grin, "I've got nothing to lose."

Kat considered me for a long time. Her direct gaze made me squirm.

"Mel"—she paused for added dramatic affect I assumed—"you don't look strong enough to make it across the shop, let alone the country." Her voice dropped to a whisper again. "You look like you're on the point of starvation. I barely even recognized you at the counter. Are you sure you're okay?"

Thrilled as I was that she noticed how skinny I had become, I couldn't help but be more than a little annoyed. Who was this girl and why did everyone think they had a right to tell me how to live my life? If this was Claire, she would have known me well enough to leave it alone. She would have known it was pointless to try to change my mind.

This was why I didn't talk to people. Or go in coffee shops.

"Listen," I said, standing up abruptly, "I've got a long way to go, obviously. I don't want to take up your whole break. It was great to see you, Kat."

I was struggling to get my backpack through the front door when Kat appeared at my side. "You need to angle it a bit more to the right," she suggested. Reluctantly, I obeyed and a second later my backpack and I were back out on the sidewalk, one of us blinking in the harsh sunlight.

"Listen, Mel, I'm sorry," Kat said, still following me for some reason. "My brother always goes off on stupid adventures and never plans anything and always leaves me and my mom worried sick. He's gotten in big trouble more than once."

I pretended she was talking to some other Mel. Was it possible to sprint with a massive backpack strapped on?

"Hey, don't speed up! I'm not saying you're doing the same thing. I'm just trying to explain why I'm so nosy!"

I stopped abruptly. "Okay, thanks, Kat. Sorry about your brother. He sounds like a real piece of work. I assure you that you've made your point. But I really have to go."

"Stay with me tonight," she said. "You shouldn't start a hike this late in the day. Are you heading to the lakeshore?"

I nodded slowly, hoping it made me look like less of an unprepared idiot. I think it had the opposite effect. "Following it down to Chicago."

"And you're going to walk along Lake Michigan Drive in the middle of the night?"

"I—" I hadn't thought about that, is what I would have said if my pride hadn't stepped in and shut my mouth.

"Stay with me tonight and start fresh in the morning, okay?"

I sighed. It had been a long day, and I was pretty sure this girl would follow me all the way to Chicago if I didn't agree. "Fine. But no more trying to talk me out of my plan, okay?"

She put up her hands in surrender. "Absolutely."

Kat gave me the keys to her apartment before heading back to work. Such a Claire thing. I could rob her blind all because she was way too nice to distrust people.

Before heading to Kat's apartment, I stopped by the ATM in the downtown university bookshop. As I waited for the ATM to process my request, I watched prospective students and their parents sift through school spirit apparel.

On the way out, my eye caught the display of postcards near the register. Slowly turning the display stand, I scrutinized all the blindingly colorful and dazzling photos of this "Grand institution of knowledge and learning," as one postcard suggested.

I had the tendency to buy a postcard at every place I could. They were like a fifty-cent work of art, and if I chose the right one, it could capture a place better than any photo a tourist could take. My favorites were the ones found in long-forgotten bins in thrift and antique stores. Postcards dating back to the early 1900s that immortalized a place I loved, if I was allowed to love a place I had never actually been to. They captured how timeless certain beauty could be, how universally loved by all. They spoke through generations.

It's a lovely thing we humans do—sending postcards. We choose the most beautiful rendition of the place we can find, include a heartfelt note about how much a person we love is missed, and the world becomes a better place. And now, for the first time in my life, I would be the one sending the postcards, not receiving them. I would be the one on the adventure.

I could feel my throat getting tight with emotion as I flipped through the display again. I was getting emotional over my own inner monologue about postcards. This was the story of my life.

But at least I felt something. Not exactly the kind of trigger I was looking for, but for a chance to be my old self again, even over a postcard, I would take it.

Exiting the shop and tucking the postcards I had purchased into my jacket pocket, I felt my phone buzz. A text from Kat:

Make yourself at home. I'll be back in an hour or so with pizza. Any topping requests?

I stared at the phone. With that, I headed back to The Bitter End, dropped the keys off with a different barista with the request to tell Kat I was sorry, then set out toward the west.

Between walking down a pitch-black road all night or trying to get out of eating takeout pizza, I'd take the road every time.

7

Dear Alex,

Don't you love this blast from the past postcard I found in the gift shop of our old stomping grounds? (Yes, they do have a gift shop now. And a new library by the looks of it. Life is very unfair.)

I'm heading out on a cross-country trek. If I don't accidentally hold my map upside down, I plan to end up at Mount Rainier. Remember? That place I would never shut up about? The place we thought we'd explore together one day? Don't worry, I'll be careful, and I'll hold your advice of "Never wipe with the shiny, three-pronged leaves" to heart.

And if you're wondering, I still can't get myself to stop missing you. Just a feeling I can't seem to shake.

Love,
Mel

I ended up polishing off the bag of baby carrots for dinner and hunkering down in a cornfield sometime around midnight to catch a few hours of sleep. I was a little worried that the thick scent of manure would suffocate me in my sleep, but if that was the sacrifice needed to outrun pizza, so be it.

What felt like a few seconds later, I woke up to the smell of manure beginning to bake in the early morning sun. An excellent start to my first full day of hiking. I was surprised to feel butterflies in my stomach as I pulled the laces tighter on my hiking boots, adjusted my backpack, and made sure my postcard was tucked away safely in my jacket pocket.

I tried to shake out the ever-present ache in my joints as I shuffled out of the cornfield and back onto the dirt road, somehow already covered head to toe in dust and blinded by the sun. I wasn't sure if my joint issues were from the constant pounding from all the running or my slow but certain deprivation of nutrients, but lately I had been waking up with the aches of a ninety-year-old woman. One would think the idea of osteoporosis and deteriorating organs would be enough to convince someone to change their lifestyle.

Stiffness aside, the day was quickly warming with the rising sun, and the road before me was flat and straight. All I had to do was keep putting one foot in front of the other and I would be at the lakeshore in no time. It had arrived—the first day of my last chance to be something.

"Be with me, Saint Christopher, holy patron of travelers. Protect me and lead me safely to my destiny." I quietly recited the prayer to Saint Christopher I had memorized during my brief stint at the Catholic elementary school where I first fell in love with the stories of the saints. I transferred to the posh private Christian school everyone else at our church sent their kids to as soon as my mom worked her magic to come up with the tuition money, but the saints and their plights never left me.

Those prayers were the closest I got to God anymore. I had recited them to myself so much throughout my life that I said them more as a reflex than anything, not bothering to think about the words. But the act of saying them was usually enough to calm me.

Today, though, I still felt an edge of anxiety coursing through me, like the lingering buzz after a static shock. So for extra measure, I threw out another prayer or wish or whatever it was into the empty, bright morning.

"Please, give me the courage to finally do something with my life. And not die trying, if possible." It was clunky and not nearly as poetic as I had hoped, but it would have to do. I took a deep breath of manure-scented air and kept putting one foot in front of the other.

There was a slight breeze that promised to offset the brutal sun, but weather hardly mattered to me. I would still be cold. Even with my jacket. Another wonderful perk of starvation.

Speaking of starvation, I decided to plan out my eating for the day. The amount of time I thought about food was almost as alarming as how little of it I ate. I had eaten a rice cake for breakfast, and I planned on an apple for lunch. For dinner, I would have most of a Clif Bar, saving a little for my breakfast the next morning.

I never skipped a meal.

"I always make sure to eat three times a day—breakfast, lunch, and dinner," I would always painstakingly explain to my grandma and the doctors. "How can I be starving myself if I eat regularly? That doesn't add up."

Shockingly, that never convinced them. And the truth was that I only ate three times a day because I read in multiple articles that long gaps between meals leads to a slower metabolism and a slower metabolism means it becomes easier to gain weight. I was not about to fail at being an anorexic because of an oversight like that.

The occasional car passing by had turned into a steady stream of traffic over the last hour. I wondered what they thought of me as they passed by. Could they see my too-wide hips? My flabby belly? My sagging arms? The jacket could only hide so much. Did they see someone full of hope and purpose? Maybe I wasn't worth their passing glance.

I was sure that when saints still roamed the earth, not everyone took the time to look up from their personal preoccupations to watch them walk by. They could have been on their way to the market, maybe the fields, or perhaps a third place people went back in the day, and walked right by Saint Paul on his way to live a holy life as a recluse. Or looked right through Saint Prisca being led away to the lion's pit for not denouncing her Christian faith.

"Ugh, one more Christian being thrown in with the lion," they might have muttered with an eye roll. "Just another Thursday."

But they should have paid attention, because according to *Lives of the Saints*, the lion refused to eat Saint Prisca and instead bowed at her feet. Then they tried to burn her alive and that didn't work either. A beheading finally did the trick, but not before she left her mark as one awesome virgin.

That's what I wanted. Not the beheading thing or the permanent virgin thing. I wanted a life worth remembering, worth writing down. But I remained frustratingly average. I had no impressive talents, not even a whiff of a tragic backstory, and when I finally did find hardship, it was the kind I completely brought upon myself. Also, it was the most average hardship a somewhat financially stable white girl could come up with. Not exactly the stuff of saints.

I passed by yet another church and instantly thought of my mother. I realized that she would probably be extremely pleased my brain had made the connection between her and churches. She might be less pleased if I also mentioned the heart palpitations I felt whenever I thought of her. Granted, my heart had been doing the too-hard, too-fast beating thing for a while now. It was another fun side effect of starvation, but I always felt it most acutely when she came to mind.

I never felt like I fit in with my family, and I blamed it in part on me being a weird, moody little kid. But I also firmly believed my mom should shoulder some of the blame.

My parents both found God later in life. My dad found Him on the rim of the Grand Canyon. My mom found Him in a McDonald's after spending another night in jail for drunk driving. Her dad had died suddenly of a heart attack a couple of years prior, and ever since then, she felt like she could do nothing but drift along. Decisions held no moral weight for her. She did what she wanted in the moment, hoping to find some sort of anchor to keep her tethered to life. She would deal with the consequences numbly and then start the process all over again.

It wasn't a preacher or an eager evangelist who guided her to religion in that McDonald's. It was the rules and regulations sign posted next to the play place.

She read and reread the sign, feeling too disgusted and nauseous to eat the burger and fries in front of her. The rules were simple ones: No shoes in the play place, no food in the play place, children should be supervised. All the rules listed were there so every kid could have the best, safest time possible. She knew they had been written to avoid lawsuits, but in that moment, she interpreted them as a sign of love. The rules were followed because parents loved their children, and they wanted to see them safe and happy. Children followed them because they loved their parents and knew the best way to show that love was through obedience.

Mom found her anchor—guidelines. Guidelines written by someone who could make some sense out of this world, sense she couldn't seem to find.

She left her food untouched and went straight to the public library, pulling out all the religious texts she could find. By the time the library closed, she had latched on to the Bible, finding God in the pages.

Rules had saved my mother's soul, so she figured it would be the same formula for her future children.

I could never seem to follow her rules well enough. I would be close, but always fall short of exactly right. My mom laid these rules out as the path to God. If you broke the rules and strayed from the path, He would be disappointed. Just as my mom always was.

Then Claire was born, and my mom had her second chance at parenting. For every rule I couldn't follow, Claire followed it to a T. Claire was everything I wasn't, so my mom shifted her focus.

Claire would try to convince me that I had the way better deal. I tried to hate my younger sister for a while. She was everything I could never be. It should have been easy. When we were young, I would take out my jealousy on her either through icy silence or words spoken in the harshest tone a ten-year-old could summon.

One day, I found her crying in her room, her new dress streaked with grass stains. It was in that moment I realized my sister wasn't my enemy. We both knew what sort of terror a grass stain could bring upon us. I helped her clean out the stains and from then on, we were inseparable. I would always feel a mix of love and envy for her, but we were the only two people alive who fully understood the wrath of our mom.

Claire looked up to me for years, and I tried my best to live up to the admiration. Growing up, I would always encourage her to find small ways to express herself. I could so clearly see how our mom's expectations weighed on her sometimes, and I could almost hear her screaming for relief. She chose to paint, and it didn't take long to find out painting was another talent of hers.

I touched the pocket where her picture rested. I missed her. Sometimes so much it was more of a physical pain than an emotion.

When Claire was about to start high school a few years ago, my mom suddenly decided the suffocating consumerism and sin in America was not the right place for Claire to broaden her faith during her high school years. My dad always wanted to do mission work, so off to Uganda they went, leaving me alone to start college. I had seen them a total of three times since.

It still stung whenever I thought of the email I received from my mom during my first week of college. Not even a phone call. Instead, a concise email with perfect grammar.

"Dear Melanie," it had read. I have many lame skills but reciting that email from heart is probably the lamest.

In two weeks' time, your father, sister, and I will be moving to Uganda for missionary work. Your father has always felt the call and Claire needs the best environment possible to grow in her walk with the Lord. We will be boarding flight 2247 at the Grand Rapids airport with stopovers in Chicago and Brussels. Lord willing, we will arrive in Uganda on the 23rd of August. We have a car scheduled to pick us up, along with our luggage, and drive us to the village of Karamoja, where we will be residing for the foreseeable future. Claire will be homeschooled as well as taking private lessons with a local tutor from Germany who has also been called to mission work. We will call once we are settled if cell service is available.

Blessings,
Mom

I never asked any questions. I just sent an equally formal email back wishing them luck. I remember I signed it with "Sincerely, Melanie" instead of "Love, Mel" because that level of intimacy no longer felt appropriate. I called my sister the next day and made sure she knew I loved her. I managed to keep it together through the whole conversation, only to have a breakdown afterward that lasted almost seven years with no sign of slowing down.

Their departure should not have affected me as deeply as it did. I had no right to feel betrayed. I was eighteen when they left, and college is supposed to be a time to start fresh. Millions of kids cross countries and oceans to attend school without their families nearby. Millions of empty nesters fly the coop as soon as that last kid completes orientation week. Their leaving was not a betrayal. It was not a tragedy. It was not a unique sort of pain. I met kids at school who never knew one of their parents, who lost a parent, who were estranged from their siblings. I met kids with real problems, and they could get through the day without crumpling.

"What am I doing wrong?" I asked the late-morning sun as I trudged down the road. What part of me was missing that prevented these trivial events from destroying me? Something told me whatever that missing part was, it was the same part that I needed to finally gain my mother's approval.

But I had no idea what that part was. Or how to find it.

The sun was directly above me when I passed the crossroads that always marked the halfway point on our drives to the lakeshore. I had chosen to walk the dirt road that ran parallel to the main highway all the tourists took to Grand Haven. Alex and I would always take the dirt road when we drove. The friendly argument before we got very far played out the same every time. I would beg to take the scenic route and he would shake his head responsibly, reminding me how bad dirt roads are for the car's shocks. Not to mention all the rocks flying up were bound to scratch the paint.

"You sound like you're forty-five years old." I would laugh, then gesture dramatically out the window. "It's a beautiful day, and we both know the scenic route didn't earn its name by accident."

"I don't think that counts as an argument when you made up the name yourself."

"Oh, come on. We're young and this car is a piece of junk anyway. What do we have to lose?"

"Hey," he'd say, giving the dashboard a loving pat. "She can hear you. Don't listen to her, girl. You've still got plenty of life left in you."

"And don't you want the life she has left to be one worth living? Not plodding along on boring old Lake Michigan Drive?"

He'd rub his neck with one hand, trying and failing to hide the beginnings of a smirk. "Believe it or not, it's not the worst reasoning you've ever presented . . ."

"Plus, we can have the roads to ourselves. No traffic whatsoever. And we both know how you feel about traffic."

If it was an especially perfect day, that would usually be the point in the conversation when he would give in. We might have gone another round or two on an overcast day, but eventually he always turned onto the dirt road. I'd take that as my cue to roll down all the windows and put in the CD I reserved for drives on back roads, ready to sing along obnoxiously and only pause to point out any cows we passed. And even though the two of us and the interior of the car were all covered in a fine layer of dirt by the time we reached the lake, he would be smiling and trying to catch his breath from laughter in the end.

I knew I should save my phone for emergencies since I had no idea when I could charge it next, but the endless stretch of dirt road was too quiet.

I stopped to fish an apple and my headphones from my bag. I drank a few ounces of water while still kneeling in the dirt and listened to the whine of the cicadas. A barely perceptible breeze shifted through the long grasses on either side of the road. Dust swelled and danced around me. For a moment, the endless cycle of dark thoughts quieted, and

I could have sworn I caught a glimpse of my old self, full of freedom and laughter. But she was gone with the sunlight passing behind a stray cloud.

I began walking again while I opened my phone, ignoring the several notifications of calls from an unfamiliar caller with a Grand Rapids area code. I tapped the music app and found the "Back Roads" playlist I had digitally converted after the CD player in my car stopped working. I bit into the apple as a familiar song filled my head and memories flooded my heart.

"How can one person feel so many things at once and not explode?" Alex had asked me once after I told him this particular song made me want to cry happy and sad tears all at once.

"How can a person drive down a dirt road and not feel all the feelings? You're telling me you're not picking up on the somber, wistful vibes this dirt road is throwing at us?"

He would laugh, and his laughter became my checkpoint. It kept me in line whenever I began to take myself and my emotions too seriously. It made me turn my face to the sun and laugh right along with him.

I rolled through the playlist again and again as the miles passed. There was no laughter to stop me from sinking into the songs. Nothing to stop the sadness leaking into me. I welcomed it like an addict. But as the music played on, I continued to feel nothing more than shadows of emotions. Barely perceptible glimmers of what these songs used to make me feel. Even the sadness I felt for the loss of these emotions was shallow. The hunger had dulled everything, even hunger itself.

8

I became aware of the road dust covering me from head to toe only when I reached the lakeshore and saw the setting sun painted across the expanse of Lake Michigan. The intense primal urge to jump in the water was almost irresistible. But plenty of people still roamed the shoreline, and there was no way any of them would be seeing me without a full set of clothes.

I found an empty bench near the footpath at the edge of the beach and sat down heavily. I winced when my tailbone hit the bench a little harder than expected. I would be feeling that bruise for weeks. My body healed itself at a snail's pace these days, if it healed at all. I still had a few bruises on my arm and hip from when I passed out in my apartment stairwell two months ago. Maybe I'd start calling them birthmarks.

I took out what remained of my water and a Clif Bar. Not exactly my dinner of choice, but it was one of the only travel-friendly foods left in my pantry. I had bought these back before I had done my research on ingredient lists and nutrition labels and discovered with horror that there were so many healthier options out there. Most bars I wouldn't even consider because of their empty calories and exorbitant amounts of sugar. Some of the pricier bars had way too high of a fat content because they were practically just nuts glued together with a sugary substance. But once I had figured out Clif Bars weren't the absolute healthiest option I could choose, I shoved them in the back of the pantry and promptly forgot about them.

The realization that I would have to eat them again terrified me for a while, but I didn't have the financial luxury at this point to throw them out. I had decided on the way that to make up for the higher calorie and sugar content, I would eat only half the Clif Bar for a meal. I did the math and with my increased levels of fitness and my cutback on calories for other meals, it would all balance out.

Typically, I would start my day with a bowl of plain oatmeal. Just good old water and oats. Oatmeal used to make me gag, but I got used to it after a while. I'd learned a body can get used to almost anything after a while. For lunch I would have two rice cakes and ten to thirteen carrot sticks, and for dinner it would either be half a can of low-calorie vegetable soup or a salad with veggies and no dressing. Other than the rice cakes, my eating plan would have to change on the road. It made my heart race just thinking about it, but I took a few deep breaths and reminded myself that there were many ways I could be flexible without letting my calorie count rise. I would be fine.

I opened the Clif Bar wrapper carefully and slid the bar onto my lap. With as much precision as I could muster, I gently broke the bar into two somewhat even pieces. I slid the larger piece back into the wrapper, folded it up, and placed it back in my bag. I would save the larger half for the morning because my metabolism was faster then, meaning the calories would burn off quicker.

As I took small, slow bites, I watched the lingering beachgoers. Well, I didn't watch them so much as judge each woman's swimsuit-clad body, deciding whether or not I should feel jealous of her figure or grateful I at least wasn't *that* fat.

I used to watch people because the little sliver of their lives I witnessed fascinated me. I would try to fill in the gaps and give them interesting backstories. Now I sat here nibbling half a Clif Bar and judging people's bodies with more hate and cynicism than I thought I was capable of.

Once I had finished my dinner, I went to fill my water bottle up again at a nearby water fountain. While I waited for the world's slowest stream of water to fill the bottle, a group of college-age girls emerged from the bathroom, shrieking with laughter.

"I mean, he's been all over you the entire day!" said a blond in a bikini top and tiny jean shorts. "And don't forget that text he sent you last night."

"Oh my gosh, I already told you! That was nothing!" a brunette squealed, tossing back her windblown hair. It had the coveted beachy look to it, even though the water was salt-free. "We always text like that. We're just friends!"

The brunette was a terrible liar.

"Yeah, right," said the blond. "We all know he's obsessed with you. I almost guarantee he'll offer to pay for your ice cream at Kilwin's tonight. Just watch."

The girls continued to shriek out peals of laughter as the brunette gave an awful rendition of a girl in denial. I watched them walk away. Their long legs, their tiny waists, their toothpick arms wrapped around each other in the unbreakable bonds of sisterhood.

I tried not to hate them as I screwed the lid back on my water bottle and returned to my bench. I wasn't being fair. The girls weren't even that bad. They were only guilty of falling in love and eating ice cream without a care in the world. Never fearing a broken heart or no longer fitting into those tiny jean shorts.

I had always been wary of friend groups. That wariness over time tended to blossom into swift and harsh judgment on my part.

They presented their bonds of friendship as unbreakable, unbendable, and unable to accommodate any outsiders. One couldn't exactly just decide to immerse themself in one of these groups. It had to occur through a series of lucky incidents and random coincidences. Watch any sitcom ever.

These friend groups—they had this shared history that became cast in a rosy light over time. It was something an outsider could never fully share. They'd let you in so you could be their audience for their wonderful, quirky, and oh-so-hilarious family of friends. You would be there to validate their greatness, but you would never have what it took to get on the team.

At least, that was my experience. Up until my mom stopped caring about what school I attended and I could leave the toxic cliques made up of girls who had been together since preschool. Their private Christian school upbringing should have taught them to love and accept everyone, and they did, as long as everyone looked and acted like them.

I understood the irony of my judgment of most friend groups because they once judged me. But I was tired, so tired, of trying to believe the goodness in those people. And it wasn't just my body that took its time to heal. I was certain my heart had never fully recovered from their rejection.

I took a T-shirt out of my backpack and folded it into a makeshift pillow. I looped a backpack strap around my wrist and settled into a not-so-comfortable napping position on the bench, facing the water. I figured I would try to get a few hours of sleep, then make my way down the coast in the middle of the night to avoid getting into trouble for walking on privately owned beachfront property.

I could see the girls near the water's edge. They were packing up their belongings while laughing with a few guys. Their laughter was echoed by the waves, creating the soundtrack to a life I once had. My eyes drifted toward the brunette. She was with the guy who must have been her crush. They were both laughing. She was laughing so hard, she apparently needed to hold on to his shoulder to steady herself. He was looking at her through his laughter. It was such a look of pure adoration that I had to agree with the blond—he was obsessed with her. No way she would be paying for her ice cream tonight.

I kept hating them as long as I could, but as I drifted closer to sleep, I gave up and resigned myself to wistfulness. That was once me out there. A little less obvious and a lot less good at flirting, but the feelings had been the same. That look he gave her, I had seen the same look before. It had been for me and no one else.

The setting sun had painted the moment in a golden light in my memory. I remembered the jolt in my heart as Alex's hand brushed against mine when he offered me an extra T-shirt to wear. My own was soaked with lake water. Even back then, I never took off my shirt to swim. I remember the soft, worn cotton against my skin and the comfort in knowing I was wrapped in his scent. I could carry the essence of him with me, even for a short time.

I remembered glancing up and being mesmerized by that look, my heart completely surrendering to him in that moment. And as the same sun set behind the same beach, the same girl who had that moment years before fell asleep. Although this time, she was a bit lonelier and a bit more broken. But I had to believe that somewhere, that same girl still lived.

9

Dear Alex,

On my way to the beach, I stopped by the tackiest gift shop I could find to pick out this postcard. I realize I used to make plenty of grand, sweeping declarations that I had neither the time nor patience for tacky, money-grabbing shops with no creativity such as these, but I couldn't afford the $4 for a vintage postcard so you'll have to settle for "Greetings from the World's Largest Musical Fountain!"

Out of the millions of times we've been here, how is it possible we never took the chance to see the musical fountain?? I would have seen it tonight, but I knew it would have felt wrong without you there too. This place already feels wrong without you. Luckily, we never made it very far west so the rest of this trip

I can forge new memories. However, I know that somehow, you'll be there all the same.

Love,
Mel

P.S. Remember when we went on a run around here, got totally lost for what felt like days (but was actually more like forty minutes), then we were so relieved we survived that we each ate three burritos from the burrito shack? Followed by a four-hour nap on the beach, of course. That was pure madness. We sure had some good times.

I could see the Chicago skyline through slightly blurred vision. I'd always had perfect eyesight, and I might have been more concerned about the sudden lack of twenty-twenty vision if I had any energy to spare. Spots had also started to dance in front of my eyes. I shook my head, trying to make them disappear. I just had to keep my focus and I would be in Chicago by nightfall.

I gave myself a figurative pat on the back for my map-reading skills. Granted, all I had to do was make sure the lake stayed on my right and I knew I would reach Chicago eventually, but what other twenty-four-year-old could survive out here without their map app? I'd like to thank self-reliance and a very dead phone.

It had been six days since my nap by the beach. Six days of constant walking through sandy forests of skinny pines, on quiet shorelines, and over paved bike paths. When the exhaustion hit me on the third day, it hit me harder and deeper than ever before. My body went from aching to throbbing to screaming to eerie silence. Standing up usually took multiple tries. My breathing had turned irregular, and I felt the rapid spasms of my heartbeat with more regularity and intensity than I was used to.

I had spent the prior few nights sleeping on dunes near the lakeshore. I would wake up sandy and covered in bug bites from horseflies and mosquitos, but I barely felt them. Same with the layers of sunburn I continued to get on my face, hands, and legs. Sunscreen had not been on my packing list. I had spent fifteen minutes trying to decide whether or not to take a bathroom scale, but the thought of taking sunscreen never crossed my mind.

I worried a bit that I would soon be on trails and no longer have deserted dunes to sleep on each night. I had felt safe in the tall grass with no people or animals around to bother me, enough light from the moon so I wasn't left in complete darkness, and no sound but the water lapping onto the shore. Nothing like the sounds in the woods that could all belong to something coming to murder me. I would probably have to spend a good number of nights in the woods in the future. No tent. Too many trees for moonlight to filter through. Nothing but me and all those sounds. Maybe I would get lucky and they would drown out the sounds in my head.

I had been on plenty of camping expeditions in my day. I had even completed several backpacking trips with my dad and some with Alex in Michigan's Upper Peninsula that had lasted a week or more. But I had never gone without a tent. The rational part of my brain knew that the flimsy poles and thin fabric of a tent would in no way stop anything that wanted to hurt me, but still . . . Now I would be a convenient human burrito, all wrapped up and ready to be any animal's midnight snack. Geez. I would have to get creative. Or just stop being such a baby. People did this sort of thing all the time. I would be fine.

Burritos, my gosh. When was the last time I had one of those? I thought back to a few months prior when I made myself a vegan burrito. Well, more like a bunch of vegetables wrapped in a leaf of lettuce instead of a tortilla. It hadn't tasted great, but that was never the point anymore.

Shredded chicken. Beans. Melted cheese. Guacamole.

I shook my head and my vision spun. The apparition of the magic burrito vanished. What was I doing? I didn't even like burritos all that much. *For Pete's sake, Mel, pull yourself together.*

Who was Pete, anyway? Was he such a good guy that we do all these things for his sake? Is it Saint Peter, maybe? Saint Pete . . . No. Not nearly a noble enough name to fit such a title. I'd have to go by Saint Melanie. Saint Melanie who died not as a martyr but as a starving idiot on her way to the West Coast. Didn't even make it to Chicago.

"Focus!" I yelled at myself. My voice sounded rough and slow from disuse. When I made it to Chicago (and I *would* make it to Chicago), I would need a plan. I would sleep on a park bench tonight. People slept in big city parks all the time, I was sure of it. And by this point, I was so covered with dirt and sweat and so stooped from the weight of my backpack that everyone would assume I was homeless and flat-out ignore me.

Technically, I thought with a start, *they would be right*.

Regardless, that was the plan. I was dimly aware that it wasn't a great one, but I couldn't bother to come up with anything better.

I still had half a rice cake left, which I planned to eat that night. I had found a few strawberry patches along the way but other than that I had been hovering around four hundred calories a day. Although my ability to add numbers had also begun to suffer. I knew every day I was trying to cut that number down even further, and I knew that was the reason I couldn't walk faster than a snail's pace, but I couldn't seem to stop myself.

This emptiness was a different kind than I was used to. It felt more permanent, more unforgiving. The thought of death flickered in and out of my consciousness, and I didn't have the willpower to push it away.

This morning when I woke up in a grove of trees not far from the Blue Star Highway, I had started to tie my hair back when I pulled away several clumps. I used to have pretty okay hair. It was dirty blond and full and easy to work with. That hair had slowly turned into a stringy, limp mess that I now always wore up because wearing it down made me look like the witch from *Snow White*.

Now it had begun to fall out. But in my mind, the trade-off wasn't even a question. I would so much rather be bald and skinny than have a head full of hair and be my normal fat self. I was vain, so much so it might actually kill me, but I was selectively vain.

That doesn't make it any better. That just makes you a walking contradiction, I told myself, wiping sweat from my face with a shaky hand. Right, and I had started this super great habit of violently shaking most of the time.

Walking. Walking. Walking. Going nowhere fast. Going nowhere at all. Going, going, gone. Gone with the Wind. *Wind and the waves. The ocean. I'm nowhere near the ocean. That's an overgrown lake, that's no ocean. No ocean, no fish. No fish, no seafood. No seafood. No Red Lobster. Chaos everywhere.*

I could no longer string two cohesive thoughts together. I let my mind roam and focused everything I no longer had on putting one foot in front of the other in some semblance of a straight line.

I had actually laughed when I saw the clumps of hair this morning. A while back, soft, fluffy hair had started to grow all over my body. Dr. Clifford had smugly pointed this out during my first visit.

"It's called lanugo," he said. "This is your body's way of trying to conserve heat because you have too little body fat to keep you warm."

But all I had heard was "body fat" and registered that I still had some.

So I was turning into a bald, fluffy shell of a human. Maybe I would change my plans and join a traveling circus instead. Did they still have a freak show in circuses? Were circuses still a thing?

Circuses, circles, squares, tangent lines. Geometry, math, mathematicians. I could be a mathematician. I could fall in love with a mathematician. He would count out his cereal every morning. I would watch him and eat nothing. Do nothing. Not math. Math isn't for me. But the mathematician and his cereal . . .

I had to stop and rest again. I was not the kind of person who stopped and rested, but I didn't seem to have much choice in the matter. My body stopped for me while my brain continued to ramble on a route to blankness.

I sat on a bench and looked around. It took me a lifetime to blink several times and realize I had been here before. It had been the middle of winter, but I walked down this very path, my hand in Alex's coat pocket because I had forgotten to pack my gloves.

"Honestly, I'm impressed you remembered to pack your coat," Alex had said. "I have never met someone as good at forgetting things as you are."

"To be fair," I countered, "you were the one who reminded me to bring my coat."

He smirked. "I know, but I was going to let you believe otherwise."

"No way! If I'm going to keep my title as 'The Best Forgetter of Things Great and Small,' I need all the help I can get. Don't try to take this honor away from me!"

That got a laugh out of him, and I walked even closer until his heat and mine were the same.

But he had been wrong. I wasn't the best at forgetting things. I couldn't manage to forget anything about that day. A day that used to be considered an "ordinary Saturday."

"This is Burnham Park." I whispered it like a question, while blinking up at the sky. The skyline of Chicago was to my back, the lakeshore was in front of me, and the last remnants of the sunset spread out to my left. I was already *in* Chicago. How in the world had I gotten here? I tried to fish through my memories for the last few hours and came up blank. Absolutely blank. Did God send angels to get me here? Like some celestial Uber? I figured the chances of that were slim. Celestial Uber aside, I wasn't at a point in my relationship with God where we did each other favors.

I sat there staring at my shaking hands, trying to form a thought, trying to wake up my brain and work through this. *Pay attention*, I commanded. But I got no response.

This bench might be safe, it might not. I couldn't grasp a good sense of the area. Maybe I should just keep walking. Right past Chicago. Never resting until I reached Washington.

Although I liked Chicago, it would be a shame to leave so quickly. Chicago, the Windy City. But it wasn't actually windy, that's not why they called it that. I couldn't remember why they did call it that, but I knew it wasn't because of the wind. There was that Great Fire in 1871 and the World's Fair in 1893. They had the meat-packing industry and Upton Sinclair's novels and the Magnificent Mile and dark and gruesome and redeeming stories down every alley and cold, brutal winters and hot summers . . .

I was circling again. I stood up quickly, trying to shake my thoughts back into place and demanding my body into action. But my vision went from blurred to spotted. The spots grew until there was nothing but blackness.

10

"Honey, can you hear me? Come on now, wake up. Come on, honey. Let's wake up now."

The words swimming through my brain belonged to an unfamiliar voice. At first I thought I was back in the hospital, but something didn't feel right. This resurfacing to consciousness felt a little sloppier, a little less starched than when I woke to find myself in a hospital room.

I had the slightest notion that my shoulders were being shaken. *I'm up, I'm up*, I tried to say, like when my mom used to shake me awake for the third time on particularly rough school mornings. But I wasn't quite there yet. I couldn't find my voice to fit the words.

A shock bolted through me so suddenly that my eyes flew open, and my lungs filled with a sizable gasp of air usually reserved for near-drowning victims. I was soaked and breathing fast. Had I actually *been* drowning?

"Told you that would work," said another unfamiliar voice, deeper than the first.

I turned to see a man and a woman kneeling next to me. The woman looked at me with such relief I felt like she must know me from somewhere. Strangers didn't look at each other like that. The man was screwing on a lid to a half-empty Dasani bottle.

"You all right, honey? You feeling okay?"

I tried to speak but the words came out in a coughing fit. I tried again. "I'm okay. I'm guessing I passed out?"

"You were out cold," said the man. He shoved the water bottle inside a backpack that was even bigger than mine.

"I'm so sorry." I attempted to sit up more. The woman placed a strong hand on my back to steady me.

"Are you sure you're okay to sit up?" she asked with so much sympathy, my throat tightened with tears.

I nodded. "This happens a lot. I'm really okay. I'm so sorry I scared you. But thank you so much for your help. Really, you're both my heroes."

"This happens a lot, huh?" The woman examined me closely, then turned to her friend. "She's so pale, Jim. And look, she's shaking. Pull out that granola bar you got earlier."

A Nutri-Grain Bar appeared from Jim's pocket. The sugary bar was pretty much a glorified Fig Newton. I sat up straighter, panic rising.

"No, no. I'm really okay. Thank you though. I don't want to take your food. You've already done so much. I can handle it from here. Really."

"Honey, you gotta eat something," the woman explained calmly as Jim unwrapped the bar. "It looks like you haven't eaten in days. My daughter used to have fainting spells every now and again because of low blood sugar. We've gotta get that blood sugar up."

I shook my head and tried to form a rational excuse, but my thoughts were so fuzzy. My elbow hurt badly from the fall, and the pain seemed to be all I could focus on. "Please," I whispered, tears threatening. "Please, I'm fine. Please don't make me eat that."

I sounded pathetic. My eyes caught Jim and the woman exchanging glances before they clouded with tears. I could not start crying. I could not possibly sink that low. Jim tucked the bar somewhere in his jacket, and the woman gently took my hands in hers.

The gesture surprised me, but I didn't pull away. Instead, the feeling of her warm hands against my icy cold, shaking ones caused my resolve to slip. Tears began to fall slowly. One tear, two . . . then the floodgates opened. I sobbed openly and unattractively on the ground as the woman gently let go of my hands to scoot next to me and wrap me in a hug.

Finally, I could feel myself returning back to normal. I felt worn out and empty in a way I wasn't familiar with. It was how I used to feel after a long, difficult run when I still took care of myself. Full of righteous, cleansing exhaustion. I used the sleeves of my sweatshirt to wipe snot and tears from my face. There was no possible chance of salvaging any of my dignity now.

"So, if helping me regain consciousness wasn't enough, I've also managed to thoroughly freak you out." I tried to laugh, but my voice was too hoarse. It sounded more like I was choking. And here I was thinking I couldn't possibly become any less attractive. "I feel like an apology would just sound stupid at this point."

They were both on the ground now, one on either side of me. I noticed I was on the grass, a few feet away from the footpath and the bench. Had I walked over there? Was I carried? I had no idea. Both of them were looking at me.

The woman watched me intensely and Jim looked incredibly anxious. Poor Jim.

"Honey, something big is going on with you," the woman said. "You don't have to tell us everything, but you've gotta tell us something so we can help you. If we don't know what's going on, we can't help. And although you may think otherwise, you need us right now."

I appreciated how she kept calling me honey. Growing up, I would hear my friends' parents call them honey or sweetie or a nickname meant for no one else. My mom never called me anything other than Melanie.

"I'm not going to a hospital. If I tell you, you have to promise I won't end up there," I demanded like a five-year-old.

The woman didn't hesitate. "No hospitals. We promise."

I studied the two of them. The only thing I knew about these two was that Jim liked Nutri-Grain Bars, and they were the kindest people I had ever met. Seemed like a pretty safe bet.

"I'm on a sort of . . . pilgrimage. Or journey or whatever you want to call it. I'm hiking to Mount Rainier. In Washington. State, not DC . . ."

Jim's eyebrows went up. "Where'd you start from?"

"Grand Rapids, Michigan."

His eyebrows stayed raised. "Yikes. Haven't made it very far, huh?"

"I am aware."

"You're walking to the West Coast?" the woman asked, looking me up and down with the concerned glance of a mother. "No offense, honey, but you don't look well enough to walk all that way. But you probably could have guessed that by now."

I sighed. "I'm more prepared than I look. I haven't been feeling great lately, but I'm in decent shape, I have my route mapped out, and I have everything I need in my backpack. Granted, I might have pushed myself too hard today. I'll admit that. I think a good rest tonight is all I need, and I should be ready to start out again tomorrow morning."

The woman narrowed her eyes at the backpack, then turned back at me. "What's your name, honey?"

"Melanie. People call me Mel," I said automatically.

"Mel, my name is Leslie. I want you to be honest with me here, okay? Did you pack food in that bag?"

I nodded, my face hot. I felt a little spark of anger in my chest, ready to ignite like it always did when people questioned my eating habits. But then I remembered how she had held my hands so gently and looked at me like I mattered. The spark quickly died.

"Is there any food left?"

I nodded again. A coward's nod.

She crossed her arms. "How much?"

"Plenty." I couldn't look at her. How old was I? "I told you, I know what I'm doing."

"Show me."

I peered up at her then, trying to act innocent as my stomach tied itself into knots of anxiety. "What?"

"Show me all the food you have left. My babies have all grown up and gone off to live their own lives, but that doesn't mean I'm done being a momma. If you're not eating right, I take that as my own personal responsibility."

For the first time, I took her in. A fleeting moment passed where I was actually proud of myself that it had taken me this long to notice someone's weight.

Leslie was a large woman, probably around 210 pounds. She had soft, brown eyes, her hair was hidden beneath a purple silk scarf, and she was wearing a good amount of clothing for such a warm day. I wondered if she did so for the same reason as me, because she hated what was underneath. But something about the way she carried herself, even sitting on the ground, made me doubt it.

I grudgingly rummaged through my pack. I knew exactly where my last remaining half rice cake was, but I was stalling. I glanced over at Jim. I rarely bothered to notice men's weight, adding sexism to my list of sins, I supposed. But Jim was so painfully thin, I couldn't help but notice. He wore a pair of dirty jeans and a Chicago Cubs T-shirt that looked three sizes too big. His hair was a mess, and his giant glasses could use a cleaning. He still seemed anxious, and I couldn't help but instantly like him.

I pulled out the half rice cake and handed it to Leslie without a word.

"This is it?"

"I was going to get more food soon," I protested weakly.

"What else have you been eating besides rice cakes?"

I checked off the items on my fingers. "Clif Bars, some apples, strawberries . . ."

"And?"

I shrugged. "That's all I need. I don't have a big appetite."

Leslie inspected the rice cake, then handed it back to me.

"You realize you're never gonna make it to Washington if you keep starving yourself, right? It's not a matter of willpower. It's a matter of absolute fact."

I said nothing. I crinkled the rice cake wrapper and avoided eye contact while my face burned hotter and hotter.

"Hey, now." Leslie put an arm around my shoulder. "I know it's hard. I know this isn't something I can cure with a lecture. But you've gotta do what you have to, to keep yourself alive. You got yourself in a situation now where you don't have the luxury of caring what you weigh or how you look. You've gotta worry about nothing but the things you never had to worry about before. Food, shelter, safety, survival. That's it. You can't afford to take on any more than that. You either accept that or die."

I looked up in time to see Leslie motion to Jim with a slight raise of her chin. He hesitated for a moment before pulling out the Nutri-Grain Bar again and holding it out to me with apprehension.

I took it and held it in my still-shaking hands. It was blueberry flavor, but I knew it would taste nothing like blueberries. This wasn't part of my eating plan. I hadn't factored in these calories. These empty, sugary calories . . .

But I also couldn't imagine trying to stand up right now, let alone walk. My head was still swimming, my body still shaking. Leslie's words could not be ignored. It all came back to that pyramid. Triangle? I wasn't sure. But I knew its name: Maslow's Hierarchy of Needs. It was one of the few tidbits of knowledge from high school that had stood the test of time.

If a person didn't have their basic needs met (food, shelter, water, rest, safety, etc.), then they wouldn't be able to motivate themselves to any higher level of existence. Things like love, belonging, connection, and self-esteem were completely out of the question. I had reduced myself to the lowest human form. I could never hope to achieve anything even remotely noteworthy if I continued to ignore the basic elements of survival. My legacy would include a bachelor's degree in nonprofit administration from a thoroughly average college, a two-year-long career at Wendy's, and dying unceremoniously of self-inflicted starvation in a park.

My life had not turned out like I had imagined it, but I could not let my death follow the same sad decline. I told myself I would walk to Mount Rainier, and when I said I would do something, I always followed through. At least, that was what the old Mel did. I was stuck between two acts of stubbornness: a declaration that I would never gain weight and another to walk across the country. It was a crossroads between life and death.

But it wasn't. Not really. I was giving in to my drama again. My declaration had never been not to gain weight, it had been to never be *overweight*. I had been so stupid and careless up to this point. I wasn't a dumb person. Obviously if I'd learned anything over this past week it was that I was no genius, but I could hold my own.

I was smart enough to trick my diseased brain into accepting the exact caloric intake that would keep me safely in the *underweight* range while safely away from starving to death. I had read a *Runner's World* article a few years back on Scott Jurek, ultramarathoner extraordinaire. He ran the Appalachian Trail on a one hundred percent vegan diet. He was a twig by the end and never once came close to dying of starvation. If he could figure it out, so could I.

"You're right," I said finally. I took the Nutri-Grain Bar from Jim with a grateful smile. I took a bite. My heart raced as I did, but I began to relax as I played my new mantra over and over in my head.

I am not going to allow myself to get fat. I am not going to allow myself to die. This is all part of the solution.

"You're right," I said again before taking another bite. It was the best thing I had ever eaten. Granted, most things consumed on the verge of starvation taste like the best thing ever eaten. "I need to take better care of myself. I will. I'm going to go to the store as soon as I feel up to it and sort this all out."

Leslie smiled cautiously. "You're not gonna throw this up as soon as we walk away, are you?"

I shook my head. "I'm not a puker. I just don't eat."

She gave my shoulder a tight squeeze. "I'm proud of you, Mel. It'll be a journey, but you're taking the first steps. You'll start to realize the further you go how many things are more important than that number on the scale."

I almost corrected her. *No, see, I figured out this plan where I'm still not going to get fat, but I'm not going to die either. It involves being more strategic about my eating . . .* This wasn't the first time I felt the need to assure someone I would not become overweight, that my revelation did not mean I was going to join the ever-growing percentage of obese Americans. But I thought better of it and gave her a smile and a nod instead.

"Do you want us to come with—" Leslie's voice was cut off by a deeper, harsher one.

"Are these people bothering you, miss?"

I looked up to see a police officer staring down at me. I waited for Leslie to answer. Hopefully she would explain the situation vaguely enough for the cop to consider follow-up questions a waste of time.

But when Leslie turned to me with a slightly alarmed

expression instead of answering, I realized the cop had been talking to me. I gaped at him, shocked.

"No, not at all. I wasn't feeling great, and these two stopped to help me. They practically saved my life with this Nutri-Grain Bar." I was a little hesitant to admit to eating a Nutri-Grain Bar—what if he thought that was how I ate all the time?—but I figured it would help move the process along.

The cop's gaze shifted from Leslie to Jim, eyes narrowed and hands near his belt. "I recognize you two. I thought I told both of you not to hang around this park anymore. Care to explain why you chose to ignore me?"

What in the world . . .

"We weren't in the park," Leslie explained. Her voice was clear, and she stared hard at the cop. "We were crossing that street over there when we saw this young girl collapse. No one else was around to help, so we ran over. We're gonna leave as soon as we're sure she's all right."

I took a second to really look at Jim and Leslie. Leslie's extra layers for a too-warm day, Jim's giant backpack, his dirty glasses, both pairs of scuffed-up shoes with soles barely hanging on . . .

They were homeless.

Like, truly homeless. Not the "walking away from an apartment I had paid off until the end of the month homeless" like I had the nerve to call myself.

And I had refused to eat *their* food because I was worried about getting fat.

They had found me nearly starved not because I couldn't afford food but because I simply refused to eat it.

The cop knelt down in front of me. "Miss, do you need

me to call an ambulance? Would you like me to tell these two to leave?"

I stared at the cop, trying to process the shock of all this at a speed my foggy brain wasn't capable of. I shook my head. "No, thank you. I'm fine. These people have taken great care of me. I'm going to hang out with them for a while."

He stood up hesitantly, his mouth a thin, firm line. "All right, then. I'll be patrolling the park and keeping an eye on you, though, if you need anything."

"That's really not necessary," I said. But he ignored me and gave both Leslie and Jim a pointed look before walking away.

A moment of awkward silence passed between the three of us. What does a person say after something like that?

"I'm so sorry I ate your food." I winced as I spoke the words.

Jim shrugged. "I hate Nutri-Grain Bars, so the whole thing worked out nicely."

I blurted out a laugh and Leslie snorted. The tension might have evaporated if I had just left it alone, but I didn't.

"I can't tell you how sorry I am for burdening you with my mess," I went on. "A mess that I entirely brought upon myself. Especially when there are . . . When this isn't even grounds for a real problem. It's all in my head. And I'm sorry that cop was terrible to you. I'm sorry you had to deal with him because of me. I'm sorry you had to spend your time trying to help a spoiled girl who decided on a whim to walk across the country because she has no real issues to worry about and nothing better to do. But I'm really so grateful for you both." I wrapped my arms around myself, the feeling of mortifying embarrassment that involved wanting the earth to open up and swallow me whole still not totally gone.

"Good Lord, have you got all those apologies out of your system yet?" Leslie rolled her eyes. "First of all, honey, you didn't *make* us do anything. We chose to help you because we saw a person in trouble. That's what decent people do for one another." She squeezed my shoulder. "Second, you've gotta stop making light of your problems. It's straight up annoying to listen to and a waste of all our time.

"Everyone has problems," she went on. "Whether it's in their head, in their bones, or all around them. Doesn't mean they're not real. Doesn't mean they don't hurt and that they don't need to be taken seriously. I think all this downplaying you're doing is a big reason why you ended up passed out here in the first place. I'm not here to judge whatever journey you're on. Just like I don't think you're gonna judge me for mine. I don't know the source of your pain. But I know you have pain, same as me. And that's all that matters."

I was crying again. Not as hysterically this time, but it was still hard to see Leslie's resolved expression through the tears. "I know I practically just met you," I said hoarsely, "but I've firmly decided you're one of the best people I've ever met. You too, Jim. Both of you are in the top five, for sure."

Leslie pulled me in for another hug. "You've got strangers caring if you live or die. That's reason enough to take care of yourself, isn't it?"

"Good a reason as any." My voice came out muffled against her coat. God knows I wanted to believe that.

11

I stood off to the side of the busy produce section and tried to organize my thoughts. I had ducked into the first grocery store I saw, determined to follow through with my plan.

But I quickly realized it was a predominantly Asian specialty food store and most of the items were way out of even pre–eating disorder Mel's comfort zone. So I kept walking and ended up at Trader Joe's.

I had been burning more calories a day than my original estimation since I hadn't factored in how much energy it would take just to keep upright with my monstrous backpack. I did some unreliable math in my head a few times and ended up with a daily caloric intake to aim for.

Even without my scale, I knew for certain I had never been skinnier. My hip bones felt sharper, and I could count my ribs easier than ever. Of course, there was always more to lose. There was the lower belly flab, the arms . . .

No. This is what I needed to survive. Besides, if I kept up my current level of fitness, I could repeatedly assure myself I wouldn't gain a pound on this new diet. For insurance if I ever had a rest day, I would cut my caloric intake down that day by seventy-five percent. Easy peasy. Keep death at bay and look skinny doing it. The real American Dream.

It will all work out. It will all be fine. I sent the thought heaven-bound in case God needed reminding that my new plan was a responsible one that deserved to succeed.

"Through God's strength to pilot me, God's might to uphold me, God's wisdom to guide me . . ." I muttered the lines from the prayer of Saint Patrick under my breath almost without thinking to calm my nerves as I made my way into the belly of the store.

I needed food that would fit in my backpack and wouldn't go bad. And I needed a large enough quantity of it to keep me alive. I walked over to the dried fruit, nut, and bar section with trepidation.

Nuts and seeds terrified me. Their calorie and fat contents were sky-high, and even though I had read plenty of scientific studies that proved "Fat doesn't make you fat," I still let out a tiny squeak of horror when I read the nutrition label.

Fat doesn't make you fat. All the experts said so. It was the sugar and salt that were to blame for the endless parade of obese Americans. Besides, I couldn't think of a better option that checked off all my requirements at the moment.

Like ripping off a Band-Aid, I quickly grabbed three bags of raw almonds and threw them in my basket.

An hour and a half later, I walked out of Trader Joe's with a fully charged phone and watch, courtesy of an over-the-top helpful cashier, three bags of almonds, no-sugar-added dried apples, raisins, whole wheat tortillas, almond butter, three bags of muesli, ten Pro-Bars, eight cans of tuna, and two chocolate bars for Leslie and Jim. I had a much heavier pack and a significantly lighter wallet, but for the first time since leaving home, I was able to muster up real confidence.

The sky had grown dark by the time I left the store. Only a few lingering streaks of purple were left in the inky-black sky. The city lights hid the blanket of stars I had slept under during my nights on the beach.

I made my way back in the direction of Burnham Park, hoping to find Leslie and Jim. They had encouraged me to spend the night near them, a guaranteed safe place to sleep. With the night fast approaching and the city cast in shadows, I was more than ready to take them up on their offer.

I found them with relative ease thanks to the two of them standing near a main intersection and shouting my name when I came into view. I smiled and quickened my pace to reach them like I was reuniting with old friends. It was a relief to be in a place so big and loud that no one took any notice of me, even when two people were bellowing my name across a busy intersection.

Leslie and Jim led the way to a smaller, quieter park a few blocks away from the lakeshore where law enforcement turned a blind eye. The three of us spread our sleeping bags out behind a grove of bushes while I heard other groups settle in for the night nearby.

Afterward, I passed out the chocolate bars and took twenty almonds and a few dried apple slices for myself. The three of us sat down together, two of us enjoying the snack and one trying to calm the rising panic as she ate almond after almond.

"So," Leslie said, leaning back until she could prop herself up on her elbow, "why Mount Rainier? I'm sure you don't have to walk all that way to see a mountain. Or if you're looking to walk a long way, why not take a route like that one in California or through the Appalachians? My daughter went on a hiking trip to those mountains a few years back. Couldn't stop talking about them."

I gratefully took the opportunity to stop eating. "I wanted to do something different, some adventure I could make entirely my own. Sure, it's not as noteworthy as the PCT or the ACT, but that's kind of why I like it." I looked down at the remaining six almonds in my hand.

"As for the destination," I continued, "there's something special about Mount Rainier. It's not just a mountain to me. Ever since I first saw a picture of it as a kid, I had this feeling I belonged there. And that wasn't a feeling I got a lot back then.

"The more I learned about it, the more I felt called to go there." I ate another almond slowly. "Native Americans have called the mountain a few different names. One is *Tahol*, which means 'mother of waters.' It's the highest mountain in the Cascade Range, the highest mountain in the state of Washington. It's filled with all sorts of life. The mountain has two volcanic craters, massive glaciers, and a bunch of rivers that originate from those glaciers. That one mountain gives life to so many different species of plants and flowers . . ." I trailed off. "Sorry. You can probably tell I haven't talked to many people lately."

Jim was folding the chocolate bar wrapper into an intricate shape. "What are you hoping to find when you reach it?" he asked, glancing up at me with curiosity.

I let the question hang in the still night air for a few beats. How could I put it into words? I could say something lame like, "I'm hoping to find myself." But that wasn't right. I knew who I was already, I just struggled to still be that person. I was hoping for a reintroduction between me and my old self. But that felt like too small a reason for this undertaking. I was out here to find purpose beyond myself, whatever version of me that might be.

"I'm hoping to find sense in my life's story," I answered honestly. "And hoping the next chapter will be illuminated. So many life-giving things originate at Mount Rainier. You can trace the patterns of streams turning into rivers all down the face of that mountain. And seeing it all from such an angle puts everything in perspective. So maybe I'm looking for some perspective in my story."

Leslie shot me a look. "You think of your life as a story?"

I shrugged. "Don't you?"

She laughed without humor. "Nope, can't say I do."

"Maybe it's stupid," I admitted, "but I really do see everyone's life as a story. I spend most of my time stuck in daydreams, stories playing all day in my head. That way everything has meaning."

"I'm stuck in my head most days too," Jim said, nodding. "It's better than the real world sometimes. More things make sense when you can turn them into stories."

I nodded back.

Leslie rolled her eyes. "So that's why you're never listening to me, huh?" she said to Jim. "You're too busy running around in that head of yours, playing make believe?"

Jim and I shared a small shrug of the misunderstood. I felt my heart warm. "Maybe you just need to find more interesting things to say, ever think of that?" Jim replied as he zipped open his sleeping bag.

"Oh, you're a real funny guy, huh? I'm sure your make-believe friends or whatever think you're a real riot."

Jim chuckled softly as he turned away from us. "G'night, ladies."

"Night, Jim," I responded while scooting into my own sleeping bag. The grass below me was soft and forgiving. The sky above me was obscured by a halo of light from a nearby streetlamp. The soft conversations of passing park-goers mixed into the far-off melody of traffic, inviting my eyes to close and my tired body to relax. In the warm, hazy moment right before falling into sleep, I took stock of my life and found it a little bit fuller.

I woke in the pale gray light of early morning. I snuck off to the nearest breakfast place and bought Leslie and Jim a couple of breakfast sandwiches each and coffee drinks that sounded fancy, but I honestly had no idea if they'd be good. I dropped their breakfast off where they were still sleeping, Jim snoring softly. The offering looked pitiful considering everything they had done for me. Without a second thought, I took out my sister's painting of Mount Rainier and placed it under the bag of food. It was the most valuable thing I had to offer, and I hoped it carried the weight of my gratitude.

I walked with renewed purpose through the drowsy city. We had come here for Alex's twenty-first birthday. The city had been so full of promise then. I remember I could almost feel its energy in the sidewalk beneath my feet as we held on to each other all the way back to the hotel. The streets we walked down had seen horror and heartbreak, famine and failure. But the city always came back stronger. I thought

I had felt the resiliency in the very pulse of the city, and it seemed to match our own heartbeats.

I'd been so stupid.

What did I have back then to feel resilience toward? I had no idea what resilience even looked like. But now I knew, and I knew I had never been resilient toward anything in my entire life. If I focused, I could still feel it in the city, its breath. In and out. In and out. But it didn't match my breath.

I glanced at women my age as they passed me on their way to work in giant office buildings with stunning views. Their heels clicked and their slimming blouses caught the first rays of sun. They were all beautiful. Resilient and strong and beautiful. They all had such bright futures that they would earn, and their stories would be told and remembered.

I began gasping for air. No, not today. I would not let myself sink today.

12

Dear Alex,

Check it out! I made it to Chicago! And I only passed out once. Not bad, right? How cool is it I was able to find this postcard of the 1893 Columbian Exposition right here in Chicago?? Anyway, could you imagine watching the first ever Ferris wheel being built? Or seeing millions of electric lights for the first time ever? People have lost far too much of their sense of wonder. If I sound like an eighty-five-year-old woman, GOOD. Those old ladies know a thing or two.

I decided to be an adult and not starve to death on this hike, so I bought real food! I know that may sound surprising since I still hold the unofficial record for the most Cosmik Fries eaten at HopCat, but trust me, for current Mel this is a big deal. So we can cross starvation off the list of things that might kill me, but we should probably add blisters to the list because I'm pretty sure a few of the ones *on my feet have grown large enough to kill. I know, attractive as always.*

And as always, I hope you're well and thriving.

Love,
Mel

Sleeping in the wilderness wasn't as bad as I expected.

After leaving Chicago, I found my way to the American Discovery Trail, giving my map-reading skills a figurative high five this time around when I did so. The plan was to take the ADT until I could cut north and meet up with the Ice Age Trail. That would take me through Wisconsin until I found the North Country Trail.

I was happy to find that, for the most part, the trail was flat, well-marked, and well-maintained. The land had been shaped by glaciers, the informational signs along the way told me. The massive hunks of ice had left smooth earth and fertile soil in their wake. The great midwestern prairie unfurled around me, interrupted only by the occasional blue heron or flash of dazzling sunlight off the surface of the nearby Illinois River. The path before me would be paved one day, dirt the next. But the expanse of clear sky above my head was nearly constant. There had been the rare misty rain shower that passed within minutes, but other than that the sky had been a solid, cotton candy blue.

The new groceries had been doing their job of keeping me alive and walking. I counted my ribs several times a day and tapped my hip bones with my fists to make sure they were still as sharp as before. At the end of each day, as the light began to fade, I would set up camp and carefully measure out the remaining calories I needed for the day. I would slowly eat my handful of almonds or can of tuna as the dome of sky and prairie grasses darkened above and around me. The ritual of coming to rest each day in step with the natural world had a calming effect, one I started to look forward to.

The layers of dirt and sweat covering my body grew steadily throughout each day. I had stopped being able to smell myself a day or so back, which was a kind mercy. My sunburns had thankfully begun to morph into a tan, but I figured it was still safe to assume a skin cancer diagnosis was in my future. My blisters had blisters, which made me walk with a limp for the first mile or so after each rest. A kind hiker had walked by when I was peeling off my socks, and he offered me some duct tape for blister prevention. My feet would never be the same, but at least the duct tape had stopped them from getting much worse. Also, six out of ten toenails had turned black.

My back still ached when I took off my pack at night. I could feel the soreness of the previous day's hike deep in my bones when I woke every morning. But each day, the pain lessened a minuscule amount. Just enough to make me feel a jolt of pride in this body I was trapped in.

The strangest, most surprising part of the last few weeks on the trail was the silence. I thought I knew silence when I lived alone in that basement apartment, but it was nothing like this. Days would go by, and I would pass only a handful of people or a quiet community whose few residents wanted even less to do with me than I did with them. Other than the hiker with the duct tape, I never exchanged more than a quick "hello" or "good morning" with anyone I encountered. When my phone died and I no longer had music as an escape, I would count my breaths to keep my mind occupied.

I don't know if the realization happened slowly or all at once, but the relentless quiet morphed into the sounds of an Illinois prairie all around me. I hadn't paid them any attention before. They weren't the roaring city sounds I was used to. These sounds didn't belong to the modern world. Each day, I found my mind and body a little more in tune with the noises around me. The crickets harmonizing, the grasses whispering with a gentle breeze, a heron's wings brushing the surface of the river. It all blended into background music. Sometimes I would even catch myself humming along.

I remembered reading once how we are constantly surrounded by God's Spirit. It's like our breath, a flame, the wind, a womb. It permeates every part of the human existence, and to be a witness to it, all we need to do is *pay attention*.

To have that kind of connection to God . . . to feel Him as close as the air in my lungs instead of a distant figure beckoning to follow and obey was as unimaginable as me waking up the next morning and polishing off a stack of chocolate chip pancakes. Besides, even if I could imagine it, paying attention to anything other than the calories eaten versus calories burned hadn't been something I was capable of for what seemed like centuries. I forced myself to focus, not on the Spirit of God that was apparently all around me but on the days that stretched out before me.

As the great midwestern prairie morphed into a landscape of sandstone canyons, waterfalls, and the deep pockets cast by trees, I began to be able to work through thoughts with such clarity it startled me. There were even moments where I could tell myself, in the crystal clear voice of my conscience, that the numbers on a scale meant nothing. That the world was this endless treasure hunt of hidden places and sun-dappled woods, but I was too busy spending my life staring down at a scale to notice. I would try to hold on to those beautiful moments with a death grip, but they always managed to slip away. I would discuss these moments of clarity with my one and only constant companion, hunger. Hunger wasn't much for conversation though, besides the normal rumblings.

I set up camp one night at a crossroads. Soon, I would be venturing off the ADT to follow a hodgepodge of trails north to Wisconsin. The days tended to blend together out here, and I felt a little shocked at how far I had already come. Although the word *overwhelmed* came to mind when I thought of how far I still had to go. It didn't help that I had chosen to camp in Starved Rock State Park. Whether the hollowed-out canyons were meant to represent all I was leaving behind or foreshadow what lay ahead, I wasn't sure.

To avoid detection from state park employees who might enforce the twenty-dollar camping fee, I walked past the waterfalls and gaping canyons carved from glaciers to reach a secluded spot near the river. The Illinois River had become my hiking buddy, and I wasn't sure how I would sleep without its lullaby. As dusk seeped into the woods and I slowly picked through twenty stale almonds for my dinner by the light of the rising moon, my mind drifted to my favorite game. I would imagine food I would never eat but could still vividly remember tasting. I played this game constantly, imagining every detail, every second of the experience.

Lately, the food of choice had been LAY'S Classic Potato Chips. The pop of the bag when it was first opened. The rich, salty smell that would reach me and immediately make my mouth water every time. Peeking inside, I would see golden slices of sunshine nestled happily together in delicate layers. So many to choose from, the land of plenty all in one bag. I'd reach in and carefully select a wish chip, folded in half to make a perfect, satisfying crunch. As soon as the salt and the oil touched my tongue, something almost primal in me relaxed, satisfied. The crunch was so crisp, like the sound of dried leaves underfoot on the sidewalk come late fall. I could almost feel the oil and salt left behind on my fingertips as I imagined myself reaching back into the bag for another, this time with slightly less-contained urgency.

LAY'S potato chips had been a camping food. My mom never allowed them in the house, but they were always packed in the car on camping trips with Dad.

So in this particular food-obsessed daydream, I would be sitting on the hard, unyielding surface of a picnic table bench while, beside me, my sister stuck the inaugural hot dog of the annual camping trip onto a pronged skewer. She did this with such care and concentration—her edible work of art. In front of me, my dad fed the fire cautiously, daring it not to go out now that the flames licked the rusty grate. He would walk over to me, eyes still on the fire, looking away only long enough to register the open yellow bag in my lap.

"Oh man," he'd say, cupping his hands in front of me, "pour me some of those." And I would oblige. They served as his trophy for building the roaring fire before us. He would sit next to me with a sigh of satisfaction. Above us, a billion stars. A million galaxies. We would watch the fire dance.

"Not a bad fire, huh?" he would say between crunches. I would eat another chip, listening to the symphony as the wood snapped and hissed and crackled. I would tell him that it was the best fire I had ever seen. And I would mean it.

All that from LAY'S potato chips.

I popped an almond into my mouth and gazed up at the trees, trying to imagine I was back around that campfire. Over the past few days, my dad starred in most of my resurfaced memories. Everything about the woods reminded me of him, and despite trying hard not to, I missed him terribly. He taught me everything I knew about navigation, charting the stars, and surviving in the wilderness.

Whenever I would walk through the woods by his side, our surroundings became larger than life. It was a talent he seemed to possess. Everything became brighter and grander when he walked into a room. He brought out the best versions of people without effort.

Whenever I was driving my mom crazy, he would use whatever free time he could spare to take me out to a network of trails near our house and we would walk for hours.

"Places like these are where you can let your imagination run wild," he would tell me, gesturing at the endless expanse of trees. "Maybe not at night though. Might end up scaring yourself to death if you don't rein in that imagination of yours once the sun goes down."

He had been right too. The first few days on this trail I had occupied my time imagining I was fleeing a medieval dungeon after being tortured for crimes I didn't commit. I was making my way through the woods to be reunited with my true love, who had promised to come to our field of clover every day until I returned. But at night, the once-friendly trees turned to shadow men and every twitch of the wind was some spirit coming to steal my soul.

After a while I didn't have the energy to fear the darkness.

With half of my dinner almonds eaten, I wrangled my sleeping bag from my backpack and looked past the treetops to the bruised evening sky. I'd be able to see a million stars tonight, and it was because of my dad that I'd know many of their names.

He wasn't all perfect. It's something a person can't help but realize once they get older.

I've heard others say things like, "I finally started to see my parents as flawed people. It made them so much more relatable."

But I didn't need my father to be relatable. I needed him to be my guiding light. I needed to believe it was possible to be accepted by such an incredible person, because didn't that mean I could also be incredible? Beyond that, my father had been my shining example that there was more than one way to earn the love of God.

I spread out my sleeping bag on the soft earth and lined up my remaining ten almonds in a neat little row in front of me. Just me and the river and ten of the world's stalest almonds. Not the traditional American family meal, but I was used to that. Most family dinners during my childhood ended up as theological debates between my dad and me with Claire playing the role of cheerleader for whatever side seemed to be winning. My mom played the role of the seen-but-not-heard housewife perfectly and would often excuse herself to clean up the kitchen.

Our dinner discussions were so formative that when I took debate classes in high school, I was shocked to learn that most people didn't know how to form a solid argument. More than one teacher tried to recruit me for the debate team, but I always declined. I had plenty of practice at home already.

Popping almond number eleven into my mouth, I unlaced my boots, stripped off my horrendous socks, and headed down to the river. It was probably good all the light had nearly faded so I couldn't see the monstrosities my feet had become. Honestly, they were probably more blister than foot at this point.

Standing calf-deep in the icy water, I looked up at the moon and held as still as possible for as long as my body would allow.

When I was younger, my dad made me believe we could debate and still love God. We could question and doubt, yet still receive His love. But when the real fights began to break out between my mom and me, suddenly arguing was not allowed. "She's your mother," Dad would so often begin as a way to shut down an argument. "It is your place to honor her."

The debating, the constructive arguments . . . Apparently they held no real weight. At the end of it all, my mom's word was law. And since her word never wavered, did that mean I wasn't eligible for God's acceptance if I *did* waver?

Even the core of my dad's goodness shifted in my eyes as I grew older. When my dad wasn't fiercely arguing, he used that wellspring of fierceness to fight for the marginalized. The nonprofit he had helped start once he returned from the Grand Canyon had been one of the most successful homeless outreach and assistance programs in the state. There was always another person who needed help, another soul to save from the streets.

I couldn't exactly voice my sadness that my dad spent more time helping the marginalized than his not-so-marginalized daughter, but that didn't stop me from feeling it. And then I would hate myself for feeling sad when I actually had a dad who loved me and kept a roof over my head and helped the homeless. I would wonder what it was that allowed him to keep his drive, to keep his passion burning bright every day. I would vow to ask him, then realize I wouldn't see him for days. And the whole maddening cycle would start over again.

Standing there in the pale moonlight, I shivered. I wondered how many shooting stars I'd have to see tonight to make my dad appear back at my campsite.

It was hard when the parent who understood me wasn't always around. My mother had stopped trying, and Claire, although kind, often viewed my choices with something between admiration and bewilderment. But my dad was different. He would see my differences and love me even more for them.

At least, he did once. I didn't know how he felt about me now. A deep silence had stretched between us for years, nothing more connecting us than the few obligatory surface questions: How've you been, how's work, how's the weather. I knew deep in my heart that the silence meant he was embarrassed at how far I'd fallen.

Trudging back to my sleeping bag and the last of my dinner, I was transported back to the last camping trip my dad and I took before they left for Uganda. It was on the two-mile trek out to Nordhouse Dunes that he stopped abruptly. I ran into him, but his steady arm caught me right before I hit the forest floor.

"Are you okay?" I asked. "Why'd you stop? Oh no, we didn't forget the chips, did we?"

He smirked and patted the tote bag he carried. "Don't you think I'd be sprinting back to the car right now if I had?"

"Fair enough. So what is it? Finally too old to make this hike without resting?"

He tousled my hair, completely ruining the ponytail that took me all of twenty seconds to tie up. Then he draped an arm around my shoulders and gestured toward the trees.

"Do you know why immersing ourselves in nature is so important?" he asked.

"Because it stops us from becoming mindless zombies who stare at screens all day?" I guessed.

"Because it reconnects us to our true selves. It strips away the stresses and strains of the civilized world."

Nowadays, I was Starved Rock. I had become the echoing canyon, empty and hollowed out. Nothing but negative space. Maybe that's how he saw me now as well. But maybe that could change. Maybe one day I would see myself as the Illinois River, sparkling and roaring and full of life. And then, maybe, he'd see me as the river too.

I could do it, Dad. I could turn back into a river for you. No more minimum-wage job. No more sleepwalking through life. I'm going to be great, just like you always knew I could be. One day after this is all over, we'll sit down together and I'll tell you all about this. And you'll look at me like you did when you first saw the Grand Canyon, and we'll both know that I finally made it.

13

Dear Alex,

I made it to Madison yesterday! Can you believe it's the farthest west I've ever ventured? Until tomorrow, probably. This place is known for its domed state capitol building (as shown). It looks the same today despite the sepia-tone of the postcard. I'm starting to believe it's not actually vintage . . . It's also famous for being on the less-impressive side of Lake Michigan and hosting a nauseating amount of Midwest charm. At least seven people have said "good morning" to me already, which is really saying something about the over whelming politeness of these people because I look like I crawled out of the sewer and have a fierce hunger for human brains. It's the sort of environment in which we were raised to believe the American Dream flourished. Places like these are deep in our roots, but this was never the sort of life we wanted, was it? A life so comfortable, so familiar that it *becomes stifling? I still imagine what that life we dreamed up would look like. It makes me feel so many things, but it mostly makes me feel alive. I'm sorry every day I couldn't be what we imagined.*

Love,
Mel

I looked at the sepia-toned postcard for a long time before tucking it into the pocket of my backpack beside the others. The day was growing warmer, so I courageously rolled up my sleeves to the elbow before rummaging through the largest section of my backpack for my lunch.

It was lucky I had arrived in Madison when I did, because my food supplies were nearly spent by the time I saw the dome of the capitol building. The last few days I knew I was only eating about half the calories I needed, and I had begun to feel that familiar exhaustion settle in my bones. I covered fewer miles and could feel my heart pound and race more than usual.

And, of course, I had mixed feelings about the whole thing. On one hand, I had been reintroduced to the solid, steady comfort that accompanied a body well cared for. A body that radiated strength instead of exhaustion. When I started cutting my calories, the swell of energy that coursed through me every time I climbed a hill vanished. I missed the dull, hard-earned ache in my muscles when I woke instead to the sharp, concerning pain in my stomach and bones. I missed the feeling that my daily hikes left me full instead of empty.

But at the same time, I felt the sting of excitement whenever I easily counted my ribs. When the sharpness of my hips felt like they would slice right through my skin. I felt a thrill when I imagined I could almost feel the pounds melting off of me with each mile.

I knew in no time at all, the dark and twisted part of my brain would fully take over again like a virus, eating away at all the goodness I had absorbed in the midwestern prairie grasses and through the waters of Wisconsin's glacial lakes. So as soon as I found a grocery store, I practically sprinted inside before I could talk myself out of it.

Afterward, I wandered onto the University of Wisconsin's campus. I thought I might attract less attention with my giant backpack and disgusting clothes (college students had more important things to worry about than laundry). After a bit of exploring, I found myself on The Terrace—a welcoming little patio space with brightly colored chairs and tables facing a lake. Only a few people milled about since it was a weekday at the beginning of summer break, so I happily claimed the table closest to the water.

I pulled out the vegan burrito bowl I had bought from the Qdoba next to the grocery store. It had been a while since I had food that didn't come in a wrapper or a bag and was above room temperature, so it made sense that when I popped open the lid, the smell of cooked food hit me with such a force I audibly groaned from impact.

I hadn't eaten at a restaurant in close to six months, but before I went cold turkey, I would still occasionally visit places like Qdoba, where customers could keep a very close eye on exactly what was being put in their meal and nutrition facts were readily available. I knew I wasn't anywhere near close to being able to calmly walk into a restaurant where I hadn't thoroughly researched the menu ahead of time, but maybe if I worked my way backward I would one day be able to walk through any old eatery establishment like a normal person.

I mixed together the beans, brown rice, and vegetables with reverence, barely able to contain myself from inhaling it all Cookie Monster–style. When the pink-haired girl behind the counter had asked if I wanted guacamole, I hesitated so long and stared so intensely at the bright-green vat of mashed avocado I think I scared her. Eventually, I asked for it on the side.

Now I opened the lid on the tiny container cautiously. Sometimes I could satisfy my urge to eat something simply by smelling it. Unfortunately, that tactic didn't work with guacamole. The bright green mash gazed up at me expectantly, almost begging me to give its life purpose by enhancing my burrito bowl.

I really needed to eat something.

I did the math in my head. I'd had only an apple for breakfast. If I added the guac now, I could cut back on dinner and therefore save more food for the road. I would still be well below my calorie limit, even with the predicted decrease in mileage today.

I nodded to myself, convinced, and tried to serenely scoop out the guacamole. I wanted to give off the air of someone who eats burrito bowls all the time and not someone who just escaped a bunker.

Eat slow, give your body time to process the calories. Stop when you're full. Don't overeat.

I took my first bite and everything around me ceased to

exist for a second. Starving myself would be much easier if food didn't taste this good. The flavor brought back memories of summer nights and backyard patios. I thought for a second I might cry but decided to take another bite instead.

I ate as slowly as I could, trying to focus on my surroundings to distract me from the miracle of beans and rice in front of me.

I watched a few seagulls swoop and dive over the water. For some reason I couldn't put my finger on, watching them made me miss my mom with a sudden fierceness. Since I couldn't be trusted not to cry over a burrito bowl, let alone my own mother, I looked for another distraction.

My gaze was drawn to an older couple standing along the water's edge. The sound of their bickering caused others to look up as well. The man was holding a map and wildly pointing out toward the lake while the woman (not nearly as thin as me—at least forty pounds heavier) shook her head and also gestured forcefully at the lake. I stared too long, and the woman caught my eye before I could duck my head in embarrassment.

"Excuse me? Excuse me!" To my horror, she was coming closer with a series of purposeful strides. I opened my mouth to spew some nonsense explanation for my stares when she reached my table and put her hands on her hips.

"Um, I'm really sor—"

"You look like you know your way around here," she interrupted, looking me up and down with narrowed eyes. I knew I had a skewed perception of my appearance, but I had no idea what she could have possibly seen to make her believe I was an expert on anything. "Can you please tell my husband that"—she pointed to the body of water to our right—"is *not* Lake Michigan?"

I glanced over at the lake and cleared my throat self-consciously. The woman's husband was walking toward us like he was approaching his own execution.

"Um, no. That's not Lake Michigan. That's Lake Mendota." I weakly gestured toward a sign near where they had just been standing. "At least, that's what it says on the sign."

The woman threw her hands up in victory. "I *told* you. We're at the wrong lake! I knew it was supposed to be bigger than this. That's why I'm in charge of directions."

"All right, all right." The man huffed. "Must've read the map wrong. Looked like a big enough lake to me."

The woman rolled her eyes. "He's not as clueless as he sounds," she said to me. "He never actually believed this was the lake. He's hungry and would rather get lunch than keep looking for the right one."

The man accepted this with a shrug and surprised me by pulling out a chair at my table and easing into it with a sigh. "I'd be much better at finding lakes with that chicken salad sandwich in my belly."

The woman gave in with a dramatic groan and also took a seat at the table. Self-consciously, I pulled my own food a little closer to me. My body tensed for them to say anything about the size or contents of my meal, but they only had eyes for the chicken salad sandwiches the woman pulled from her backpack. She neatly laid out two sandwiches before her and her husband, along with a bag of chips and two Diet Cokes. The man took a gigantic bite of the sandwich and fell back into his seat, eyes closed.

"You sure do make the best sandwiches, Linnie."

She snorted, but something in her face softened. She turned to me. "This isn't the first time George has acted dumb in the name of lunch. I should know the signs better by now, considering we've been married fifty years. But all the man needs to be happy is a good sandwich, so it's not like I can complain."

"Fifty years?" Together for fifty years. I couldn't even imagine what being alive for fifty years would feel like, let alone fifty years with someone else beside me.

She put her grievances with her husband aside long enough to beam at me. "Yes." Celebrated our fiftieth back in April. This is our trip to celebrate. Well, it's supposed to be. We haven't gotten very far."

"Where are you headed" I asked before taking a tentative bite of my food. Neither of them said anything about my meal or my appetite. Still, I continued to eat with caution.

"To all five of the Great Lakes," George answered, his mouth full. "We heard they're really something to see. We're from South Dakota. Not much to see there."

I smiled, warming to these two already. "I don't think you'll be disappointed. The Great Lakes are incredible. On some of the beaches, you'll think you've stumbled upon the ocean. I think the lakes are even better than the ocean, personally. No sharks or salt to bother you."

Linnie put down her barely nibbled sandwich and turned to me. "I hate the beach, but that's what our friends back home said. They said the Great Lakes have all the good parts about the beach and none of the bad. I don't believe it myself, but George has been dying to see them. I chose our last three national parks to visit, so it's only fair he got to choose this trip."

George had finished his sandwich and was eyeing Linnie's hungrily. She handed him half, and he kissed her on the cheek before accepting.

"Well, the farther north you go, the more beautiful they are, in my opinion," I said, closing the lid on my half-finished lunch.

"How many have you been to?" Linnie asked.

"Only Michigan and Superior. But Lake Michigan is completely different up in Northern Michigan than it is in Southern Michigan. Plus, there are way more shipwrecks to learn about the farther north you go, which I can never resist. Nearly every tiny Northern Michigan town has a shipwreck tour or museum to visit. I swear I've done every tour and visited every museum at least twice."

Linnie raised her eyebrows and grinned. "Got a thing for morbid stories, huh?"

I shrugged. "It's only a little weird. I have yet to murder a sea captain or anything."

Linnie tossed her head back and laughed wildly. I smiled.

"George, we're sticking with this girl for a while. I want to hear more about these shipwrecks. Finally, something about these darn lakes that sounds interesting."

"Fine with me," George said, polishing off the last of the sandwich. "We've got nothing but time."

Linnie snorted. "Not at our age, we don't." She opened her bag of chips and motioned her head toward the building behind us. "Are you a student here?"

I shook my head, wondering if they had somehow miraculously not smelled me by now or were only being polite. "No, I'm from Grand Rapids, Michigan. I'm just passing through."

"On foot, by the looks of it," George commented, balling up his already-empty chip bag.

Linnie shot him a look. "George, where do you get these ideas? Why in the world would a young girl like her walk here?"

George shrugged. "Maybe she likes walking, but she sure doesn't look like she drove here."

"George! What in the world—"

"He's right, actually," I interjected, afraid Linnie was seconds away from launching across the table at her husband. "The reason was more like I didn't have a car or money to fly, but I do like walking."

I caught a smirk cross George's face before he brought the Coke bottle to his lips. "Told you," he said, satisfied.

Linnie glowered at him, then turned her menacing expression toward me. "You *walked* here? Do you have any idea how dangerous that is?"

"Linnie, you can't talk to the girl this way. You don't even know her. You don't even know her name!"

Linnie stood, hands on her hips. "I don't need to know her name to know she's being completely irresponsible and foolish!"

I probably would have been offended by this conversation if it weren't so utterly entertaining. I leaned back a bit and watched George and Linnie fight it out. From the short time I'd known them, bickering seemed to be the fuel of their relationship.

"This sounds like what Mikki wanted to do last summer," George argued. "You remember, hike that trail along the Appalachians? And how much good did it do when you told her the same thing you're telling this girl now?"

"A world of good! She was made aware of all the flaws in her plan. My disapproval is what led to her being so prepared! She never would have made it that whole way if I hadn't brought all those issues to her attention. For goodness' sakes, the girl was only planning on taking one pair of socks!"

"And she also didn't talk to you for six months, if I recall."

"That's because she was too busy taking my advice and preparing for the trip. And you can't exactly call up your grandparents in the middle of the wilderness, can you?" Linnie adopted the world-weary look of someone carrying the burden of being right all the time. "Well, she could have, because of the emergency tracking phone I took it upon myself to mail to her, but that was only for *emergencies*. She called us as soon as she got back from that hike, and you know what she said to me after you got off the phone?"

"I'm sure you're gonna tell me whether I guess or not," George mumbled.

"She said, 'Grandma, I never got the chance to thank you. Without your advice, I never would've made it to the end of that trail. I would've died out there. I'm sorry I didn't listen to you sooner.'"

George gave a huge laugh. "There is no way, no way at all she said that to you, Linnie. You can't tell a lie to save your life."

"Well, she nearly said it! And I know that's how she felt. I could hear it in the tone of her voice!"

"Right, just like you can hear Stella listening in to your conversations with our grandkids?"

"Don't you dare, you've heard the breathing yourself! Just last week you said I was right about that!"

George put his hands up in defense. "I don't think I ever said—"

"Well, I should really get going . . ." I stood awkwardly. "But it was really nice meeting both of you."

Linnie stepped in front of me, arms crossed. "And where do you think you're going?" Despite her temper and her menacing glare, she was about as intimidating as a duckling. "There's no way I'm letting you walk back to Michigan. George and I are heading there soon enough, and you will ride back with us."

"That's very kind of you," I said, trying hard not to laugh. "But I'm actually heading out west. To Washington State. Mount Rainier, to be exact."

Linnie visibly paled and muttered something under her breath that I first thought was a prayer but soon realized was a long, unbroken string of curses.

"Oh boy." Sensing danger, George rose from his chair and took hold of her arm. "Linnie, let's take a breath. Let's try not to get too worked up." He gave me an exasperated look that said, *Now you've done it.*

A half hour later, I found myself in the same seat where we had met, waiting for Linnie and George to finish talking through my situation. I had no idea what kept me glued to this chair. These people had no power over me. I had the freedom to get up and leave whenever I wanted. And yet, here I sat.

I watched the two of them, arguing back and forth in increasingly loud whispers. They seemed to fall into arguments like it was second nature. But instead of making me cringe at the pitfalls of marriage, it held my fascination. There was no hate in their speech. The tone they had with each other wasn't desperate or full of rage because, through each argument, they seemed to know they were ultimately each other's ally. They were two equal partners with differing opinions (on practically everything, it seemed) who would rather talk through it than board up their walls and never discuss it.

Their relationship was startlingly different from my parents'. I could not even begin to imagine what my parents would have to talk about once my sister moved out. Their children had become their common denominator over the years. Only on a handful of occasions could I remember them discussing anything else. Truth be told, it would be perfectly normal if they went an entire week without saying anything more than a "good morning" and "good night" to each other.

My mom's interests were being a homemaker and following the Ten Commandments without question. My dad's interests were debating the Ten Commandments and anything outside the home. I predicted coldness and distance in their future.

Finally, Linnie and George came back to the table. Linnie's expression was still stormy, but at least she looked less pale.

"Okay, here's the agreement we settled on," George said. I marveled at the fact that I was in no way involved in the creation of this agreement. "You'll come back with us to our hotel for the night. We've got a nice room at the Hilton with double beds. You can shower if you'd like, and we'll take you to get a new set of clothes and some extra supplies you'll need for your journey. After a good night's sleep, we'll let you continue on your way."

He paused for a breath or dramatic effect, I wasn't sure which. "In exchange, you will join us for dinner tonight, and we will have a discussion to make sure you have thought this whole plan through. Linnie will most likely be leading this discussion. Do we have a deal?"

I shook my head. "I'm not looking for any charity. I'm fine with the supplies I have."

George considered me and sighed. "Young lady, I don't think you realize what bad shape you're in."

I burned with shame for a second until I realized he wasn't talking about physical fitness, just my overall state. I could live with that. All my favorite heroines wore worn and dirty clothes and could have probably used a shower.

"If you want to make it to Washington, you're gonna need better supplies. No way around it. That cotton sweatshirt of yours and those shoes won't get you to Minnesota, even. If you want to make it, you'll accept our charity. Plus, if you don't"—George gestured toward Linnie—"frankly, you'll break the poor woman's heart."

I glanced at the two of them. They looked like they were plucked straight from a 1990s travel brochure, complete with polo shirts, midcalf socks, visors, and fanny packs. I almost laughed at the absurdity of this whole situation. *I could shrug this off and walk away*, I thought. But even though I didn't expect to find impromptu parental figures in Madison, Wisconsin, here they were. And I couldn't say I hated it.

"All right," I said, nodding. "Deal."

"So . . . you're from Grand Rapids." George said this with an air of extreme caution. He was probably afraid to hear me confess some other life-threatening activities I was involved in that would surely give his wife a heart attack.

We were in a low-lit, comfortable corner of a local brewery. It was the beginning of the dinner rush, and by the looks of the constant stream of people shuffling through the door, we were lucky to have gotten a table. George had hardly been able to contain his excitement about this place.

"Great reviews on Tripadvisor—says they have the best burger around. And you should see the fries. They looked seasoned in the photos, which always takes them to a whole new level."

"Sometimes I think this is more of a tour of Midwest breweries than a tour of the Great Lakes," Linnie commented with a raise of an eyebrow.

George had shrugged. "Who says it can't be both?"

I was sitting across from them, hiding behind my menu. Another meal out had not been the plan today. The menu didn't provide nutrition information, although I could guess how many calories most of the menu items contained, and it was enough to make my stomach flip.

Breweries especially made me uncomfortable. They tended to favor fried foods and massive portions. Plus, the nutrition information was never available. I glanced around quickly to judge the weight of everyone sitting around me. Ninety percent were overweight, and everyone weighed more than me. That didn't make me relax though. They probably became so overweight from eating at this very place. Just like I was about to do . . .

And to think I used to love going out to eat. A night at a brewery with Alex and friends had once felt like the most natural and comfortable thing in the world. Now I wasn't even comfortable in my own skin and especially not in a place like this.

It had also been in the plan to walk at least six more miles today, but all the steps I had taken were from running up and down the seven flights of stairs to George and Linnie's hotel room a few times (I told them I had a pathological fear of elevators), strolling through the local REI as they shopped for my supplies, and walking approximately a mile total to get to and from the shore of Lake Michigan. We eventually found the Great Lake after George and Linnie realized they mixed up their Wisconsin cities and the three of us took a quick road trip an hour and a half east to Milwaukee. At the sight of the water, George whistled lowly and offered an appreciative "Well, look at that." Apparently, that meant he was wildly impressed.

I tried not to fidget in my seat like a five-year-old. This was not the plan. If I wasn't very careful and didn't think of something to make up for the lack of exercise, it was completely plausible I could gain at least five pounds tonight.

No, it was not plausible. Not even possible. *You* know *this.*

But did I really want to take that risk?

From snares of the devil, from temptations of vices, from everyone who desires me ill . . . I played another few lines from Saint Patrick's prayer in my head while counting my ribs behind the giant menu. It didn't have quite the calming effect I was hoping for.

I tried to take a steady breath and lowered the menu a bit. To my surprise, I found George and Linnie staring at me. Had I been thinking out loud? Did they catch a glimpse of my insanity?

"Is something wrong?" I asked.

"No, no. I was just asking about you being from Grand Rapids. Not even asking, really, only stating a fact . . ." George trailed off.

"Oh! Yes, sorry. I think I zoned out for a second there. Absorbed in the menu. Man, how will I ever choose?" I gave an awkward, high-pitched laugh. "But yes, I'm from Grand Rapids. Born and raised. This is actually the farthest west I've ever been."

I glanced back down at my menu and caught sight of a word near and dear to my twisted heart: *salads*.

Thank God.

"And what exactly caused you to pack up and leave?" I could tell Linnie had been waiting to ask this all day. "It can't just be because you have a death wish. You didn't have to walk across the country to fulfill that."

"Linnie . . . We talked about this," George cautioned, resting a hand on her shoulder.

Linnie brushed him off. "George, I've spent the whole day talking to this girl about everything under the sun except this, the whole time thinking, *Well, she actually seems to be a rather interesting, quite intelligent young woman besides that one thing I'm not allowed to talk to her about.* We agreed I could bring it up at dinner. I've done my part. We're at dinner. So it's time for me to say my piece."

The server returned with our drinks before she could begin. By the time the server had finished handing George his craft beer and me my glass of water, Linnie had polished off almost her entire glass of wine.

"Keep them coming, my friend," she said to our unimpressed server. I had a feeling he had seen one too many wine-happy seniors in his time.

I took the opportunity to return to my menu. I landed on the garden salad (I could pick out the croutons and, of course, ask for dressing on the side) and a side of vegetable soup. I felt like the soup added enough to avoid suspicion, but still minimal calories so I could stay below my limit for the day.

A realization came to me as I remembered something I had passed in the hotel lobby. A gym. With treadmills. I relaxed instantly. After George and Linnie went to bed, I would sneak down to the lobby and get a solid six-mile run in. Maybe seven, just to be safe. That would get me back on track. I smiled with relief.

"This isn't funny, Mel!" Linnie nearly yelled, causing me to jump. "This is a very dangerous thing you have chosen to do. Do your parents even know you're out here?"

"My parents are in Uganda. And I'm twenty-four, Linnie. I've been making my own decisions and accepting the consequences of those decisions for years. I appreciate you looking out for me, but this is something I need to do."

Linnie rolled her eyes. "What is it with you millennials and these journeys you feel like you have to take? Life itself is enough of a journey. What you *need* is to buckle down, get a job, raise a family, and along the way you figure everything else out. You're not going to find out anything worthwhile when you remove yourself from the real world."

"I'm not some freeloader who's never had a job in her life," I shot back, feeling my anger rise for the first time that day. "I've done everything from scrubbing toilets to compiling reports to asking, 'Do you want fries with that?' I had my future planned out, I had dreams of raising a family, and I had someone to dream with. But all that left me with was proof that I'm the biggest screwup that ever existed." I set my menu down on the table.

"I've been reminded time and time again that I'm not worthy of that future family or even a crappy minimum-wage job flipping burgers. So yes, Linnie, I need to do this. I need to prove to God and anyone else who might still care that I'm worth something. And I'm sorry, but nothing you can say is going to change my mind."

Linnie was silent for a moment. I realized I had been talking louder than I intended.

"You're not at all prepared," Linnie ventured weakly.

I smiled. "Can't use that argument anymore, I'm afraid. Not after all the gear you bought me."

George put an arm around her. "Sounds like she has to do this, hon."

Linnie looked down at her glass for a long moment, then suddenly leaned over to rummage through her purse.

She pulled out a pen, and on her napkin she wrote an address and three phone numbers in neat, purposeful handwriting. She slid the napkin across the table to me.

"That's our home address, each of our cell phone numbers, and our home phone. I don't know exactly how long we'll be gone, but our daughter is staying at our house while we're traveling. If you find yourself in trouble, call us. If you can't call us, send a letter to our home address. Our daughter will let us know when it arrives, and we'll come to help you, whatever you need." She took a deep breath. "You may feel like you have to do this, but you don't have to do it completely alone."

I folded the napkin with great care and tucked it into the pocket of my new lightweight jacket. It was more of a symbolic gesture. I'd create a new contact in my phone after dinner since there was no way I wasn't going to lose that napkin. "I'll remember that," I said, feeling a surge of love for the two strangers who sat across from me. "Thank you."

"Well," Linnie cleared her throat and straightened. "Now that that's behind us, let's talk shipwrecks."

I grinned and pulled up YouTube on my fully charged phone. It felt strange to know the time and date again.

"Ever heard the song 'The Wreck of the Edmund Fitzgerald'? Because you really don't know the depths of a Great Lakes shipwreck until you've heard it. No pun intended."

14

SOMETIME IN EARLY JUNE

Dear Alex,

Why is this written on a postcard advertising Milwaukee, you ask? If you know anything about Wisconsin geography, you'll know that Milwaukee is not in the right direction. Well, it just so happened I got myself stuck in the middle of an argument between a husband and wife who've been married for fifty years, and four hours later, I was traveling with them to Milwaukee in the back seat of their rental car. This was after they bought me new hiking clothes, boots, socks, a tarp, and the world's smallest tent. Then they continued to bribe me with dinner and tried to talk me out of my trip.

Life's kind of nuts. But it's also better than anything to know there are genuinely good people out there who buy complete strangers dinner and a new pair of socks. I now have their home address and I vowed to visit them one day after I've made it to the West Coast or survived a shipwreck. (We bonded over shipwrecks. It was a whole thing.)

I have a confession: I have this new habit now of barely functioning until I get in my daily allotment of exercise. (It's something I picked up after you left, along with a few other unhealthy habits. Totally not your fault. Just a few more creative ways I like to self-sabotage.) So I snuck down to the hotel gym once they had gone to sleep.

Alex, I ran seven of the fastest, angriest miles I have ever run. I was thinking about their fifty years and how we could have had fifty years if I could have only pulled myself together. That could have been us touring the Great Lakes and breweries. That could have been us looking after random girls trying to walk across the country, bickering the whole time out of love.

I looked at myself in the giant mirrors lining the walls afterward and wondered what you ever saw in me. I know I'm not much to look at now, but I couldn't even see a shadow of what you claimed to adore. I hated every inch of my reflection so fiercely, wishing it had been enough to make you stay. Wishing it was enough to make me not understand you leaving.

Love,
Mel

P. S. Sorry this turned into five postcards instead of one.

"The times they are a-changing."

I read this out loud, staring up at the giant mural of Bob Dylan on the corner of 5th and Hennepin in downtown Minneapolis.

Minneapolis had surprised me. There was art *everywhere*. It filled parks and covered walls and packed museums. There was life in every corner of the city. Every block felt fluid, moving toward something better and bolder.

I had spent a whole day roaming the city. Yesterday had been rainy, and despite my new rain jacket, I didn't feel like starting the next leg of my trip sopping wet. Instead, I passed the day slowly, wandering through any museum with free admission I could find. I spent lifetimes staring at paintings of times gone by, wondering what sort of person I would have turned out to be if my story belonged to a different century. I let the art fill me up with senses of longing and desire and bravery and destiny, created from stories that didn't belong to me, but settled in my heart all the same. It was so wonderful, almost cleansing, to be full of feeling again, even for a few short hours.

I had been planning on stopping by Saint Paul before continuing west, when the mural caught my eye.

It showed three profiles of Bob Dylan, and in each one he grew older. And although his eyes turned increasingly sad, the colors splashed around him told a different story. I wondered if age had snuck up on him, or if he had felt every second of the process. All that talent, all that glory, and below all of it he was still only a man who let the rise and fall of life leave lingering sadness in his gaze.

I *did* feel like the times were changing. Even just a little. As I stood looking at the mural, I stood tall. I had not arrived in Minneapolis as starved as I did in Madison. Linnie and George had spent a small fortune on the instant meals that fit neatly in my backpack. All I had to do was add water and eat. They were perfect, the calorie count so exact. I would eat half of one at breakfast, the other half at lunch, and a handful of dried fruit and nuts for dinner. Although I had to deal with my muscles growing stronger and more pronounced, I was still able to count all my ribs whenever I checked, wrap a hand around my upper arm, and feel that my hip bones were still sharp as razors. I wasn't fat, I wasn't dying, and I couldn't deny the strength I felt.

My routine on the road had become so familiar that there had been some days when it had even felt comfortable. To the best of my abilities, I was in control of my life. Taking charge and, finally, succeeding. All this, and I hadn't even left the Midwest yet.

"That's not art, you know," I heard a voice say from behind me. I turned around to see a woman leaning against a stroller, staring at the mural with contempt. She looked to be around my age and was, to my horror, possibly even thinner than me. I instantly disliked her.

"Why not?" I asked, curious.

The baby in the stroller let out a gurgling laugh. The woman quieted her with a pacifier.

"A person can't take someone else's words and persona, add a few splashes of color, and call it art. There's no creativity in it. No originality."

I glanced back at the mural. "I heard once that there were no original ideas, just old ideas rearranged and reinvented. Besides," I continued, looking back at her, "I only have two qualifications for art. It has to have required talent, and it has to make me feel something. This mural checks both those boxes."

She shook her head. "You're just like everyone else."

I bristled. That was the second worst thing she could have accused me of. Right behind being called fat.

"Oh, and I'm supposed to think you're different because, what? You're a self-proclaimed art critic? Wow, never met one of those before." My words surprised me. I typically wasn't one for confrontation with strangers.

She just rolled her eyes. "Yeah, because I really care what you think of me."

I stared at her for a second. This girl was unbelievable. Who did she think she was with her loose black tank top, ripped jeans, twig arms, and more piercings than I could count?

Then I had the answer. She wanted to be the one in a million instead of one in millions. She thought she was different, but she was only a slightly more gothic, much more artsy version of me. No wonder I didn't like her.

I crossed my arms. Maybe it was the lack of showers as well as squatting to pee in the woods these past few weeks that had made me forgo all the rules of civilized social interactions and tact.

"I think you do care what I think of you," I told her. "Actually, I know you do. You care about what everyone thinks of you, even though you try your best to act like you don't. You do everything in your power to make yourself unique, then wonder why you don't belong anywhere."

Her only reaction was the ever-so-slight raise of an eyebrow. The baby made the gurgling noise again, but this time she ignored it.

"Yeah, I get it." I held out my hand. "Mel Ellis. Fellow self-proclaimed outcast."

She hesitated, and I understood. I certainly would have hesitated if a dirt-covered stranger who just made some fairly bold statements about my character flaws wanted to shake my hand.

Eventually, she took it. "Jackie Stevenson."

"All right, Jackie," I said after releasing her hand. "If this isn't art, what is? I've been to most of the art museums around here, but I have a feeling you don't approve of that 'art' either."

"Absolutely. Most of the art in there is totally sexist and misogynist. None of it paints the world as it truly is. That's my job as an artist, to sketch the world in its most bare form."

"You're an artist?"

"I am."

Of course she was. "What kind of work do you do?" I asked. "You mentioned sketches?"

She eyed me warily, then shrugged. "Yes, I sketch. People, mostly."

"What kind of people?"

She grinned wickedly. This girl was a weird one, that was for sure. "The worst kind. I was actually on my way to get a few hours of sketching in." She looked me up and down, sizing me up. "Come with me, and I'll show you."

"Um . . . I really should be going . . ."

She raised an eyebrow, looking at my clothes. "Where? On a camping trip or something?"

"No, not exactly. It's . . . Never mind," I eyed the slate-colored sky. I had been worried about the weather all day, and it appeared only to be worsening.

"Do you sketch inside or outside?"

"Inside."

I turned my attention back to her. "Is it free?"

"What? My art?"

"No, the place where you sketch."

She suddenly did an excellent impersonation of a tortured artist. "Besides the price you pay with your soul, yeah, it's free."

"Geez. Okay. Well, it looks like it might rain again soon, so I guess I could spare a few hours."

Jackie nodded and asked no follow-up questions. She began to push the stroller. "Good. You desperately need exposure to impactful art. Your taste in murals tells me as much."

It was my turn to roll my eyes, but I followed after her all the same. "Has anyone ever told you you're kind of pretentious?"

She shrugged. "Has anyone ever told you that you have terrible taste in fashion?"

I looked down at my dirt-covered, baggy clothes. "Got me there."

She glanced in my direction. "It's not that I don't get the grunge look, I do. It's that none of your clothes have any *shape* to them. There's no flow to your outfit, no personality. It's an important way to reflect your spirit, you know?"

If nothing else, this should be an interesting way to pass the time, I thought reluctantly.

"The Mall of America," I repeated again. I turned to Jackie, who was seated on the bench next to me. She was pulling out her sketch pad and pencils. The life of the mall roared in my ears, bustling and buzzing all around me. I felt like I had to yell to be heard. "Really?"

"Also known as the corrupt heart of America," she replied, flipping to a clean sheet of paper. "You see people for who they are here. If you take the time to look, that is."

People were staring, but I was more or less used to that by now. Something about my shabby clothes, off-putting smell, and backpack that looked like it was about to swallow me whole won me mostly sympathetic-bordering-on-pitying looks. I'd get the rare hostile glare, exactly like the one the guy with the mullet and the sleeveless American flag T-shirt was shooting me now. Like my very existence offended him. But he passed without much more than a sneer, and I did my best to shrug it off. I was getting better at that as my hike wore on. I turned my attention back to Jackie, who was sharpening a pencil with careful and precise effort. I had a feeling I was in the company of someone who also knew what it was like to be stared at.

Before she touched the pencil to paper, the baby started to fuss. Jackie tried the pacifier, but the baby just shook her tiny fists and let out a cry of frustration. Jackie sighed and unclipped the infant from her stroller and abruptly handed her over to me.

"Here," she said, passing me a bottle. "She's hungry. You feed her while I sketch."

"Um . . ."

"It's easy, see? You hold her in your arms like that—"

"No, I know how to feed a baby. I used to take care of my little sister all the time. It's just that . . ."

"What?"

"Nothing. Never mind."

"All right, then."

I held the warm, soft little body close to my own as she drank sleepily from the bottle. Her warmth sank into me as she nestled deeper into the crook of my arm. I sucked in a breath and looked up, trying to break the spell.

We were sitting on the outskirts of a food court and Jackie had zeroed in on a middle-aged couple staring at their phones, two half-eaten plates of Chinese food between them. Silence ensued as Jackie focused on her subjects and I tried not to fall in love with the little human in my arms.

"So, what's her name?" I asked finally, repositioning the baby on my shoulder so I could burp her.

"Who?"

"Your— The baby."

"Oh," she said, not looking up. "She doesn't have one yet."

I studied the baby. She was at least four months old. Far too old to not have a name.

"Why not?"

She looked at me for a fleeting moment, then back at her work. "It's not my place to name her. She should name herself, like I did when I left home. She's her own person. I'm not going to start off our relationship by making that huge decision without her input."

I waited for Jackie to tell me she was joking, but she said nothing more and went back to her sketching.

"So . . . What do you call her in the meantime?"

Jackie sighed, annoyed. "I don't call her anything. If I have to refer to her, I call her the baby. It'll work just fine until she can name herself."

I gave the baby a look that I hoped telepathically said, "*Moms, right?*" She cooed her agreement.

I readjusted the baby, and she began to drift off to sleep. Her long eyelashes brushed her perfectly round, perfectly spotless cheeks. The contrast of her tiny soft body against mine, sharpened by hunger, made me marvel that we were even the same creatures. I was tempted to bring her closer to me so I could smell her head and brush a hand through her soft, fine hair. But I resisted. Not an acceptable thing to do in public with another person's baby.

Unsurprisingly, the warm, soft bundle of pink asleep in my arms brought back a flood of desire to have my own family someday. I had so often dreamed of that future when I had Alex by my side. After he left, I couldn't bring myself to imagine a similar future with someone else in his place. I still couldn't, still stubbornly and stupidly believed he was the only one for me. But I imagined my own baby all the same. One I could cradle in my arms, sing to sleep, love unconditionally. One I could raise to believe she was worth everything to me just for being who she was.

Of course, that future was a long way off. And a significant other wasn't the only thing I was missing. I hadn't had my period in close to six months now. Starvation wasn't kind to the reproductive system, and I had often worried I'd caused damage that would not so easily be undone.

"This one is just about finished for now." Jackie's voice cut through my thoughts. "I'll probably add a few more details once I'm back home, but you get the general idea." She moved closer to me and held out the sketchbook so I could get a better look.

The middle-aged couple were featured in the bottom

right-hand corner of the page. The expressions on their faces, lit up by their phone screens, were a mix of defeat and mindlessness. The uneaten Chinese food sat abandoned between them. The rest of the page was filled with their posts on social media: "Mall day with my love!" "Can't get enough of the Chinese food <3" Their smiles were plastered on, their happiness so filtered I could feel the fakeness even through the black-and-white sketch. There was no doubt about it, Jackie was talented.

"Wow," I said. "You really weren't kidding when you said you were an artist. This is amazing, I mean, it looks just like them, but I don't know . . . more raw. More vulnerable." I peered up at her. "You've met my two criteria. It took talent and it makes me feel something.

"My sister's an artist too, but not like this . . ." I handed the sketchbook back to her. "Congrats, this is officially art in my eyes."

She nodded as if she was affirming everything I had said. She flipped through several previous pages for me to look at. Each one featured a bleak look at humanity. A group of girls making fun of someone trying on clothes, a child in tears being dragged by his mother while she gabbed on her phone, a middle-aged man shoplifting, a woman crying on a bench surrounded by bags and bags of designer clothes. I glanced at Jackie.

"These are all amazing, but they are all so . . . dark. Geez. Are they all like this?"

"Of course. That's what I see when I come here. That's what consumerism does to people. Places like this are ruining our world. They are corrupting us from the outside in." Jackie tapped her pencil against her knee and stared daggers at the mallgoers. "These people need someone to capture their sins in raw form so the darkness they add to society can be exposed."

Yikes. I pursed my lips. "Humanity has its share of monsters, sure, but we aren't all bad. I'm sure this place has its share of stories about generosity and kindness and love. I refuse to believe it's all ugliness. What about redemption?"

She scoffed. "You're seeing what you want to see, not what's actually there."

"Aren't you doing the exact same thing? When was the last time you looked at these people with the intention of finding the good instead of the bad? When was the last time you withheld judgment?"

I shrank back a little at my last accusation. When was the last time *I* withheld judgment? The first thing I did with anyone I met was judge them on their weight and instantly measure their worth. I shook my head slightly. Good Lord, the sketches Jackie could do of me.

I sighed. "I'm sorry. It's not fair of me to judge you for judging others. I get what you're doing, and I believe you are ultimately trying to do it to help others. But can I make a suggestion?"

Jackie narrowed her eyes for a moment, then waved her hand. "Go ahead."

"Do two sketches. One of what you see and one of what you wished you saw. Give people something to work toward, not just a reason to despair. You're so talented, people will see themselves in your work. They'll see their flaws, then they'll see the good that is possible within them. It might motivate others to change for the better."

"What are you, some sort of self-help television personality?" she said, mocking me. But she was already studying her sketch, flipping to a blank page, then flipping back again.

I smiled and admired the sleeping baby in my arms. I could hear rain falling hard on the roof above us.

"You know, I think she looks like a Norah," I said to Jackie. She didn't even bother to look in my general direction before rolling her eyes.

"Yeah, I'll be sure to mention that to her when she's trying to decide."

I laughed harder than I should have. There was something about this moment that made happiness well up inside me, spilling out into laughter. Jackie had already started sketching the second piece. I rocked the baby gently as I watched a beautifully happy middle-aged couple appear on the page, not a phone in sight.

"These could be in a museum someday, little Norah," I whispered loudly to the baby. "The exhibit will be called 'Redemption at the Mall of America' and your mom will have to thank a random stranger she met standing next to the tacky Bob Dylan mural for the inspiration. What a day that will be, huh?"

"You're the worst," Jackie muttered. But I could see a trace of a smirk pass her lips as she gave life to a lo mein dinner on the page.

15

The wooden pew was digging fiercely into my tailbone and spine, but I didn't care. I was too preoccupied with staring up at the domed ceiling, letting the immensity of it sweep me away.

I wasn't used to spending long periods of time in conversation, so weariness and exhaustion quickly settled in after I parted ways with Jackie. She offered to let me spend the night on her couch, but I thanked her and said I needed to be on my way. More than anything, I was ready to be on my own again.

I had slowly made my way through the starless night down the rain-soaked streets to end up outside the doors of the Cathedral of Saint Paul by daybreak. The cathedral wasn't on my way, but I couldn't pass up a chance to see it. Besides, I never turned down an opportunity to get an extra ten miles of walking in.

The doors opened thirty minutes prior to the morning mass. People were slowly trickling in, some lighting a candle and whispering a prayer before finding a seat. The candles flickered and cast dancing shadows along the walls, as if they were doing their part in communicating with God.

The first time I had visited a Catholic church had been with Alex and his family. I had grown up in a sleek, modern megachurch that consolidated their efforts into tapping into mainstream Christianity with trendy music and catchy series titles. Their attempt at marketing Christianity certainly got people in the door. But the longer I stayed, the shallower the whole industry felt. I didn't find the substance behind the flashing lights and fog machines.

This was not the case with Alex's church. As soon as I walked into the cool darkness of the chapel and glimpsed the light filtering through the stained glass, the pillars reaching up toward the heavens, I felt smaller than ever before.

This is a house of God, I remember thinking for the first time.

Since that had been only the second time I met Alex's parents, and the two of us hadn't been together very long, I refrained from dramatically falling to my knees. But there was no hiding my enchantment for that sacred ground. Everything that surrounded me was a symbol of something greater than myself. Lives lived for God and His glory were forever remembered in stone, paint, and glass. The best among us, immortalized and constant reminders of who we could be for God.

This cathedral was even more grand than Alex's, and I was so much less worthy of being in such a place. I had come here to gather my strength for the stretch ahead of me, to remind myself again of why I set out in the first place.

What waited ahead of me was a long stretch of unfamiliar country where I didn't have a set trail to follow. I would have to wind my way haphazardly to the North Country Trail, and if I wanted to avoid weeks of wrong turns and misdirections, I needed to be on high alert. No more comforting routine, no more falling into daily rituals. I would once again be out of my comfort zone.

The thought demoralized me instead of inspiring courage. I had felt so strong in Minneapolis, but in the house of God, I was forced once again to face how far I had fallen. The strength left me as soon as I walked through the doors of the cathedral. It was a shallow strength, like the faith in my old church. It had been based on nothing but false stability and all stripped away as soon as I was reminded of what I truly was.

I didn't believe I was a bad person. I also didn't believe I was a particularly good person. I was never a rule breaker, but I was never great at following *all* the rules. I had no real handicaps, no real talents. And that was the bare truth I had to come to terms with every time I found myself in a place like this, surrounded by images of those who earned the favor of God. I had been in church long enough to know that I had God's love no matter what, but just because someone was forced to love you because they made you didn't mean they had to be proud of you or even like how you turned out.

My parents had made that much clear.

Everyone I loved looked at me and wanted someone great, the best version of me. They *deserved* that version, and I couldn't give it to them. And I knew I couldn't let any of them back into my life until I proved my worth to them.

I hoped God would come around first. He had a reputation for being the most forgiving. I wasn't there yet though. But I believed I would be one day. I had to. Maybe I'd need to climb to the top of Mount Rainier, but I would get there. And I would come back, back to everyone, and be welcomed with open arms.

I walked out of the cathedral while the notes of the last

hymn still hung in the air. The early morning fog had evaporated, the sun shone brightly, willing this day to be a good one. It would be above my head before I knew it. It was time to continue moving on. I didn't stop walking as I moved farther and farther away from the cathedral. I took a zigzag path to avoid stopping at traffic lights. I knew that if I didn't keep my feet moving, I would go running back to the comforting darkness of the cathedral. I would spend the rest of my days hiding out in the pews cast in the deepest shadows, eating nothing but communion wafers, surrounded by the saints. I would be the beautiful and mysterious myth of the cathedral, and people would come from all over to catch a glimpse of me. My very presence would cause them to turn to God. My disordered eating would turn to fasting. It would be selfishness-turned-holiness because of the walls surrounding me. And slowly, after a long time, I would feel like I belonged in the house of God. I would feel like I was home.

But no, my road back to God stretched out to the west. I was certain of it. This would either be the greatest triumph or failure of my life. Either way, it would be great. It would be a marker of my life, a point of remembrance, an event of value.

"Through the strength of heaven," I began, reciting my favorite part of Saint Patrick's prayer. The song of the choir of Saint Paul's cathedral still rang in my ears as I walked down sun-drenched streets.

> Light of the sun
> Splendor of fire
> Speed of lightning
> Swiftness of the wind
> Depth of the sea

Stability of the earth
Firmness of the rock
I arise today.

I finally allowed myself to stop walking when I stood in the middle of a grocery store aisle. Communion wafers would not get me to Washington. I ran my hand up my ribs, counting each one methodically. I surveyed the aisles and mentally cataloged seven people who were bigger than me.

I built up the nerve to reach out and take the bags of muesli and almonds from the shelf of breakfast foods. Then I lingered in the aisle, pretending to study the nutrition facts on a box of granola bars while I waited for the other people in the aisle to make their selections.

They were all overweight, much more overweight than me. Their BMIs almost made me feel genuinely thin for a moment, until I remembered one wrong choice of sugary cereal and I would meet the same fate. I was always right on the verge of obesity, a fact I was more sure of than anything else in my life.

I watched as my fellow grocery shoppers selected boxes of Cookie Crisps and Honey Bunches of Oats, Luna Bars, and peanut butter made with hydrogenated oils. Not one of them chose the muesli or raw almonds I had selected. And that's how a psychotic anorexic with little to no human interaction finally concluded that the food she pulled from the shelves would not make her fat.

At the checkout counter, I added a few postcards to my pile of groceries—a couple of the Minneapolis skyline and one of the cathedral. I had so much I needed to write in each of the tiny white spaces. Luckily, I had an abundance of unknown trail ahead of me to figure out how to begin to say it all.

16

Dear Alex,

If you've ever wondered if the middle of Minnesota is scenic, let me save you some time and money and disappointment—it isn't. Lots of corn. Lots of fields. Plenty of cows, so that's cool. Not much else though. Not much else at all.

I sleep in cornfields most nights and haven't run into any trouble yet. If I can avoid thinking about The Children of the Corn, I can usually get in a solid few hours of sleep. I would give you a number, but the concept of time and dates left me somewhere a hundred miles back. I'm usually woken up by the first sprinklers of the day and am back on my way before anyone's the wiser.

Remember how we'd spend our summer nights on the roof of that run-down old apartment I had on Houseman Ave? Every time we climbed up there through my bedroom window the roof would sag and bend so severely, we swore it would be *the last time. But night after night, we kept going up there to stare past the glare of the city lights and the fog of pollution, fixing our eyes on the multitude of stars. I see the same stars out here most nights. There are millions more of them, but I still recognize our favorites. The ones that used to hold our gaze as we planned our lives together.*

Love,
Mel

P.S. They really should make these spaces on postcards bigger. Maybe I'll go into the postcard business when this is all behind me. I'd revolutionize the place.

Dear Alex,

I sometimes imagine that when you first told me you loved me, we were staring up at the stars together, feeling like the only two people in the universe. But that's not true, is it? No, you told me on a Tuesday morning right before you dropped me off for my nine thirty class. I had told a terribly bad joke that made you laugh like corny jokes always did, and through that laughter you simply said, "Mel, I love you." That was it. Flawless and to the point, like everything else you ever did.

I've gone over that day, that car ride, and that joke enough times that I'm certain it's been imprinted on my heart, and yet I still don't know what about that entirely ordinary moment made you decide it was the right one. My own declaration of love (which I made a few emotional and panic-stricken days later) pulled out all the stops. I waited until it was a rainy night and made sure our favorite song had played on the drive back to your place. I was wearing the blue dress I knew you loved. When we ran to get inside, I pulled you close and kissed you, like it was the most spontaneous thing in the world and not something I had been obsessively planning for days. When we broke apart, I told you I loved you too. You laughed and it was suddenly just you and me again, the fanfare melting away. You kissed me again and said, "I knew it was going to be something dramatic."

You know what's funny though? When I think back to that time, the first thing that comes to mind isn't the rain or the dress or the car or the music. It was the look on your face when you told me you loved me and when I told you I did too. That's all I see. It's the irrefutable evidence I have that I was once a version of me that could be worth everything to someone.

Love,
Mel

I didn't walk through the full heat of the afternoon. I shuffled. The temperature had risen brutally over the past few days, making the dusty road before me shimmer and pulse under the relentless waves of heat. The most beautiful part of Minnesota—its brilliant blue sky that stretched over the emerald fields of corn from one end of the earth to the other—had become a deadly enemy. It offered no relief, no escape except the stray wisp of cloud that stayed only a few moments before continuing on its journey.

I had been filling up my water from garden hoses belonging to farmers who asked few questions but weren't shy about staring openly at this creature that had washed up on their property.

But I hadn't come across a house in quite a while, and my remaining water was running dangerously low. I was trying to save the last few drops for an all-out emergency. I was drawing near to that point, but I figured I still had a few miles to go until I reached full desperation.

I had only really been in corn country for a few days. Before that I hiked over dramatic bluffs and through stream-cut valleys, feeling possibility and progress after every geographical change. Then, a few mornings ago, I smelled the farmland before I actually saw it. Fertile soil, like the earth after a hard rain. At first I was entranced. There was a quiet here even more profound than what settled in the forests. The lives of the people here were unassuming, the roads were dusty and barren, the sky was overwhelming and endless.

But that's how it started to feel after only a few short days—endless. I couldn't even differentiate between the rare farmhouses I passed by on occasion anymore. I just wanted some sign of progress, some break in the landscape to assure myself I wasn't walking in place. It was enough to make a person's sanity begin to slip.

The last few days hadn't been the best nutrition-wise either. Every night, I had been using heat exhaustion as an excuse to cut my evening meal down to nearly nothing. In the past three days I had eaten a total of thirty-five almonds, one can of tuna, and two handfuls of muesli. That familiar hollow, below-empty feeling permeated every muscle on a near-constant basis now. I knew I was running on fumes, and I knew this could be easily fixed, but my mind was becoming too muddled to do anything about it. My resolve to overpower my dark side was as exhausted as the rest of me.

And my feet. Yikes. I was due for a new pair of shoes, even though I wondered if there was much point since the blisters had long ago turned into calluses, and the majority of my toenails had called it quits back in Minneapolis. Also, after weeks of shedding skin like a snake, due to round after round of sunburn, I had a farmer's tan dark enough to cause permanent sight damage if viewed next to my ghostly pale feet and thighs. Let's just say I wasn't about to win any beauty contests.

I was deep in thought, imagining myself far away from here. Imagining Puget Sound.

The water from Rainier's melting glaciers fed the Sound. Cool and crystal-clear water. I loved the images that body of water brought to mind. Darker and more brooding than any lake, yet far more intimate than the ocean. A sound was glimpses of silvery waters beneath low-hanging clouds, the far-off cry of a whale, soft waves lapping up against weathered docks breaking the rare silence of the modern world. To me, a sound was where people went to be alone but never felt alone. They went to feel comfort from the land on either side, but still hear the slight whisper of the unknown shifting with the waters.

It worked to take my mind off the heat and the dust caking my lips until the noise of a vehicle slowing behind me jolted me back to reality. I looked up quickly to see an expensive-looking, cherry-red car. It was too shiny and new for this backcountry road baking in the dry summer heat. Underneath the sweat and dust, the spidey sense all solo females share pricked at the base of my neck.

I glanced nervously back up the road. I had been following this dirt road most of the day and had been passed by only a handful of cars. No houses were in sight. I kept my head down and continued walking, hoping the driver would get the message and speed off.

Instead, the car pulled up next to me. The tinted passenger-side window rolled down, revealing an attractive man in a gray T-shirt and jeans. He flashed the whitest teeth I had ever seen in an unsettlingly large grin.

"Hey, there," he called out. "Need a ride somewhere?"

I shook my head, not stopping. "No, thanks. I'm enjoying the walk. Thanks anyway."

Still, he didn't drive off. "Pretty lady like you shouldn't be wandering these roads all by yourself. No one's out here for miles. Someone bad could come by and no one would even know."

I really hoped I was only imagining the sly tone of his voice. But my senses were on high alert. No one called a woman in oversized clothes this covered in dirt and sweat "pretty" without ulterior motives. I glanced around subtly. Corn surrounded me on both sides. If it came to it, I would take my chances in the fields.

A thought came to my head suddenly, something I had read in a survival guide with my dad before one of our thru-hikes. It was the section about what to do when you see a bear. You could either play dead or do everything in your power to act bigger and stronger than the bear. I think the choice depended on the type of bear, but since playing dead would get me nowhere good in this situation, I rashly decided to give the other method a try.

I stopped and turned to meet his gaze. He was still leaning over, that terrifying smile plastered on his face.

I offered him my own terrifying smile in return. "Oh, I'm not worried about that," I said slowly.

His grin flickered. "You should be. There are some bad people out there. Why don't you just let me—"

I cut him off with a shrill laugh. "Bad people out there? You think I'm afraid of bad people?" I rushed the car and clamped my hands down on the open window, making sure there was enough distance between the two of us that he couldn't grab me.

He jumped.

"You have no idea the things I've done!" I screamed, making sure saliva flew everywhere. "You have no idea what I'm willing to do! No one messes with me and lives to see tomorrow. No one ever has, no one ever will!"

I let out a scream of fury that caused crows hiding in the crops to take flight. I kicked his car hard, then again and again with such crazed intensity that I barely registered that he was driving off. Before I knew it, the car was a red dot on the horizon, and I was once again alone, panting in the dust. My face was so dry and cracked, it hurt when finally I smiled.

I was still shaking slightly when I heard the music. The dirt road beneath my feet had turned to asphalt and cars now passed by every other minute. The gradual return to civilization made me feel a little safer, but my heart still turned to ice every time a car seemed to slow before passing by.

After all these weeks, that was the first time I felt true fear. I marveled at that for a moment, thinking back to all the people I had met in dark woods and on abandoned streets. Maybe people were genuinely good, not the judgmental monsters I had made them out to be in my head.

Even still, the run-in with the man in the cherry-red car had been my wake-up call. I had let my guard down far too much, trusting I was perfectly safe in the middle of nowhere with no one to have my back. Slowly losing touch with reality due to hunger, dehydration, and heat exhaustion was not a valid reason for creeps to leave me alone. *You have to stop walking with your head in the clouds, Mel. And pay attention.*

Pay attention. Pay attention to that rare gust of wind, and maybe even catch a glimpse of that elusive Spirit of God. It certainly felt like it was sent from heaven, mercifully cooling every inch of my exposed skin, even just for a moment. But there was something else in the wind—the sound of music and the smell of something sweet and heavy with memories.

The farther I walked, the louder the music became until I was standing in front of the gates to a full-blown carnival. It was such a bizarre sight after seeing nothing but cornfields for the last few weeks that at first I was certain I had finally reached the level of heat exhaustion where mirages are a real concern.

It was kind of an odd thing for a mirage though. And that

sticky, sweet smell was so strong now that I took an almost involuntary step toward the gates.

It stayed put. Looking as real as anything. I took a few more steps until, by some invisible force of fate, I was in front of the ticket counter.

A bored high schooler glanced up from his phone, then did a double take.

"Whoa. You look awful," he remarked candidly, eyebrows raised.

I smiled, feeling tension I didn't know was there ease from my shoulders. Now there's a statement I could trust.

"Believe me, I know." I gestured to the fairgrounds behind him. "What is this place?"

"It's the North County Fair. Happens every June. Biggest event all year, 'cept for the Thanksgiving parade and the ice-sculpting fair." He let out an awkward little laugh. "You must not be from around here if you haven't heard of the fair."

I nodded a little too long.

He took an almost imperceivable step back in the tiny ticket booth. "Are you sure you're all right? You don't look all right."

I kept nodding. "I'm fine. How much is a ticket?"

"Well, entry is five dollars, and each ticket is fifty cents. You'll need a ticket or two to ride most of the rides."

The breeze picked up again, carrying another wave of that sugary, familiar scent. Maybe that was what the Spirit of God smelled like. But if that was the case, why was it so familiar?

"What's that smell?" I asked.

"What?"

"Can't you smell it? It's sweet and familiar, but I can't put my finger on it . . ."

The kid honestly looked terrified by this point. "Um, it's probably the caramel corn. They've been making fresh batches all day. The fair's famous for it."

Caramel corn. No wonder it smelled so familiar. It was the only sweet food Alex ever ate. That was such a weird fact about him, come to think about it. He hated chocolate and couldn't stand ice cream, cake, or pie, but offer him caramel corn and his eyes lit up and the bag was empty within minutes.

I remembered I had attempted to make him a batch for his birthday one year. Because I had close to zero culinary skills and lacked the patience to cook caramel the right way, the whole thing had taken me seven attempts and a whole day of my life. The final result could hardly pass as caramel corn, but he was thrilled all the same. That was probably the best gift I ever gave him—homemade caramel corn that was more kernels than popcorn or caramel.

The boy cleared his throat, and the trance was broken. How long had it been since I last spoke? If the look on his face was any indication, far too long.

"All right, then," I said. "I'll pay for entry and for enough tickets to ride your best ride. Which one is that?"

"Definitely the Falcon. It's the only coaster here, and it has a great drop. Nothing else here is worth your time anyway. It's two tickets to ride. So six dollars total." The boy held out his hand expectantly, looking thrilled at the opportunity to end this interaction.

I pulled out a few crumpled, sweaty bills from my pocket, carefully counted them out, and placed them into the boy's outstretched hand.

He handed me the tickets with a smile of absolute uncertainty. "Hope you have . . . fun."

"Thanks," I replied, then headed through the gates.

I walked straight through the carnival, ignoring the bright colors and electric lights that blurred at the edges of my vision. I ignored the smell of hot oil, the sounds of laughter, and the shrieks of happiness. I went straight to the roller coaster and came to a halt at the back of the line. I spent that extra dollar for one reason only: a memory I suddenly wanted so badly to revisit. And I would find it only at the top of that coaster.

The line was surprisingly long for the middle of the day. Although upon second thought, I realized I had no idea whether it was a weekday or weekend.

To bide my time, I did what I always did these days in public settings. I picked the women out of the crowd and determined who was or wasn't thinner than me.

My gaze settled on a group of girls who appeared to be smack in the middle of their high school years. They wore tiny shorts and cropped tank tops like it was the unspoken uniform of young, pretty females acting older than they actually were.

Most of them were not quite as skinny as me, I concluded with a dark and shameful smirk. There was one girl, though, who had toothpick-thin arms and an unimaginably small waist. She had to have me beat.

I was too exhausted to try to fight my next line of thinking. Why was she thinner than me? Did she have a more effective eating disorder? I watched her take a giant bite of a slice of greasy pizza. *No . . . That can't be it. She must work out more than me. I should really start running some of my daily miles, increase my fitness levels so I can compete with her.*

Or maybe she just had a crazy-fast metabolism. I scrutinized her. It didn't appear she had reached puberty yet. *Oh, you wait, girl. Once you hit puberty, that pizza slice won't be so innocent. You'll be bigger than me in no time.*

This wave of toxic thinking hit me with so much sadness, I felt my knees buckle. I doubled over, trying to fight back tears of self-hatred.

"Hey lady, are you okay?"

I turned my head, expecting to see a little boy. Instead, I ended up needing to straighten and looked up into the face of a giant of a man with a soft smile on his face who appeared to be in his late twenties.

I smiled back weakly.

"I'm okay, thanks for asking."

He wasn't looking at me exactly, and his eyes kept darting around, like there was too much wonder surrounding us to take in. He rocked back and forth on his heels.

"That's how I look when my tummy hurts," he said solemnly, still not looking at me.

"I guess it hurts a little, but I think I'll be okay." A realization dawned on me suddenly. I smiled at him and changed tactics. "What do you do when your tummy hurts?"

He rocked back and forth on his heels a little faster. "My mom gives me Tums. They don't taste very good."

"No, they don't. I think they taste like chalk."

He laughed in a halting, uproarious laugh. A few people turned around to stare.

"You can't eat chalk!" he exclaimed. Then, without warning, he switched subjects. "I'm riding the Falcon. I've already ridden it six times today. But I've got four more tickets, so I can ride it two more times. Then tomorrow, Mom said I can get ten tickets. So tomorrow I can only ride it five times."

"That's still a good number of times," I said encouragingly. "Is it your favorite ride?"

He bobbed his head. "Yes. It's the best ride ever. You go up really high, then you go down superfast. Faster than Superman."

"Dang, that's fast."

"Yes," he agreed, head still bobbing. He bent down and whispered loudly in my ear. "Want to know a secret?"

I stiffened a bit but nodded anyway.

"If you make yourself extra big when they come to check the lap belts, you'll be a bird."

"Um," I started, confused. "I'm sorry, I don't think I understand."

He tried to explain it again, this time through a series of charades, but I was still completely lost.

"How about this," I suggested, "we're almost to the front of the line. I'll ride next to you, and you can show me, okay?"

He considered this for a moment. "Okay. But we have to wait for the front seats."

I grinned. "No arguments here." I looked up at him. "I'm Mel."

"Like Mel Gibson? Like *Braveheart*?"

I laughed. "Sure, like *Braveheart*. What's your name?"

"I'm Tom. Like Thomas. But I like Tom better."

"Tom it is, then."

A few minutes later we had exchanged our tickets for the

coaster's front-row seats. I went to pull down the lap bar, but Tom put out a hand to stop me. He shook his head like we shared a dark secret.

As the carnival employee started checking lap bars at the back of the car, Tom motioned for me to move all the way to the edge of my seat. I followed suit.

When the employee got to our car and pushed down on the lap bar distractedly, it barely moved. As soon as he left, Tom slid back in his seat, chuckling under his breath. I slid back too. There was about a foot of space between me and the lap bar, rendering it nearly useless.

"Now when we go down, we'll fly like birds," Tom said excitedly.

My heart flipped. "Oh my gosh. That's brilliant!" For reasons I would never know, I remained terrified of gaining five pounds when I wasn't the least bit afraid of dying a fiery death on a rickety roller coaster due to a useless lap belt.

The ride groaned, and we began our slow ascent to the sky. The car shook terribly. Tom was rocking back and forth with the force of so much pent-up excitement I wondered if we would fly right off the tracks.

But with a painful crawl, we went up and over the peak. Then time and space were suspended in one fantastic moment before we plummeted back down to earth.

I rose from my seat, nothing but the raised lap bar separating me from the air and the sky. I closed my eyes and raised my arms as my heart rose in my chest. And I flew. I was free from everything that ever weighed me down for five beautiful seconds. My head and heart filled with nothing but summer air.

I fell back hard on the seat when we prepared to climb again, then threw my hands up once more to catch the second drop. The third drop was smaller. The whole structure seemed to shudder beneath us. But I still caught a bit of that intoxicating freedom on the way down.

We slowed down as we approached the loading dock. Tom was whooping and laughing next to me. I tried to catch my breath and pushed my mess of tangled hair out of my face so I could feel the sunshine.

"Wasn't that so cool?" Tom asked, almost too excited to speak.

"Pretty much the coolest thing I've ever done," I said. "Thanks for showing me how to fly."

He beamed. "Now only you and me know the secret."

"I won't tell anyone, I promise."

He seemed to believe me and settled back into his seat. "I'm gonna go again."

"That'll make eight times, right? The last ride of the day?"

"Yes, but tomorrow I will ride five more times."

"Well, that's a good thing to look forward to."

The teenagers unloading the cars behind us were in no hurry. I followed Tom's example and sat back in my seat, my breathing returning to normal. The thrill of flight already receding to memory.

"Does your mom like roller coasters?" I asked Tom.

He shook his head. "No way. She says she's not brave enough like me."

I smiled. "My mom loves roller coasters. You would never guess if you met her, but she was crazy for them when I was growing up. Every once and a while, she'd wake me and my sister up to tell us we were going to an amusement park like

Michigan Adventure or Cedar Point for the day. She'd do it without warning and wouldn't say much the whole drive there. But as soon as she felt that first drop, she would laugh and scream the entire way."

Tom wasn't listening. He was looking back at the track, already planning his next trip. But I felt the need to go on.

"I always wanted to sit next to her so I could see her face once we came to a stop. Her eyes were always so bright, her hair so wild . . . She looked more real than ever before.

"Thrill rides were her drug of choice, I guess. I asked her about it once, when we had just finished riding the Millennium Force at Cedar Point, and she was in the best of moods. She told me she gets to feel reckless without any of the consequences." I shrugged. "Kind of made me sad for her, you know?"

I gazed up at the sky and saw gulls swooping down to collect scraps of carnival food. They dove straight down without fear, like my mother in those few fleeting moments. I wished I could see more of her like that.

I wished I knew her at all.

That night, I stretched out beneath stalks of corn and a blanket of stars. Hunger exhausted me and also kept me wide awake. Ironically, I had a bag of caramel corn within arm's reach. Apparently I only purchased overpriced carnival snacks for the sake of nostalgia.

I couldn't leave without buying a bag. Even though there was no Alex to give it to, it felt like a missed gesture of love all the same. I knew if I ate a piece, it would be like summoning his presence. Almost as if he was right beside me, telling me how weird it was we were in a cornfield eating caramel corn. But then all I would be left with would be an empty bag, an aching loss, and probably about three extra pounds.

I imagined him next to me for a moment, just one moment.

When he would lie beside me on the couch, already asleep during the opening credits of a late-night movie, I could feel life radiating off of him. Sleeping or waking, he buzzed with warmth and a wild, unsettled beating heart. Even unconscious, he encapsulated the scope of the living with every breath. It had kept me anchored to the earth, reminding me what an incredible thing it was to be alive.

I watched a shadow of a bird or bat pass above me and my thoughts drifted back to the first drop of the roller coaster. I imagined my mother again, hair wild and eyes bright. How real she looked in the fleeting moment.

But what did that even mean? What was "real" for my mother anyway? Was being uninhibited "real" for someone who was always guarded? Was laughing with joy "real" for a person who believed we were meant to experience joy through suffering?

I tried to summon an image of her while keeping the memory of her on the roller coaster close at hand. People always said I looked like her, which never seemed to please her. I could remember fractions of her smile in all her poised and perfect photos. It was my smile, the one I used to see in the bathroom mirror or in the rare photo I allowed to be taken.

She was far more beautiful. Looks like ours transformed into beauty when paired with size zero dresses and an air of refinement, neither of which I could manage. But from the shape of her nose to the color of her eyes, there was no doubt she was a part of me. The trouble was, I had no idea what part that could be.

I would see pictures of her on Facebook every now and then. Pictures of family outings, dinners with friends, smiling with a group of local missionaries. I would stare at those pictures for a long time, zooming in on her features and trying to figure out who this woman was that I had always called my mom. I tried to figure out what was going on behind that familiar, shy smile, but I could never manage to do so. I always came to the same conclusion: I didn't know my own mother.

It was possible I never knew her. She wasn't a person to me when I was a kid, just Mom. And now that the time had come for me to recognize her as an individual, the time where I could relate to her struggles and ask for advice and feel the same weight of the world on my shoulders, she up and left. For all I knew, she was out there in the world "rediscovering herself" as someone who was so much more than just a mother, and I wasn't there to reintroduce myself along the way.

She had always seemed so one-dimensional to me. She was my mom who told me the rules and expected me to follow them. She loved me based on my ability to do so. She was the rock of the family. Never wavering, never changing. Something that never seemed to require closer examination. But what if that view of her wasn't fair? I never gave myself the chance to dig a little further below the surface.

A soft breeze rustled the stalks of corn. I could say all the same things about my view of God, I realized. If my parent who created me wasn't one-dimensional, how could that be the case for the God who created me? But it was a realization too intimidating to contemplate under a naked sky.

It wasn't fair that I made all these assumptions of my mother's depths, I suddenly realized. It wasn't fair that I never gave her the chance to prove those assumptions wrong. It was possible that the chance simply never presented itself, but it was just as likely that I wasn't looking for it. But whatever the reason, here I was. Trying to piece together my mother with thousands of miles between us.

I was suddenly overwhelmed with the urge to know everything about her. I wanted to sit next to her, close enough that I could see every line on her face she had earned in life. The conversation that would follow wouldn't be about me. Nothing about how I should act, but everything about who she was. I'd say, with great courage, "Mom, tell me about yourself. Tell me everything. Anything you can to lessen this distance between us."

But that couldn't happen right now in a Minnesotan cornfield. In the meantime, maybe these hazy memories that refused to leave my heart could be put to use. Maybe I could sift through them, piece by piece, and find shards of the real woman who raised me. Maybe even begin to shrink the distance between myself and the God I claimed to know in the process.

17

MID-, MAYBE LATE JUNE

Dear Alex,

I bought you a bag of caramel corn from a county fair the other day. People go a little crazy for the stuff here so if you're ever contemplating a move, Middle of Nowhere, Minnesota, might be your sort of place. This postcard I found shows the fair the year it opened, and honestly, not much has changed over the past sixty years. I eventually came to the conclusion that it was impractical to carry a bag of caramel corn with me my entire life, so I buried it with great reverence in a field in hopes it will grow a caramel corn tree you can take your children to visit one day.

"Here, kids," you'll say as they carefully pick golden kernels from the tree's branches, "this is where that girl I used to date, you know, the one in the mental asylum, buried the caramel corn she bought for me, even though it had been *nearly a year since we'd broken up. Really dodged a bullet there, didn't I, kids?" And they'll laugh along with you and enthusiastically eat pounds and pounds of caramel corn with you and your supermodel wife. If you're feeling up to it, maybe send me a package of caramel corn from the tree for me to plant more all around the grounds of my mental asylum so I can feel like I still have some sense of purpose, okay?*

Love,
Mel

I emerged from the woods like a zombie, shocked by the asphalt beneath my feet. I was at the end of a cul-de-sac. Porch lights provided dim puddles of visibility to wade through as I blindly made my way down the road.

It had been a rough week, to put it lightly. I had been in high spirits after the fair, especially since I happened to wander through a small town with totem poles and American flags fluttering from every porch where I could finally buy more food, charge my watch, and fill up on water that didn't taste like it was coated in lead. Fully stocked, hydrated, and happy, I waved a hearty goodbye to the corn. I was filled with such a powerful sense of accomplishment when I came across the first trail marker for the North Country Trail that I unintentionally ran the next two miles. The land was flat and the weather cooler. All I'd have to do was follow it all the way through to Bismarck, North Dakota.

Wide prairie wetlands sloped gently into pockets of woodland. Seas of tall, wispy grasses were broken only by wild trees and deep crystal lakes. Choruses of frogs and crickets became my anthem as Minnesota finally gave way to North Dakota.

I spent a good deal of time each day trying to take my revelation in the cornfields to heart. I strained to pay attention to God's Spirit around me, trying to feel His presence in the Red River Valley and the vast grasslands of eastern North Dakota. It was a nearly impossible thing *not* to feel when walking into a sunset of such rich reds and purples that every other color was made to look like imitations. I didn't get the flood of knowledge of God I was hoping for. But God sent a flood of a different, more traditional kind.

That flood took the form of an endless torrential downpour.

The best thing about North Dakota so far had been its wide-open sky. The horizon stretched on and on, nothing to separate me from the heavens. But under open skies is not the ideal place to be during a weeklong downpour.

Far too often, the rain came down in such massive quantities I couldn't see a foot in front of me, resulting in several wrong turns a day. I saw no one (because who in their right mind would be out in this weather?) and heard nothing but the ceaseless hammering of raindrops against my hood. The grasslands had turned into fields of slippery mud that provided no traction whatsoever, so the rain would wash away the mud from my clothes just in time for me to fall again.

My progress slowed to a crawl. I think the rain lasted a week, but the truth was I had stopped keeping track of the days. It could have easily been two weeks, a month. Every day bled into the next. The only way I could mark the passing of time was by my declining physical and mental health.

Half my food supply turned to mush, but I was so demoralized I didn't need much more of a reason to justify eating less. It didn't matter though. The world around me was and forever would be an unnavigable mess of mud and thick mist.

There were a few mornings when I needed a couple of tries to get to my feet, which were constantly pruny and probably well on their way to developing gangrene. The new boots I had no choice but to splurge on after the fair did nothing except rub exciting new blisters. My limbs were like ice. My heart pounded after the simple task of standing. I had a tarp and my tiny tent, but the ground was already so saturated with rain, and I was so completely soaked through, that it hardly seemed to matter. I shivered constantly, and my teeth often chattered so violently that I couldn't see straight. I was beginning to forget large pockets of time. I would wake up in the morning with no recollection of putting up my tarp. I would lie down at night unable to piece together the day I just survived.

I wouldn't say I was about to give up entirely right before I stumbled into that neighborhood. Giving up was something I didn't do. But I could say with confidence I would have just kept stumbling around a bit until I simply dropped dead. My brain had ceased to possess the ability to make any decisions, rational or irrational, by that point. I had stopped pulling out the map or checking my compass because those actions took too much thought and effort. Every step I took now was simply an automatic response.

So I really was just a few meals of brains short of being a full-blown zombie when I stepped back into the real world. I couldn't fully register the shock of it all, so I kept walking—the only thing I still knew how to do.

It must have been relatively early in the evening, because almost every house I passed had lights blazing in the windows. The rain was still falling, but at a more forgiving pace than it had been for most of the day. I could see lives played out like on a TV screen through the wide, rectangular windows. It was borderline invasive, but I didn't care.

When Claire and I needed to get out of the house, I used to drive us to an unfamiliar neighborhood. We would park the car at the end of the street and walk up and down the sidewalks, pointing out our favorite houses and imagining out loud what our lives would be like if we lived there. When she left, Alex and I carried on the tradition. Dreaming up more details of our shared future out loud with each house we fell in love with. When Alex left and the winter brought darkness and bitter cold, I wandered the same streets alone and watched the families' lives play out through the windows. It brought me such an intense, intoxicating mix of sadness and comfort.

I watched two boys chase each other around a living room, each one wearing a different football jersey. I watched a woman and a young girl at a piano, slowly plunking away notes I couldn't make out. I watched a man set two places at his kitchen table with great care. He folded the napkins into triangles and gently laid a fork on each one. He filled two glasses of water and carried them over to the table, followed by two plates the color of a robin's egg. He checked his watch and disappeared from view as he bent down to check something in the oven.

"Can I help you?"

I jumped. A woman holding the largest umbrella I had ever seen had appeared a few feet away from me. She held a leash in her other hand, and I looked down to see a sopping wet, shaggy dog who stared at me unblinking, wagging his tail violently.

The woman didn't exactly look upset, but she certainly didn't look pleased to see me either. From what I could make out, the two primary emotions she was struggling between were concern and confusion. With painstaking effort, my brain woke up enough for me to realize that the house I had been staring into and the man I had been staring at probably both belonged to her.

"I'm so sorry," I said in a hoarse voice I barely recognized. "I was just out for a walk. Your . . ." I glanced desperately back at the house. A collection of framed landscapes caught my eye. "Those pictures on your mantel are so beautiful. I couldn't help myself but stop to have a better look."

I tried to walk past her, but she held up her hand with the leash to stop me. I wasn't sure if it was illegal to stare into people's homes. Probably. At least when they arrested me I would finally be out of the rain.

"You're out for a walk, huh?" she asked doubtfully.

I shifted from one soggy foot to the other. "I like the rain."

She gave a short laugh. "Could have fooled me." She peered under my hood, trying to get a better look at my face. I pushed back the hood with the hopes of being seen as helpful and further convincing her I wasn't here to murder her and her family.

Something like shock passed her features. "How long exactly have you been out for a walk?"

"A few minutes or so," I said without hesitation. "But I think I'll head back home now." I turned to walk the other way, but this time she grabbed my arm. The dog took this gesture as an invitation to sniff me.

"I don't think it's a good idea for you to walk back in this weather. I'll drive you home. What's your address?"

"Oh, no it's really okay. I live just around the corner. It wouldn't make sense for you to drive me."

"Just around the corner? Are you with the new family that moved in a few days ago? 384 Poplar Street, right?"

I nodded, relieved. "Yeah, that's us. Still getting the lay of the land. We love it here so far though."

Through her scowl she somehow grinned. Her grip on my arm tightened. "Yeah, there is no 384 Poplar Street. Why don't you come inside and give my husband and me a more believable version of why you were standing outside our house in the pouring rain looking like you're at death's door?"

I let her lead me to the garage, too stunned that I had fallen for such a predictable trap to do much else. She balanced the umbrella on her shoulder as she punched in the garage code. Still gripping my arm, she led me around the parked Ford and up the steps to the door of the house.

Even though I was finally free from the rain, I barely registered the change. I could still hear it thrumming in my ears. I wondered if I would ever stop hearing it.

But the warmth of the house slowly seeped under my jacket. Sunny yellow light filled the hallway. I could hear music playing down the hall and the scents of a home-cooked meal drifted in from the kitchen. I imagined potatoes, roasted vegetables, maybe some chicken, definitely fresh-baked bread . . .

"Matthew!" the woman hollered, grabbing a towel from a nearby hook. The dog shook and water went everywhere.

"Ah, come on, Charlie!" The woman enveloped him in the towel, shaking her head as she dried his fur. She unclipped Charlie from his leash, and the dog went bounding down the hallway with seemingly no particular destination in mind.

"Matthew!" she called again, slipping off her rain jacket. "Can you bring a few towels?"

I looked her over involuntarily. No, it was completely voluntary. It was my gut reaction, my second nature even when I could barely see straight from exhaustion. She was nowhere near as thin as me, I concluded. I felt the familiar relief, but it was swallowed up by crushing self-revulsion in no time. I glanced at her again. She was all curves. Beautiful curves that swooped into one another. Even in the cramped entryway, she held herself with an air of confidence that left me stunned by her beauty. She wasn't thin, but goodness, she was flawless.

The man from the window appeared a few moments later, carrying a stack of towels.

"Wasn't able to get to Charlie before he shook again, huh?" He noticed me then. "Uh . . ."

"I found her standing on the sidewalk out front, staring into the house. Said she was looking at the pictures on the mantelpiece, but I caught her in a lie when I asked where she was from. So who knows what she was actually doing. I'm in a charitable mood though, and she's probably the saddest-looking thing I've ever seen, so I figured I'd give her a second chance to explain herself before I called the cops."

The three of us stood there in the tiny hallway for a beat too long. The sound of the water falling to the floor seemed amplified.

"Matthew, those towels would probably be a lot more useful if they were drying something, not laying folded in your arms," the woman remarked, walking over to a small bench so she could take off her boots.

Matthew gave a quick shake of his head, snapping back to the present. "Right. Um, here, let me help you with your bag and jacket."

He reached out, but I slipped the backpack off my shoulders before he could reach it. This was already weird enough without someone helping me take off my clothes. I held a hand out for a towel, which he handed over quickly. I placed the backpack on the towel so I wouldn't make the floor any more soaked than it already was. My shoulders ached fiercely, but so did everything else.

After a few uncomfortable minutes of stripping in front of strangers, I stood there in my drenched long sleeve and pants, trying not to shiver. I glanced down at my feet. They were two giant prunes, but I sent up a silent prayer that there didn't appear to be any signs of gangrene. Matthew handed me another towel, and I took it gratefully.

"Thank you," I said, mortified.

"Are you all right?" he asked me, trying to look at my face. I could feel his wife looking at me as well.

"Probably not. Actually, definitely not. But I will be," was all I could offer. "I'm so sorry I was looking in your house. I give you my word I'm not here to rob you. I just needed a distraction from the rain."

"Rain, which, by the looks of it, you've been out in for quite a while," the woman said. Her arms were crossed defensively, but the edge in her voice had vanished.

"I'm hiking to Washington. I'm from Grand Rapids,

Michigan. I got caught in the rain, I don't know . . . a week ago maybe? I'm not sure."

I could have made a gesture to leave right then, but I felt physically ill at the thought of leaving this warm, dry shelter to feel the pelt of raindrops on my skin once more. I could still feel them falling, pricking my skin like needles over and over . . . Out there, I was completely at their mercy.

My pride, which would normally cause me to turn up my nose at charity, had been stripped away with my dignity. I didn't even try to hide my desperation when I peered into their faces. I hoped my shaking body and the tears threatening to fall were enough to convey that I needed them more than I had ever needed anyone.

"Amy, why don't you go grab her some dry clothes. I'm going to show her the bathroom so she can take a hot shower and change."

Amy squeezed his arm and left without a word. Matthew took me gently by the shoulders, his eyes meeting my gaze.

"I'll be right back, okay? I'm going to go get the bathroom ready."

I nodded. He followed Amy down the hall with purposeful steps.

And just like that, whatever frayed string of strength I had been clinging to snapped. I fell to my knees, absolutely spent. Charlie came bounding up to lick the tears and rain running down my face.

I curled up right there on the welcome mat. The grit left by shoes dug into my cheek and mixed with the tangled, limp nest that I supposed was still my hair. The rough bristles of the mat were something so definable, so easily held on to. I gripped them like an anchor, not daring to let go and get swept up in the storm once again. I could never go back out there. I could never face what I had just barely survived again. I would live here, beg Amy and Matthew to adopt me, and become Charlie's full-time nanny so Amy wouldn't have to walk him in the rain. Matthew would set three places for dinner each night. On the weekends, we would sit on the couch together in the warm, low light of the living room and watch movies. We would be completely inseparable, a family that would never let one of us face the rain alone.

Charlie laid down next to me, his fur sticking to my wet clothes.

"You won't make me go back out there on my own again, will you?" He said nothing, and I was okay with that. I held him close, my other hand still gripping on to the welcome mat for dear life.

I didn't hear Amy and Matthew approaching. My eyes were closed too tightly to see them reach down and gently loosen my grip from the mat and Charlie. I was five years old again, and there didn't seem to be much I could do about the reverse-aging process.

I managed to walk to the bathroom, my ears still ringing too loudly with falling rain to make out much of what they said. They ushered me inside and closed the door behind me, leaving me alone in a small but neat bathroom with a checkered floor and a cheerful striped shower curtain. The shower was already running.

I pulled back the curtain ever so slightly to see the water droplets falling from the showerhead. *This isn't rain*, I told myself. *This is indoors, surrounded by plenty of safe and dry spaces to run to*. I held out my hand. And this water didn't leave an icy touch. It was soothing and comforting, wrapped in steam. Slowly and shakily, I stripped off my clothes and stepped inside.

I sat there for a long time, holding close whatever was left of me. Mostly bones and skin, by the feel of it.

"Where there is doubt, faith." I reached into the recesses of my mind for the prayer of St. Francis, the falling water making the words only for me. I wrapped them around me as a security blanket.

> Where there is despair, hope
> Where there is darkness, light
> And where there is sadness, joy.

I let this purifying water wash away the stains from the water that wanted my life as payment. And only when I became so tired I thought I was in danger of falling asleep right there in a stranger's shower did I turn off the water and step out.

"All right," I told myself shakily, "time to attempt to pull yourself together."

There was a giant fluffy towel waiting next to a neatly folded pile of clothes. Who were these people who offered showers and comfy sweatpants to random stalker girls? I dressed, put my still-tangled hair in a half-hearted bun, and went to open the bathroom door when a familiar shape in the corner of the bathroom caught my eye.

A scale.

The sight was both terrifying and comforting. I didn't even think, I just crossed the bathroom and stepped on, the cold metal stinging the balls of my feet.

The tiny screen blinked to life. Then without much warning, my whole self-worth flashed up at me.

The breath was sucked out of my lungs and came out in a choking, coughing fit. The number was astonishingly low, so low that I felt a sliver of panic in the waves of euphoria that crashed down onto me. I was at my lowest weight ever, but of course that didn't mean I couldn't be skinnier.

The room swam a bit. These dizzy spells had become a frequent event. I knew this was not the weight me and my healthier alter ego had agreed on back in Chicago. I knew that number on the scale had consequences. But I couldn't sweep away the shallow excitement it brought. I gripped the edge of the sink as the dizzy spell passed, fighting back a sob. My heart was torn to pieces that the number on the scale made me want to jump with joy but left me too drained to even stand up straight.

When I recovered, I opened the bathroom door and ventured slowly down the hall, trying to think of what exactly to say to strangers who had front-row seats to one heck of a meltdown and still decided to save my life. When I caught snippets of a hushed conversation, I stopped.

"She looks like she's escaped from a prisoner of war camp or something," Matthew said in a low voice. "You saw how skinny she was, Amy. Who knows the last time she's eaten. Something is seriously wrong with her, and you want to kick her out?"

I was beyond thrilled, ecstatic actually, over the news that these strangers thought I was skinny. The rest of the conversation hardly even registered.

"I'm not suggesting that! All I'm saying is we should turn her over to someone who knows how to handle this sort of situation. You said yourself that there's something wrong with her. She needs professional help, not an accountant, a dentist, and a golden retriever."

Now that was cause for panic. I wanted them to think I was thin, but not to the point of needing professional help. I tiptoed back down the hall, then walked to the kitchen, making sure my footsteps could be heard.

They instantly stopped talking. I found them standing together awkwardly in the middle of the kitchen, doing a terrible job of trying to hide the fact they had been talking about me.

"Thanks for the clothes," I said. "And the shower. That was, well, I'm not even going to try to describe what a relief that was. I thought for a long while that I was never going to be warm again." I leaned against the doorframe, not really sure what this situation called for. "I was prepared for rain, but not like that. It just wouldn't stop." I shook my head. "It's enough to make a person go a little crazy. But I'm all right now, scout's honor."

The expression on Amy's face made me certain she didn't believe that for a second. Matthew looked at me like I was a puppy that had just been kicked.

"Why don't we all eat some dinner and talk through this a bit more?" Matthew suggested. "I'm sure you must be hungry." Amy shot him a look.

Panic momentarily shocked my system. I still couldn't fully identify the mouth-watering smells coming from the oven, but whatever it was, I knew it was rich and calorie dense. "Oh, no. I couldn't. I'm sure you only made enough for two."

"Not at all," Matthew said, turning toward the oven. "We

cook only a few meals a week here, but in big enough quantities to have plenty of leftovers."

Of course they do, I thought while taking in the room. It was like I had stepped into a catalog page for The Container Store. I had never seen such an impressive level of home organization. The handles of the cooking utensils matched—spatulas were red, spoons were blue, whisks were green . . . The napkins in the napkin holder were folded neatly, the spices were in alphabetical order. It only made sense these people knew how to meal plan, this was what put-together adulthood looked like.

Matthew put on a pair of oven mitts that matched the apron tied around his waist, opened the door, and peered inside. I could see a golden baguette and something cheesy in a casserole dish. My stomach twisted with nerves.

"Looks like we're about ready here. What can I get you to drink . . . Um, wow, we don't even know your name . . ."

"Well, that's pretty understandable considering how I introduced myself to the both of you. I'm Mel, and water suits me just fine."

Matthew smiled. "All right, then, Mel. Water coming up. You and Amy take a seat and dinner will be out in a sec."

I sat at one of the places that wasn't set for dinner and Amy brought me a plate and cutlery. She took the seat across from me, no doubt so she could peer into my soul. She was making a valiant effort.

"Grand Rapids to Fargo," she said. "That's quite a ways to walk."

So I was in Fargo. Right on track. Honestly, I was blown away that I had managed to keep walking at all, let alone in the right direction. I offered her a small smile. "It certainly is."

Matthew placed the cheesy mystery dish on a trivet in the center of the table and arranged the now sliced baguette around a dish of butter. A salad with tomatoes, carrots, cucumbers, croutons, and what looked like balsamic vinaigrette was also added to the table.

"Wow," I remarked, relaxing a bit when I spotted the salad. "This is impressive."

"Matthew's an incredible cook," Amy said, still staring into my heart of darkness. "Which is great since I struggle to make a bowl of cereal without some sort of disaster."

Matthew laughed, and I joined in politely. Amy kept watching me.

She continued to watch me as I piled my plate high with salad (avoiding the croutons) and scooped an acceptable portion of what I now saw was a baked gnocchi dish with marinara sauce, vegetables, and cheese. This left me with the excuse that my plate was too full to accept bread, thank goodness.

I tried to distract my dinner companions from my task of picking out the vegetables among the gnocchi and cheese with conversation about my journey here. My shaky willpower during this task surprised me. I had always loved gnocchi, but I had given up dozens of foods I loved without issue.

But today I was like a cartoon character, literally salivating over the gnocchi I pushed from my fork. I berated myself. The rain must have weakened my resolve. That was always the first step of gaining weight: allowing yourself a break from the limitations you have placed on your diet. Once you did that, there was no turning back.

At least my recount of my trip was going well. I walked them through each stretch of the journey, with nothing but positive imagery and assurance that I had encountered no greater problems than learning to pee in a wide-open grassland while cows looked on with interest. I seemed to be pulling off the most panic-inducing meal of my life. At least I thought I was, until Amy gestured casually at my plate.

"What's wrong with the gnocchi?"

I froze, empty fork in hand. I quickly ran through my options. I could say I was gluten free, but that would open up a whole new can of worms. I could say I wasn't a fan of gnocchi, but that seemed equally unbelievable considering they both thought I was near starvation. I sighed. The truth had to be better than anything she thought I was hiding.

"I may have a touch of an eating disorder. Gnocchi, although delicious, doesn't exactly vibe well with my constant internal struggle as to what is and is not acceptable to put in my body." I pasted a smile on my face and speared a piece of zucchini with my fork. "But I'm a big fan of the vegetables. And the salad. Don't worry though. It's completely under control. I'll admit I kind of fell off the wagon this past week because the rain nearly made me lose the will to live. But other than that, I've really been getting better."

They stared at me, then after a quick glance at each other, Matthew became fascinated with the napkin on his lap and Amy began to rub her temples like a major headache was heading her way.

"So let me get this straight," Amy said with a measured patience that seemed painful. "You're trying to walk across the country while battling an eating disorder. With no professional help."

"Right, and it's going pretty well, actually."

"You look like you barely survived a famine."

"Well, like I said, the past week or so hasn't been great. But other than that, I've made some real progress." I leaned in closer, trying to communicate the gravity of what I was about to say. "I even eat almonds and almond butter now."

That didn't seem to impress her. Matthew muttered something to his napkin I couldn't make out.

"Mel"—Amy leaned in as well—"this is not a good idea. Eating disorders are not a joke. Especially when in a state like this." She gestured toward my general existence. "People in your position need professional help. There's no shame in that. It's not a sign of weakness to accept help—"

"Listen," I interrupted, pulling away from the table. "I really appreciate how much you both have helped me, but I can't stay here if I'm going to be lectured at. I've heard the same thing a thousand times. I know there's no shame in therapy, but I've got my reasons for not wanting to go down that route. I'm coping in my own way, and I think I have the right to continue to do so."

It was Amy's turn to pull back from the table. She stood up with such force that her water glass was knocked over. Charlie was instantly at the scene, lapping up the puddle that formed on the floor.

"You have two choices, Mel." Her voice was an icy calm. We were eye to eye, and I didn't have to see a *National Geographic* special to know she was asserting her dominance over the situation. "You can either sit down and let us help you, or you can go back into the rain and cold. Yes, sure, you have the right to deal with things your own way, but if you're in our house, you need to be okay with us helping you."

To my shock, Matthew was nodding along with her. "She's right, Mel. You have your choices, but I hope you choose to let us help you."

"I'm not here to be your project!" I was yelling now. "I'm not here for advice, or to be the wayward youth you so generously save!"

"And do you know why you're actually here?" Amy asked, close to yelling herself. "You're here because you were desperate. You were desperately in need of help, and you know it! We *saved* you. And why did we need to save you? Because you can't take care of yourself!"

"It was because of the rain!"

"All right, Mel, all right." Matthew intervened, holding up his hands in a form of surrender. "You say it's because of the rain. That's fine. You've got a chance to prove us wrong." He pointed at the uneaten gnocchi on my plate. "Eat your dinner, all of it, and we'll back off."

Amy seemed to find this arrangement agreeable. She crossed her arms and waited.

I considered unleashing my inner angsty teenager and yelling, "You're not my parents!" But that would be the opposite of progress. Instead I yelled, "Fine!" like a stubborn toddler and sat back down hard in my chair, raised my fork, and hesitated.

There was silence from my audience as I stared down at the enemy—soft, pillowy gnocchi. They seemed to have multiplied since the last time I looked down at my plate.

Most of the time, anorexia came down to this: the pain of hunger versus the pain of eating. One was physical, the other purely mental. There were times before the hunger quieted to a low, constant roar that my body would cry out for food with such intensity, I would find myself doubled over in agony. It would spread to my brain, leaving a dizzying, blinding headache in its wake. It would rush to my limbs, making them heavy and unreliable. It would burn my throat, as if it was raw from literally crying out for nutrition. I would stay doubled over like that until the pain finally moved on, leaving a muted version of itself behind to keep me company until it could once again return full force to watch over me as I continued to waste away.

But as bad as that pain was every single day, it was nothing compared to the pain of trying to overcome my fears every time I forced myself to take a bite of food. I could never fully shake the image of another pound being added to my body with another forkful. That vision of me, fat and defeated, would always become clearer the more I ate. I would fight tirelessly between the knowledge that eating was actually showing signs of great strength and progress, and the somehow much more real terror that I was giving in to weakness, being tricked into letting myself go. No matter how I tried, I always surrendered to the torment of shame, spiraling justifications, and crippling inadequacies.

So that was why I found myself at a stranger's dinner table with my mouth full, sobbing as though someone had shattered my kneecaps instead of told me to eat a plate of perfectly good gnocchi. Once I finished everything on my plate, I continued to sob. I clutched my stomach, trying to force it not to double in size like some very real part of me believed it would.

"I'm sorry," I gasped. "I'm so, so sorry."

"Come on." Amy was at my side, gently pulling me to my feet. "Let's get you to bed."

18

"My sister went through something very similar when she was growing up," Amy began cautiously. I was lying on a twin bed with a purple-and-blue patterned quilt over me. The room was small and tidy with an empty dresser for guests and cubbies stocked with neatly folded matching towels and sheets. The pale green walls held photos of serene prairie landscapes, only visible by the dim light of the bedside lamp Amy had turned on. I was facing the wall, too emotionally wrecked and embarrassed to look at this woman perched at the foot of the bed who probably wasn't much older than me.

"It really . . . it really changed her. We were so close before that. But then, I don't know . . . She drew into herself. Away from everything and everyone." She paused. I could picture her staring off into a past I couldn't see.

"I thought she was so selfish. I was so angry with her for such a long time. Our parents weren't the kind of parents kids hoped for, so I really needed her. But she was all but consumed by this *thing* that I thought she had chosen to let devour her from the inside out."

I didn't say anything. There was nothing to say to that, anyway.

"I only realized how wrong I had been about the whole thing once she got help and opened up to me about it. I realized I had been the selfish one, not her."

That statement was enough to make me turn around and face her. "That doesn't make any sense. What she did . . . It was her fault. She was a victim of her own creation." I shifted to face the ceiling. "Trust me, I would know."

I heard her sigh. "See, this is why I really wish you would seek professional help." When I didn't say anything, she continued. "This is not your fault, Mel. This happens to people all the time without much rhyme or reason. It's nobody's fault because blaming yourself or anyone else doesn't change the fact that you're here now, suffering from it. You wouldn't blame the cancer patient, would you? The same rules apply to people who suffer from mental illnesses. I'm not saying this to clear your conscience. This stuff has been scientifically proven."

"From what you said it sounds like you might not be blaming your sister, but you're blaming yourself." I curled up, pulling the quilt to my chin. "You said you were the selfish one. Blaming yourself is just as bad as blaming your sister."

Out of the corner of my eye, I saw her shake her head. "That's not why I said that. I'm not to blame for my sister's illness, I know that. But that whole time I knew she was suffering, all I wanted was for her to be fine again. Fine for *me*, not for her. I felt like I lost her, and I was so angry because of it." She rested her forearms on her thighs and glanced back at me. "But because I chose to cut her out of my life instead of pull her closer, I didn't realize until it was too late that I never actually lost my sister. She was still there, but consumed by something that had gone from being a part of her to trying to define her.

Amy straightened and turned her attention to smoothing the wrinkles out of the quilt. "During her darkest times, my sister saw herself as only a number on a scale. That was it. And I saw her as only a shadow of what she once was. She needed someone, or something, to be by her side with the sole purpose of never letting her forget who she was and how greatly she was loved for that. She needed someone to remind her of all her depths, her passions, her strengths and weaknesses, successes and flaws . . . everything. That way, she would have never forgotten that whole person she was outside her weight." Her hands stilled on the bedspread. She brought them together loosely in her lap and gave me a small, sad smile. "It was everything she was, all of it, that made us love her so deeply. Not her ability to diet or what her dress size was." She paused. The room stilled around us. "And I never told her any of that. Never once reminded her of the love I had for her. All I did was leave."

The ferocious determination I saw when she met my gaze again almost made me jump. "So I'm not going to make the same mistake twice. You're right. You're not my project. But you did come here for a reason. And at the very least I'm going to do whatever it takes to remind you of the fact that you are, and have always been, so much more than that number you can't get out of your head."

I woke up the next day with the thought I had somehow found my way back to my own bed. I ran through the list of things I had to do—morning sit-ups, push-ups, and jumping jacks followed by a fifteen-mile run, work . . .

But then I remembered I didn't have work or a morning routine anymore. I was in Fargo, North Dakota, at the mercy of a couple I had done my very best to humiliate myself in front of.

I groaned and eyed the clock. 4:27. I stared out the window, confused. Although the sky was overcast, there was no denying that it belonged to the 4:27 of the afternoon, not early morning.

I had slept for nineteen hours. Longer than every night's sleep from the last week combined.

In a haze of disbelief, I walked across the bedroom, opened the door, and started down the hall with no general sense of direction until I spotted Amy through an open door to an office.

She sat behind a large, important-looking desk that was covered with frames and papers and yet still appeared tidy. She looked up from a stack of her own papers when she heard me, peering over a pair of comically large glasses.

"I slept for nineteen hours!" I blurted in a slightly accusatory tone. I was too shocked to remember to be uncomfortable around her.

Amy took off her glasses, folded them neatly, and leaned back in her seat to look at me. "Yes, I noticed. I was planning on calling the coroner if you didn't wake up within the hour."

"I didn't even know a person could sleep for that long," I marveled.

Amy gestured toward a chair in the corner of the room. The last thing I wanted to do was sit, but I obeyed.

"You're freaking out a little bit right now, aren't you?" Amy framed it as a question she already knew the answer to.

I started bouncing my knees up and down. "Just trying to get my bearings. I've become pretty used to my surroundings constantly changing."

She gave me a small smile. "That's not what I meant."

I shot her a confused look. My bouncing legs picked up speed.

"I'm guessing you're a little freaked out that the whole day's gone by and you haven't had the chance to work out."

I stopped bouncing my legs—my go-to move for burning calories while sitting.

I cleared my throat unnecessarily. "Maybe a little."

She crossed her arms. "Figured as much."

"I'm guessing your sister let you in on all our self-destructing secrets?"

"After you fell asleep last night, I called her and we talked for a few hours. She sent me a bunch of articles that really helped her. She echoed my thoughts, by the way. Said you should definitely get some professional help." She sighed. "But she said she understands that you have to do things your own way. Everyone has their own means to recovery and stuff like that." Amy made her opinion of that statement clear with a roll of her eyes.

"She's going to call each night to check and see how things are going," Amy continued. "It's kind of nice, actually. Ever since she moved to Sacramento, we haven't had the chance to talk as much. So look at that, you're helping me out after all."

"Wait, each night?" My heart struggled to find its normal rhythm. "What do you mean?"

Amy gave me a look of grave seriousness. "We'd really

like it if you stayed with us for a week so you can get your strength back. After that, go on your merry way. All the way to Washington and whatever you want afterward. But you need this." She narrowed her gaze at me. "Come on now, you slept nineteen hours last night. That should tell you something."

"I can't do that." I felt tears burn my eyes. "I can't just do nothing for a week."

Amy shook her head. "You won't be doing nothing, even though I thought and still think that would be best for you. My sister said cutting you off from all physical activity wouldn't do you any favors, so we're still going to get plenty of exercise, but not to the extreme you've been taking it." She offered a smirk. "I promise we're not going to chain you to the couch in front of the TV and force-feed you McDonald's."

I breathed. That was better, that was manageable. I could still do what I needed to keep my weight down. And I had to admit, despite the nineteen hours of sleep, my body didn't feel capable of continuing on. Everything ached and twinged. My head throbbed, my throat was raw, I still shuddered when I thought of the rain. Skinny celebrities did this sort of thing all the time. They took a little detox from their extreme diets and exercise routines so when they got back in the habit, the results were even more pronounced. This could be okay. This could be handled.

I looked up at Amy. "I can't ask you to do this for me. Don't you have to work?"

She waved a hand. "Well, if you keep sleeping for nineteen hours, I can get plenty of work done from home. Otherwise, I have a good amount of vacation days I was looking to use anyway." She leaned toward me. "Besides, like I told you last night, this is important. For both you and me. We'd be doing each other a favor by you sticking around for a week."

I snorted. "Solid argument."

She raised an eyebrow. "So?"

"So, all right." *Yes, this will be okay*, I told myself again. *It will all be okay.* "Thanks, by the way."

She stood and stretched. "All right, then. Come on, according to the less-than-reliable weather channel, we should have a break in the downpour for a few hours. Let's go walk Charlie."

19

JULY 7

Dear Alex,

I'm being kept prisoner in Fargo, North Dakota, by a sinisterly kind couple who insist on helping me reestablish whatever's left of my sanity before I continue on my way. I know, right? How dare they?

But in all seriousness, they're incredible. Their patience alone deserves to be applauded. Amy spends the most time with me, walking with me around the neighborhood and trying to coax bits and pieces of my personality back into the forefront of my mind. She keeps telling me that I've got so much to offer, but when I let myself become consumed by something so trivial as weight, I'm abandoning all the good I have to offer for something with no purpose, no meaning. And if my whole existence revolves around my weight, something that brings no joy or value to anyone, including myself, then what meaning could my life possibly have? She doesn't *sugarcoat things, which I much appreciate. She said that was something that helped her sister recover from her own eating disorder, and I guess I can see why. But you and I both know that I have tried time and time again to offer everything I have to a cause and to people I knew mattered, and where did that get me? A minimum-wage job and an empty apartment.*

Love,
Mel

"The zoo? Really?"

Amy snatched the passes out of my hands while doing an almost believable impression of a very offended person.

"Excuse me for trying to think outside the box! Aren't you as sick and tired of walking loops around this neighborhood as I am? Besides, these passes expire at the end of the month."

"Well, for the sake of expiring passes, I accept your zoo proposal." I grinned at her. "And you're right. The thought of walking one more lap around this neighborhood is enough to make even an exercise addict question her choice of addictions."

Amy snorted and rose from the table to answer the *ding* of the toaster oven. She added two slices of grainy toast to each of the plates sitting on the counter and brought them over to the table. She slid one in front of me.

Along with the toast there was a pile of scrambled eggs, two strips of turkey bacon, and four strawberries. I stared at Amy, waiting.

"All right, so here's your choice for breakfast," she said,

reaching for the butter dish placed between us. "You can either put butter on your toast or you can drink a glass of orange juice with your meal."

I considered this for a few moments, listening to the scraping sound of toast being buttered.

"I'll take that butter after you're done," I declared.

She nodded, then eyed me suspiciously. "You know you have to butter both pieces, not just one. Don't you dare try to find one of your loopholes."

I did my best to appear shocked. "I haven't the slightest idea what you mean. Personally, I love butter so much I might not stop at the bread. This turkey bacon looks like it could use some, definitely the strawberries. We might have to get another stick out for full coverage, actually."

Amy took a bite of her toast, unamused. "You done now?"

"Yes," I grumbled and grabbed the butter. I spread the thinnest possible layer imaginable on each slice of bread and took a bite.

"How've you been feeling these past few days?" Amy asked before taking a sip of her coffee.

"Better," I admitted. "I would even be bold enough to say much better."

"You sound disappointed."

I shrugged. "It's not easy to be reminded over and over again that you're not as strong as you think you are."

She raised an eyebrow. "You know that what you're doing now, fighting your disorder and taking your life back, that's true strength. What's weakness is giving in to that familiar, almost comforting need to punish yourself." She motioned toward my plate. "You're not giving up. You're fighting back. You know that, right?"

"Yeah, and I even believe it sometimes."

She smiled then asked, "Why do you think you need to punish yourself?"

She would make a great therapist, I thought. *Throwing questions out like that so casually.* I sighed. "Because I don't think the world was doing a good enough job of that on its own, I guess."

"Why do you feel the need to be punished at all?"

I was quiet for a moment, moving the eggs around my plate with my fork. "I've had every opportunity under the sun to live up to the expectations set for me. And every single time I've fallen short."

Amy seemed to be working through a response when Matthew strolled in.

"Morning, ladies," he said cheerfully, completely oblivious to the heavy weight of the room.

"Your breakfast is in the toaster, honey," Amy told him.

Matthew beamed. "What would I do without you?"

Amy rolled her eyes. "You'd probably have to put your own Pop-Tarts in the toaster. Ever consider that thirty-two might be the age when it's time to give up Pop-Tarts for breakfast?"

Matthew bent down to kiss her before grabbing his bag and heading toward the door.

"They're the unsung breakfast of champions, my dear," he said. "How about this, maybe when I lose my zeal for life, I'll give up Pop-Tarts for breakfast. Sound fair?"

"Fair enough," Amy called after him. "Have a great day!"

"You too! Both of you! Love ya, honey. See you tonight!"

And with that, he was gone. Amy watched the door as if he might reappear at any moment. Finally, she turned her attention back to her plate. She smiled to herself as she muttered something about the irony of a dentist eating Pop-Tarts for breakfast.

"You two are quite a couple," I noted.

"Been together since high school. I don't believe in love at first sight, but what I felt when I first saw him came pretty close to that."

I took a bite of toast. Chewed it slowly. "So you've always been sure? About him?"

Amy set down her half-eaten piece of toast and took a sip of coffee from a mug that read DENTISTS MAKE GREAT FLOSSOPHERS. "Since the very beginning. I was lucky, I guess. A lot of people seem to struggle to grasp that level of certainty."

"Well, how *did* you know? That you were meant to be together, I mean. How did you know there wasn't something better out there for both of you, especially when you met so young?"

She took another sip of coffee, seeming to gather her thoughts. "Well, in a world of infinite possibilities and what-ifs, I could never know for sure if there wasn't something better. If this was the best for both of us. But I can tell you this." She paused and leaned closer. "I remember at least a few of the dreams I have each night. Some fade away as soon as I wake up, but one or two always stick around for me to replay in my head. There's this scenario that's a common occurrence in these dreams. I find myself in a relationship with someone, either fictional or real. We're blissfully happy, madly in love. But every time, no matter how good the dream relationship might be, there's always a point in the dream where I think about Matthew. Instantly, I become so sad at the thought of missing out on a life with him. The dream always ends in a mix of sadness and joy, but mostly certainty. Certainty that I'm right where I'm supposed to be with the most important person I could be with. Does that make sense?"

I tore off the crust of my bread, keeping my eyes on my plate. "It does." I glanced up at her finally. "I wish I remembered my dreams."

Amy shrugged. "You have an imagination, don't you? When the time comes when you have a person in your life that you suspect might mean the world to you, try to picture your life with someone else. Try to imagine him living his own life, completely separate from you. However that makes you feel, that's your answer."

"All right, what should we see next?" Amy was squinting at the colorful zoo map in front of her.

"I don't think anything is going to beat the otters," I said. I was a little overwhelmed by everything. Amy had lent me a long sleeve and some drawstring shorts. The rain had finally stopped, bringing swarms of people to the zoo. I hadn't been around this many people for a while, and the crashing of voices started to sound like the pounding of rain against my hood.

"Well, we have to see the reptiles. They're right over there. Want to stop in before lunch?"

I watched as a mob of half-wild children were herded inside the reptile building. Add lizards, and it was the perfect combination to bring on a full-blown panic attack.

"I'm not really a fan of our scaly friends." I looked around for an escape. A shaded exhibit to my left beckoned. "I'll wait for you at that exhibit."

Amy searched my face for anything concerning. Finding nothing, she put her hands on her hips. "Only because I can't *not* see the alligators. I like Charlie and all, but I've always pictured myself as more of a gator owner."

"I think your heart may belong to the Florida swamplands instead of North Dakota."

"I'm inclined to agree with you, but until I convince Matthew that the Sunshine State is more than a statewide retirement home with swamp creatures instead of squirrels, I'll have to observe behind glass. I'll see you in a bit."

She half walked, half skipped into the reptile building. I shook my head. What a weirdo.

I sauntered over to the quiet, shady exhibit I spotted before. As I approached, it became clear why it was abandoned. According to the sign, the exhibit belonged to the gray wolf, but nothing except a few crows were visible.

Suddenly, one came into view. It walked with grace and purpose, almost gliding across the grass. Its ears twitched. I thought of Charlie's sloppy, uncoordinated gait. I was fairly certain wolves would be slightly ashamed of their optimistic golden retriever cousins.

Wolves were my favorite animal when I was younger, when having favorites of everything was still of the utmost importance. I think my love was mostly inspired by the animated *Balto* movie, which I must have watched at least fifty times. I liked the idea that when the zombie apocalypse happened, wolves would still be roaming the streets. Their self-reliance and refusal to be bound by domestication would save them in the end.

I thought I'd also do okay in a zombie apocalypse. It was this world I couldn't seem to manage. Self-reliance had always been an important attribute for me, but after Alex left, it was the first time in my life when my daily comings and goings didn't have an audience. What I did in my free time no longer affected anyone but me.

No one wondered where I was or concerned themselves with my well-being since I had pushed them all away, God included. I couldn't imagine reaching out and receiving a response, let alone a response that wouldn't make me feel worse about myself. What would God possibly have to say to someone like me? Someone with nothing of value going on in her life? Would He tell me I needed to suck it up, work harder, try again? I already knew all those things. I didn't need proof another distant figure in my life was disappointed in me.

There was a great sense of freedom that came with the loneliness. The wolves, self-reliant and untethered, must feel it too. I exploited that freedom in no time, because although my life was now one of freedom, it was also one devoid of meaning. I used my reckless, meaningless freedom to do all sorts of self-destructive things, leaving my life to rapidly descend into shadows no one cared to explore. I couldn't say I blamed them.

Sitting in the shade, I realized I was nothing like the wolf. I had no idea how to be alone or how to look after myself. If I were Balto, there is no way that medicine would have reached those kids in time. I would have been too busy running in the wrong direction to fit in a few more miles than all the other wolves.

"Would you look at that," said a voice behind me. "Denali's out and about."

A woman who appeared to be in her late seventies pointed her oversized souvenir cup toward the wolf. "She's a beauty, isn't she?"

I nodded. "She is."

"And look at that!" The woman stepped closer to me, pointing with her free hand toward what I at first thought was a rock under the shade of a pine. "That must be Cascade. Can't blame him for resting in this heat."

I turned to take in the wolf lady. She wore a shirt that read SAN DIEGO ZOO and a visor with silhouettes of African wildlife.

I raised my eyebrows. "You really have a thing for zoos, huh?"

She laughed. "I like their gift shops a little too much, I can tell you that. I'm making my way to every zoo in America. This is my home turf though. I've been here hundreds of times. Could probably name every animal in this place."

"I've heard of people visiting every baseball stadium in America, but I don't think I've ever heard it done with zoos. That's pretty cool though."

She smiled, still looking at the wolves. "It's become something of my life's work, really. Which isn't saying much when you're retired." She chuckled. "You see, my friend Lonnie and I used to visit the local zoo in every city we traveled to together. She was my best friend for fifty-three years, so we did a lot of vacationing together. We were all we had for most of our lives."

She reached into her fanny pack and pulled out a faded photo. It showed a younger-looking version of the woman standing next to me and a bright-eyed brunette in front of a monkey exhibit.

"This is her," she said. "I show her picture to everyone I can. We had a falling out, like friends do, but she died unexpectedly before we got the chance to make up. This is my way of apologizing."

I didn't know what to say to that, and she seemed familiar with that reaction. She chuckled again.

"I know it sounds extreme. I know I'm wandering. But Lonnie was my anchor. And it feels too late to find a new one." She held up a hand as if to stop the protests I wasn't about to offer. "I don't want one, anyway. I know Lonnie was the greatest blessing of my life, and I'm very much okay with surrendering any time I have left to the memory of her."

"I had to push a kid or two out of the way, but I got to see the gators." Amy's voice made me jump. "Ready for lunch, Mel?" Her gaze shifted to the woman beside me. "Oh, hi, Miss Julie. Great weather for a day at the zoo, huh?"

Miss Julie bobbed her head. "It certainly is, dear. You two enjoy your lunch. The place right around the corner has the best soft serve."

"Thanks for the advice, as always." Amy smiled. "Enjoy the wolves."

"Oh, I always do," Miss Julie said before turning back to the exhibit. Amy lightly touched my elbow and led me out into the sunlight.

"You know that woman?" I half whispered as we walked away.

"Everyone who's ever been here before knows her. She's a local legend. She tells everyone she can about Lonnie. She spends the winters traveling to other zoos, but in the summer, she's here almost every day. She can't seem to get on with her life."

"It sounds like Lonnie *was* her life."

"Good grief. You ask about Matthew and me and now this. Please don't tell me you're a romantic."

"Through and through, I'm afraid. And of the hopeless variety."

"Ugh, you people are the worst." She rolled her eyes. "Now let's keep our chitchat practical and emotionless or I might have to force you to eat some of that soft serve."

I held up my hands in surrender. "Practical and emotionless. Got it."

20

Amy disappeared into her office once we got back to the house, set on getting some work done before Matthew got home. In spite of myself, I winced when she said that. I was consuming too much of these people's lives. I had been staying with them for four days, and although they both constantly told me otherwise, I couldn't help but feel the acute burden of my presence.

It didn't escape my notice that the bathroom scale had disappeared after that first night. I surprised myself when I realized I didn't miss it, that it was actually a relief that I didn't know where it was. Amy's sister really had covered all the bases.

I felt well enough to venture on, both physically and mentally. I no longer shuddered when I thought about getting back out there with nothing between me and the sky. And even though Amy and I walked plenty of miles every day, I still felt restless. I felt eager to move on, but for the first time since I started, I felt a little directionless. I still had my destination in my head, but something was causing my heart to wander in circles. I sighed and set off in pursuit of something to calm my nerves.

With Charlie by my side, I rolled out Amy's spare yoga mat on the living room floor and started an ab routine I knew from heart. Amy said she'd allow these kinds of exercises once a day underneath her roof and always out in the open. She made it clear she had no patience for secret late-night workouts or early-morning jumping jacks and planks behind a closed door.

"Let's be adults about this, agreed?" she had said. And for some reason, that actually stuck.

After half an hour of abs and another half an hour mix of jumping jacks, lunges, push-ups, and squats, I laid down on the mat in the fading daylight, relishing my increased heartbeat I could feel even in the tips of my fingers and toes.

Charlie stood over me, panting. I sat up and ran my fingers through his fur, taking in the pictures that cluttered the mantel for the first time since the night I stood outside the house.

The pictures were all in their own unique frames. Some were painted, others were sketched, and there were several photographs. But they were all tied together by a common element—water. A neon waterpark and a murky lake. Turquoise waters off the coast of an island. Ocean waves laced in silver. I rose to my feet and walked closer to the mantel. Upon closer inspection, I saw that each piece bore the initials MT.

The overhead light flicked on. I hadn't realized how dark the room had been, and I blinked rapidly as my eyes adjusted. Charlie bounded up to Matthew, who was standing at the edge of the room with his hand still on the light switch.

"Sorry. Hope I didn't startle you," he said while bending

down to greet Charlie. "Just figured you could see a little better with the lights on."

"You would be correct about that, thanks." I turned back to the pictures. "Did you make all these?"

He joined me at the mantel. "Sure did. I love painting and sketching in my free time. Photography too, although who isn't a photographer these days?"

"They're really amazing. I've never seen anything like it."

Matthew accepted the compliment in stride. "Did Amy tell you about them?"

I shook my head.

His face lit up with the expression of someone about to share a favorite memory. "Well, Amy and I met in high school. Back then, before I realized it wasn't exactly a lucrative career, I wanted to be an artist. Amy and I hadn't been together that long, but I already knew she was the best thing that had and would ever happen to me. So one day, I took her to my studio, also known as a corner in my parents' garage. My family had gone to California a few months earlier for vacation, and I couldn't get the ocean out of my mind. I had been experimenting with different blues, any shade I could find. I had stacks and stacks of beach scenes, rivers, lakes, even puddles. She sifted through them without saying a word."

He shook his head and laughed. "I thought she hated them. But then she said the most beautiful thing anyone had ever said to me. It was the thing that made me absolutely certain about her. She told me, 'This is how it's like being with you. You make my world more beautiful than I could ever have imagined.'"

He gazed at the photos, his eyes shining. "So these are all

part of my life's work. Capturing as many shades of blue as I can for her. I'll probably fill every bare inch of space in this house before I run out of shades."

Later that night, I stared up at the ceiling above my bed, trying to sift through the emotions of the day to find the meaning in them. A blank postcard I purchased earlier that day rested on my chest. It showed the otters splashing around below inflated, colorful letters that read RED RIVER ZOO. I wanted to write about Miss Julie and Amy and Matthew. I needed to try to explain how obvious it had become that life carried meaning only when there were others to share it with. How when I slipped into this life so fully consumed by myself, I pushed away everything that made me valuable, leaving me empty. Hollow. Starving.

I turned onto my side and grabbed the pen on the table beside me. I wrote the truth down before I had the chance to change my mind.

You were the greatest thing in my life. And I don't know if I can bear to devote the rest of it to the memory of us.

I didn't even have to pull out the letter I kept in my jacket pocket. I knew the address by heart. I wrote it with a manic hand in the indicated box.

The hallway my door opened to was dark and still. It was later than I thought. Amy and Matthew had been asleep for hours. I crept to the study and clicked on the desk lamp.

The top drawer opened with a shudder. I sifted through neat stacks of sticky notes and labeled containers of paper clips, binder clips, and pushpins until, miraculously, I unearthed a sheet of stamps.

I took it as a sign of divine intervention. That this was actually a fantastic idea, and I should ignore the growing sense of dread in the pit of my stomach.

It was a full sheet of stamps and I hesitated, considering slipping them back into the drawer. Instead, I took them to my room and furiously wrote that unforgettable address down on fifteen additional postcards, slapped a stamp on each of them, gathered them up, and practically ran out the front door.

I sprinted down the street barefoot. The night was warm and sticky after weeks of rain. I had walked around the neighborhood enough times to know that a right turn onto the main road would bring me to the parking lot of the post office. Loose asphalt bit into my feet as I ran across the lot. *I probably could have paused long enough to put on shoes*, I mused. But that wouldn't have been nearly as dramatic.

I nearly ran straight into the blue, metal box. I fumbled with the postcards, opened the lid, and dumped them inside. I closed the lid, then opened it again to make sure they were really gone. They were truly out of my hands.

I waited for the wave of panic as I stood there panting, but all I felt was increasing pain in the soles of my feet as the adrenaline wore off.

It was only when I was back in the house and went to slip a five-dollar bill into the top desk drawer to cover the cost of the stamps that I felt the impact of what I had just done.

Amy was waiting for me there, sitting in the desk chair and looking at me with an eyebrow raised.

The sight of her jolted me back to reality. I was no longer wrapped in my safety net of heightened emotions the night's brooding hours tend to bring. Now the clock read 3:02 a.m., and I was the idiot this poor woman had to deal with instead of getting a solid night's rest.

Amy rose from her seat and came to stand right in front of me. Her hair was wild and her eyes bright. In them I could see something akin to pity, but not quite as humiliating. It was sympathy, I realized. It was a willingness to try and understand. She was looking at me like I knew I used to look at Claire when she was having a rough day. Like she would give life and limb to make it better.

I still hadn't moved. She considered the money, then slowly put a hand on my shoulder and said in a slightly exasperated tone, "Maybe we should talk."

21

“We met in a philosophy class freshman year of college.” I was sitting with my knees tucked against my chest in the corner of what I now considered to be my bed. Amy leaned against the wall across from me, the perfect pose of an attentive listener. She had made us both tea, and I was grateful for something I could hold in my hands.

“Well, technically we officially met when I chased him down in the hallway after a class, but obviously I had noticed him before that.” I winced. “Can I take a second to assure you this story doesn’t end with a confession of a body buried in a field somewhere?”

“Good, I was worried,” she managed to say through a stifled yawn.

“It was hard *not* to notice him,” I said, smiling at the memory. “This was Philosophy 101, a required class that just checked a box on everyone’s transcript. No one felt it was worth their time. Well, no one except Alex. He argued with nearly everything the professor said, confidently voicing his opinions on every aspect of morality while the rest of the class was on their phones or sleeping.” I laughed.

"And in those rare moments he wasn't talking, he would tap his pencil on his knee while thinking of his next retort. He was nonstop energy. To me, he was like this unlikely, kind of hopeless vigilante. Never resting in his pursuit to teach us all his infallible definitions of right and wrong." I rested my cheek on my knee for a moment, studying the patterns on the quilt.

Amy waited so I continued, "One day, we were discussing Kant's murderer at the door example. It's that scenario where there's a person outside your door who wants to murder someone you're hiding in your house. They ask you if that person is home and you can either be dishonest and tell them no or be truthful and tell them yes. It's supposed to raise the question of if we are ever justified in breaking our moral codes. No one was paying any attention, except for Alex.

I bobbed my tea bag a time or two, the still-steaming water now a deep amber. "He argued that a moral code with flexible rules isn't a code at all. It becomes completely meaningless if we only follow it when it best suits us. I thought that was completely ridiculous. And honestly, I was concerned that this kid with the unbreakable sense of right and wrong believed this. So, after class I ran up to him. I said something along the lines of, 'Would you seriously let the murderer in just so you wouldn't be a liar?' I remember he looked at me for such a long moment. I don't know if he was surprised that someone else was actually paying attention in class or trying to figure out why I cared so much.

"Regardless, he finally answered and said, 'Of course not. The greater good always trumps any moral code we have in place. I value honesty, but not to the point that it's a hazard.' So I asked him why he said otherwise in class. And he told me playing devil's advocate with the professor helps pass the hour. Then he grinned at me, and the rest was inevitable."

I could tell Amy thought this last part was ridiculous, but she remained silent. I wondered how she felt about Matthew's story. But then again, it was always different when it was your own.

"I know people say this all the time," I told her, "but when I tell you that we were great together, I don't say that lightly. Those first four years of our relationship, when things were good and everything was ahead of us, we were unstoppable. We completed each other in that precarious but soul-binding way that only two healthy people from opposite ends of the emotional spectrum can.

I flicked my gaze up at her for a moment, long enough to confirm she wasn't laughing at me. I cleared my throat self-consciously, set my untouched tea down on the bedside table, and forged ahead. "He helped me assign reason and purpose to my emotions. He helped me make decisions, gave my life direction, and encouraged me to sort out my endless and overwhelming ambitions so I could actually reach my goals. And I helped him to pick out the beauty in the world, reminding him it wasn't all garbage and suffering. I'd point out the worth in something he might have overlooked. I taught him to be less hard on himself." I shook my head. "He was so hard on himself. About everything. He worked so hard, so unceasingly, until he ran himself into the ground. But I tried to constantly remind him that enjoyment is a necessary and beautiful part of life. I'd help him open up to his emotions a bit more, stop keeping everything in so much. But we both loved each other for our desire to make the world a better place."

I could see the beginnings of an eyeroll from Amy, so I rushed to defend myself. "Yeah, I know. But we were in college, so that life goal was still totally acceptable. We both wanted to work with the margins of society. Alex in politics, me in the nonprofit sector. And we were doing it. We were doing it together, supporting one another and celebrating every new milestone side by side. It was everything. And then, and then . . ."

I was off to such a good start, but I felt myself losing steam. I had never actually talked about this next part. It was the part I tortured myself with constantly, but never the part I shared. "Then I screwed everything up. In every conceivable way, really. We were approaching graduation and I had no luck securing a full-time job. So I worked an unpaid internship at a local nonprofit and picked up a part-time job at Wendy's. It was only meant to be temporary until I got a job where I could actually use my degree. Alex had no problem getting a job. He was hired by a local politician to help run his campaign, and his career took off from there. Eventually, my internship ended. I really needed a paying job, like one with benefits and such, so I couldn't afford to take on another unpaid internship. The job search still offered nothing, so I started at Wendy's full-time."

I sighed and buried my head in my hands.

"Alex kept excelling, like always. And I came up with nothing but disappointments. He was out there every day making our city better, just like we planned to do, except I wasn't pulling my weight. At all. Our whole relationship was built on this idea of working toward something universally good and transcendent and then . . . Then everything felt imbalanced.

"So I guess I became a little depressed. I don't know. I know it doesn't seem like I had anything to be depressed about. I had enough money to get by, an amazing boyfriend, a college degree, I was healthy . . . But I felt depressed all the same. And then I would get frustrated at myself for feeling depressed, which would make me lash out at everyone around me. And more often than not, that would be Alex."

Amy sat relaxed, sipping her tea. I tried to channel some of her calm before going on. "I would accuse him of not spending enough time with me, of focusing more on his work than our relationship. He would point out that I was being hopelessly emotional over nothing. That I had become completely self-absorbed and self-indulgent. And he was right, of course. All I could argue back was that he was being judgmental and cold, which may have been true, but who could blame him? The way I was living, I deserved to be judged. I deserved no sympathy for my uncontrollable outbursts. He was living his dream and I was becoming more and more of a burden every day.

"I could feel him pulling away, and I let him." I sighed. "I did things to push him further from me because I no longer felt like I was good enough for the relationship. When he finally left, he apologized. He said he was sorry, but he couldn't lose sight of what he believed he was born to do."

I pulled my knees in closer to my chest and buried my face in them. "He doesn't even know about the anorexia," I added with a bitter laugh. "That was something I picked up sometime after he left. Besides, he had more than enough reasons to leave without it."

I raised my head but kept my gaze on the bedspread. I wasn't afraid to own my actions, but I was embarrassed to share my failures. It would be one thing if my behavior had been justified in some way, but the fact that I couldn't pull myself together when I had every opportunity in the world for success was unforgivable.

I took a breath and finally met Amy's eyes. She held her now-empty mug in her hands and her expression assured me she had heard, no, truly listened to every word I had said. "So I just sent him a bunch of postcards," I said. "Ones I've written to him over the months. They barely make sense but writing them was more meaningful than anything I've done in a long time." I released my grip on my knees to gesture toward my body. "I mean, do you think I don't realize how meaningless this whole thing is? This whole eating disorder? I can't tell you how many hours I've wasted running mile after mile, measuring out portion sizes, staring at myself in the mirror." I made a sound somewhere between a laugh and a sob.

"I've wasted so much time wasting away. Contributing nothing, helping no one, only hurting and confusing the few people still left in my life. And for what? So I can be skinny enough? Joke's on me, because I'll never be skinny enough. This sickness eating my brain will never let me stop trying to lose those next five pounds. And honestly, skinny enough for who? There's literally no one left in my life!"

I was shouting now and silent tears ran down my face. I had never said that out loud before, but some small part of me, still fighting after all this time, must have believed it to be true. It was such a simple truth. These games I had been playing with myself, this mystery weight I never seemed capable of defining or achieving—it was all meaningless.

And this was something I always did. I made a grand design

out of what should have been a simple truth. Everything had to be bold and beautiful and incredible. I had always wanted a unique life, so much so I tended to dramatize the one I had whenever I could. For crying out loud, I chose to walk thousands of miles instead of going to rehab.

"I don't know what to do, Amy." I was no longer shedding silent tears, but full-on ugly crying. "I haven't known what to do since about the fiftieth email I got telling me in some way or another that I didn't get the job. And I guess that's why I'm still stuck in these meaningless, self-obsessed loops. I lost all my meaning. I lost it in the professional dreams I didn't live out, the family I was once close to, the man I loved so fiercely and lost so completely. So I tried to create my own meaning in something, my own worth in something, but I've lost everything bigger than me in my life to find meaning *in*." I wiped at my cheeks. "Geez, maybe I've just been looking for something I could actually control in my life. And look where it got me. I couldn't even do that right."

Amy placed her mug on the bedside table next to mine. She scooted onto the bed so we had our backs against the same wall. She didn't touch me, but her presence was enough.

After I was no longer gasping for air, a long silence fell between us. Finally, she spoke. "You're still going to Washington, aren't you?"

"Yes," I said without hesitation.

She crossed her arms. "You know you might not find what you're looking for when you arrive, right?"

"I know," I said. "But at least I will have achieved something. And I think that will give me the motivation to start again."

She seemed to want to say something more on the subject but changed her mind.

"What about him?" she finally asked. "What about Alex?"

I sighed. "I think there are things I need to say to him still that don't fit on the back of a postcard." I glanced at Amy. "He lives in Montana now. In Billings. I didn't plan on visiting, and I still don't plan on it. But I also didn't plan on writing him postcard after postcard, so who knows."

She nodded and I smiled. "You're being weirdly quiet. I thought I might scare you off with that story . . ."

She gave me a clipped laugh. "I know better than to try to get someone who's blind to their own value to see their worth. It's something you'll have to find again on your own, because my words aren't going to make a difference." Amy stretched and yawned. She gave the quilt a couple decisive pats before scooting off the bed. "You're right, you've got to find your meaning again. And I think the best thing for you is to keep journeying on. You're strong, stronger than I thought you were, and I know now you'll be okay out there. But when you're out there on your grand adventure"—she paused for emphasis, looking into my eyes like she was about to share the secret of life—"keep your eyes open for meaning in things big *and* small. If you do that, you may just find what you're looking for."

I wrapped my arms around myself, my heart suddenly swelling with gratitude for this person who was a stranger to me not five days before. "You know, I think I would have died if it wasn't for you."

She rolled her eyes. "Don't be so dramatic."

22

"Well, I guess that's it, then."

I was standing on Matthew and Amy's front stoop a few hours later, packed and ready to go. It was early, so early that the sky was still a deep black and stars could be seen through the clouds.

"This better not be it," Amy countered, hands on her hips. "You promised to call every time you crossed state lines. And you better believe I won't hesitate to file a missing person report if you don't."

Matthew put his arm around his wife and offered me a sympathetic smile.

"I know, I know. I'll call, I promise." I looked at the two of them, committing the sight of them to memory to get me through the road ahead. "If I started thanking you for everything you've done for me, we'd be here for days, so I wrote it all down and left it in my room." I grinned at Amy. "It's pretty much a really sappy version of 'Thanks for looking out for me.'"

Amy's features were tight. If I didn't know better, I would guess she was trying not to cry. I hugged them all, including Charlie.

“Did you pack your breakfast?” Amy asked. “I’ll hunt you down myself if you’ve left it on the kitchen table.”

I held up the paper bag. “Got it.”

Amy gave one sharp nod. “Well, get going, then. Put some distance behind you before the sun comes up and tries to boil you alive.”

It was harder than I thought it would be to turn away from them. But I forced myself to, knowing I had given myself no other choice. I waved goodbye and walked away into the black morning.

I felt different somehow. I tried to shake it off with each mile, but the feeling stuck. My limbs didn’t seem to move as fluidly. I jumped slightly at every noise. The muscles in my back tightened up and ached almost instantly. I had become too domesticated over the past week, and more than once I found myself stopping in my tracks, one decision away from turning back to the safety and comfort of the home I had just left behind.

But that wasn’t my life. I had been an invader. No, I had to build my own life. It had to be earned. Granted, this was a bit of a roundabout way to do so, but the traditional methods never worked well for me.

So I ventured on. I walked down quiet main roads, occasionally pulling out the local map Amy had given to me.

Eventually the world showed first signs of the approaching morning. I caught snippets of birdsong, windows to bedrooms and kitchens were illuminated with a warm glow, and everything was cast in the deep-blue shade of a brand-new day.

Something about the shade of the sky brought back a hazy memory from so long ago, it could have been my first memory. It was on a morning like this, when the air was still heavy with blue darkness and sleep.

> Good morning to you.
> Good morning to you.
> Good morning, dear Melanie.
> Good morning to you.

My mother's singsong voice, reserved for only the earliest wake-up calls, cut through my dreams, and she gently shook me awake under my mountain of blankets. She loved me so much back then.

The floor was ice-cold, and my eyelids were heavy. It was the cusp of winter in Grand Rapids, and through my little window I believed the streetlight was the sun. But it was 5:30 a.m., the sun a long way off, and my mother spoke in a soft whisper like she was worried she would wake the sleeping world.

I shivered while I dressed. My mom, hugely pregnant with Claire, buttered a piece of toast for me to eat on the way to an early-morning gymnastics class on the other side of town. That was before we all realized I had about as much coordination as a jelly bean. I looked like one too. Underneath the puffy blue coat my mom had zipped up to my neck, I wore a bright-pink leotard that stretched over my four-year-old belly. I was too young to compare my body to the girls somersaulting and jumping into the foam pits. All I knew was that I liked the trampoline the best.

We must have done this exact routine a dozen times before, but I think that morning stood out because of how I felt watching the commuters fly past us on the road. This 5:30 a.m. world was unknown to me. I hadn't known darkness like this. I didn't know anyone did anything but sleep in those early hours. The world was too busy and too dark, and it all felt wrong compared to the world that I knew of sunshine and backyards and smiling faces in the grocery store. Now I couldn't make out any faces as the cars passed us by.

But then I caught a glimpse of my mother in the front seat. She was humming along to a quiet song on the radio, looking like this world didn't scare her at all. I felt the warm toast wrapped in a paper towel on my lap and the snugness of the seat belt harness around me. I knew then that as long as I had my mom around, nothing in the world could hurt me. Nothing would be too scary.

And now in the early, humid morning I watched the traffic of Fargo, still unable to see the faces as they passed. My mother was thousands of miles away. The toast eaten long ago. There was no seat belt snug around my chest.

And all I wanted, more than anything, was to not feel afraid again. To feel that unshakable, caring, loving presence that I knew without a shadow of a doubt I could count on to get me to my destination safely.

A few sunrises later, I had left the quiet residential streets of Fargo far behind for the equally unassuming city of Bismarck. Despite the familiar comfort of the brick storefronts and tree-lined neighborhoods, I felt an almost overwhelming urge to make my way back to a wilder place where the sky had no end and the voices of trees were the only ones to be heard.

From Bismarck, it was easy to find my way onto the Lewis and Clark Historic Trail. I took a deep, shaky breath after passing the first trail marker, my feet firmly planted on the dirt path. Air warmed by summer sunshine filled my lungs. I released the breath and smiled, feeling that surrounded by these windswept plains, I was the closest I could possibly be to belonging somewhere.

I continued along the banks of the Missouri River and watched fishing boats navigate the jagged shoreline of Lake Sakakawea. Right before I left the vibrant green fields and plains of North Dakota for Big Sky Country, I came to a crossroads. The powerful Missouri River continued straight ahead, deep and wide and sure. Veering off to the south, however, was its muddier cousin, the Yellowstone River, broken by islands of shrubby trees and winding haphazardly out of view. I didn't have to look at my map to know following that river would take me straight into Billings. Straight to Alex.

I thought back to the postcards, falling with finality to the bottom of that blue bin. Had they been collected? Had they already been dumped and sorted along with millions of other letters, thousands more desperate pleas and aching longings scratched out with pen?

I still wasn't sure if I would ever step foot in Billings. I knew I could no more easily stop breathing than give up even the possibility of seeing him again. I turned my back on the Missouri River and headed south.

In the time since leaving Fargo, I had missed having Alex by my side with a ferocity that seemed more animalistic than rational. I felt his absence as sharply as I did in those first few weeks he left, like a phantom limb. Being a hopeless romantic—emphasis on the hopeless—I had loved him so fully, so completely, that I had left nothing of myself behind to turn to when I was left alone. No part of my soul was left unbroken.

We had come together so rapidly and seamlessly. There was never any discussion about the growing intensity of our relationship because the progress had felt as natural as breathing. We would spend every second possible glued to each other's sides. But during the decline—*my* decline—some social or professional obligation would occasionally take my successful, extroverted other half away from me for a few hours or days. The idea of having my own space to do whatever I pleased again always made my introverted heart fill with excitement. But it would take only a few hours for the aloneness to lose its appeal.

I would miss how he would tolerate my every conceivable attempt to distract him from getting anything of value accomplished when I wanted his attention. I missed his laugh and his closeness on the couch. I missed his arms reaching out to me whenever he sensed I needed them. He had slowly, so slowly, chipped away at my chronic loneliness and the self-reliance that had encased my heart for so long.

And when that crack formed, my heart broke through and rushed out to him like thundering rapids. He turned an introvert into a being who looked forward to another person's company. He had the superpower of bringing out my truest self, and he did so by making me believe it was also my best self.

Something had shifted, I remember, that made the most anticipated time of day *our* time instead of *my* time. It was disarming and uncertain, but I let myself fall into it because it was better than anything I had ever faced alone.

Ironically, I was now searching for him against a backdrop created for the lone wanderer. Montana was a place where it only made sense that the hills were covered with not much else other than dry brown grasses and sparse shrubbery, because the sky swallowed everything up. It was a larger-than-life masterpiece painted every morning, even more overwhelming than what I left behind in Minnesota and North Dakota. The horizon spoke of limitless possibilities, the sort of thing that inspired the songs of cowboys and outlaws. I felt my singularity so acutely under that painted sky. There was nowhere to hide from myself, nowhere to run from the memories that had so resolutely shaped who I was now.

He continued to leave, and I continued to miss him. Then one day, he didn't come back. It had been necessary. I knew that truth with all my heart. Because as much as I loved having someone to miss so completely, as much as I loved having another person value my presence, I couldn't allow it to continue when he was so clearly mistaken about my worth. He deserved more than someone he had to lie to about her potential for greatness. So he left, as I knew he would. And I was left missing him, even still.

I had tried to stop missing him. Tried to outrun his memory with all those miles on the treadmill. I never tried to replace him though. It was the way of brokenhearted introverts. We don't have the energy to go out and suffer through social events. We don't see the point of including people in our lives anymore. So we turn inward, deeper and deeper, with nothing left around us to pull us out. The real world becomes a barely visited place. All the voices and conversations we need, or think we need, are right in our heads.

I used other tactics to try and move on. But once you've experienced someone who you've allowed to become a permanent resident in your soul, I'm not sure you can ever fully regain all the pieces of your old self. You'll always be longing for those arms around you, always be aware of that missing piece.

So I kept walking, all that day and the next and the next, under that eternal expanse of sky. And during that time, I found myself wondering for a moment, only one brief moment, what it would feel like to be worth so much to someone that they would walk across plains and woodlands and prairies to find me, for no other reason except that they could no longer bear the distance between us.

23

I couldn't help but stare. The vending machine was a beacon, and I was drawn to it like a moth to a flame. I could almost hear the siren song of the bright-yellow packet of Peanut M&M's reaching out to me, begging me to free it from its cage.

I put a hand against the glass like behind it was my long-lost child and not a bag of artificially flavored, chocolate-coated peanuts. I wasn't sure at that moment if I had ever wanted anything so much in my entire life.

I was doing fine with my food rations, still days away from running out, and I was eating well and often, making sure I hit the minimum required calories every day without fail.

But when I last shopped for food in the sleepy small town of Terry, the only grocery store had limited options that fit my already extremely picky food requirements. With little other choice, I thought I would simplify things by eating the same thing for breakfast, lunch, and dinner every day.

This worked out fine for a few days but became mind-numbingly boring after that. My foraging skills had been of very little use through the dry, beige hills and plateaus. It was the first time in a long time that I had to force myself to eat not because I wanted to lose weight, but because I was so completely sick of *what* I was eating.

As my beige meal plan of muesli and raisins stood in contrast to the glorious rainbow of M&Ms, I could feel my ironclad self-control beginning to slip.

I recalled the sensation of consuming those tiny orbs of happiness with hardly any effort. The crisp bite into the outer shell, the sweetness of the chocolate, the crunch of the peanut. All a perfect blend of salty and sweet. I never liked candy much, but Peanut M&M's had always been the exception.

All I had to do was put in a dollar and press a few buttons. That's all, and then they would be mine.

But where would it end? If I let myself slip now, on something so blatantly unhealthy, what even more fattening mistake would be next?

So I sighed and slipped in a dollar, hit A6, and waited for my Super Healthy Omega 3 Trail Mix to fall. Not a drop of chocolate in sight.

I sat on a bench outside the rest stop as I unhappily munched on the bland walnuts and pistachios. I tried to pretend they were M&M's, but it was no use.

It was midday and the remote rest stop was busy, which I appreciated. Run-down rest stops such as these always left me with a murdery vibe, so the more families piling out of minivans, the better.

I watched as an elderly man stooped to pick up a dog in the back seat of his car. The dog looked old, blind, and as if it would blow over in a stiff breeze. A woman stepped out of the car as well, and I could only assume she was the man's daughter. The woman headed indoors as the man and his dog shuffled over to the grassy area near my bench.

I turned my attention back to my lackluster snack, trying to give the dog some semblance of privacy. But I glanced back at them when the man picked up the dog, held him up like Simba in the *Lion King*, and told him to have a better look.

I blinked and studied the view. More desolate hills spotted here and there with deep-green, gnarled trees. I could make out the beginnings of a small town in the distance, but that was about it. Even the sky was bland today, a massive sheet of sleet gray.

After a long moment, the man placed the dog gently back on the ground and peered up at me.

"She likes the view," he stated plainly. "I think it makes her think of a giant dog park."

I looked out again. "I guess I can see that."

He let his dog sniff around, the two of them looking quite pleased. "My daughter and I are taking her to all her favorite places," he said, not looking up from his companion.

"What?"

"Bella." He indicated toward the dog, who was sniffing furiously at a fast-food wrapper. "She loves this rest stop. All the smells and snacks left over by travelers. My wife and I used to stop here every time we went to visit our kids."

"Oh," I said. "Well, she has good taste. It's a nice rest stop."

The man beamed, then bent down to give Bella a treat.

The woman returned, taking her father gently by the elbow. "Is Bella done sniffing? We've still got to make it to the ice cream place and the dog park before dark, so we should probably get back on the road."

"Hear that, Bella?" the old man said to the dog. "Your birthday party is just getting started."

His daughter only smiled, picked up Bella, and walked the two of them back to the car.

I watched them drive away, a little stunned.

I pulled out my phone suddenly, which had been dead before Fargo. I hadn't bothered to charge it at Amy and Matthew's. I told myself it was because I was too good for social media and the goings-on of the modern world, but truthfully it was to avoid any texts or voice mails from my grandma, who was back from her cruise by this point. Or even worse, from my mom. I even went as far as calling Amy from the world's last standing payphone when I crossed into Montana to avoid using my own phone.

But something about that man and his daughter made the avoidance efforts seem childish, almost cruel. As much as I often thought my existence would be easier if the matriarchs in my life didn't care about me, they did. It was a weird and often twisted sort of love, but it wasn't something I'd been able to walk away from completely.

I found an outlet under the display of brochures for local attractions. I picked up a stack and leafed through colorful advertisements for trading posts, frontier museums, rodeos, and old military forts as I waited for my phone to come back to life.

I glanced over as I heard buzz after buzz—an onslaught of notifications for missed calls, texts, and voice mails. When it finally fell silent, I stifled a groan of pure dread and picked it up.

Almost all the texts were from my grandma. The two that weren't belonged to Kat, wishing me safe travels and asking me to let her know if I was all right if I got the chance. I texted her back without hesitation. I also rattled off texts to Linnie, George, and Amy, whose contact I had just added, to let them know I was still alive and doing fine.

As for my grandma's texts . . . They started out enraged, all caps and demands and various forms of "how dare you?" But as I scrolled through the texts from weeks passed, the tone changed from furious to pleading to fearful. The last one was from a week ago. It simply read:

Just please tell me you're safe.

I bit my lip. Guilt rushed over me, making it hard to breathe. I knew she'd be upset, but I hadn't realized how worried she would be. I typed out a message, then stared at it a long time before hitting send.

I'm doing great. Sorry to worry you. I'll call when I finish what I set out to do.

I immediately sent another text, imagining my grandma's panic.

I now realize that "finish what I set out to do" was an ominous choice of words. I'm just walking a lot and ending up at a particular destination. Call you when I get there.

I leaned back against the rest stop wall. It was a pathetic attempt to patch things up, but I couldn't call her. I couldn't trust myself not to tell her where I was or where I was going. Because as much as she complained about having to drive all that way to visit me in the hospital, she always showed up. And I had no doubt that if she knew where I was, she would get in her car and not stop driving until she found me. I couldn't let her do that, to herself or to me. So a text message would have to work for now.

My phone buzzed, and a text popped up from my grandma.

Don't you EVER ignore me like that again. I know you're too stubborn to talk to me on the phone, but please text me every once and a while so I know you're all right. I don't think that's too much to ask.

Deal. Sorry, Grandma.

You're always sorry.

Just be safe.

I sighed wearily. There was always so much to be sorry for. The reasons for apologies on my part never seemed to run out.

I switched over to my voice mail, which was crowded with more messages from my grandma. I couldn't muster the courage to listen to them. Amid all her voice mails, there was one from an international number. I knew who it was, and maybe I was contemplating listening to it because I felt like I deserved to be punished.

Or maybe it was because I couldn't help but think back to that night in the cornfield, when I contemplated getting to know the woman who raised me.

Or maybe what it all came down to was as simple as some small part of me really wanting to hear my mother's voice.

I pressed play and held the phone up to my ear with trepidation.

"Melanie, I recently received a call from your grandmother." Her voice was a little warped from static, but the disappointment was unmistakable. "I don't even know what to say. I thought I raised you better than to run off like that. I know you have been having some . . . issues, but running from them is never the solution. Did you even take the time to think of how disappointing these actions are to God? The one who sends us struggles to overcome in His name? We are called to become stronger through adversity instead of giving in to Satan's cowardice." I could hear sounds of life in the background. I imagined dusty roads, brilliant sunshine, and neighbors calling out greetings to one another. My mother's voice was low. I fit her in at the edge of the scene, far enough away so no one could overhear her trying to fix her mess of a daughter.

"As always, you chose the most selfish option, never once looking to God for strength. You need to come back now from wherever you are. You need to repent and start living the life God wants for you. It's not too late to become the person God expects you to be to further His kingdom, not just another person floating aimlessly through the secular world—"

The voice mail continued on for another two minutes, but I scraped up just enough self-respect to spare myself the rest of the guilt trip. I deleted the message and scrolled up to the most recent calls to see if there were any others from her I needed to delete.

There were no more from her, but there was a voice mail dated yesterday afternoon. From Alex Martinez.

I held the phone very, very still as I tried to slow my heartbeat. Every inch of me felt like it buzzed with electricity. My nerves were suddenly so strained I worried they would snap and I would burst out laughing hysterically until I had no breath left in my body and died of laughter right there on the floor of the rest stop.

The message was forty-seven seconds long. I got up, paced from one end of the tiny building to the other five times, then sat back down. I involuntarily held my breath as I pressed play. My breath stayed locked in my body through the next few seconds of profound silence, then came out in a rush when I finally heard the voice that was still my favorite sound in the world.

"Mel . . . I got the postcards. Your postcards. All of them."

I felt close to bursting into tears. It would be easier than listening to the rest of his message. I had very little dignity left to maintain anyway.

"I don't really understand what's going on, but I want to see you. Please. I've wanted to see you . . . Just please tell me where to meet you. If you don't want to see me, I understand. But please let me know that you're safe. Keep sending me postcards or even a text. Anything to let me know."

There was a pause then. It went on for so long I thought I might have reached the abrupt end of his message.

"I miss you too," he said finally, making my heart twist into knots. "Every day. And it seems to be getting worse with time, not better." He sighed, and I imagined him on the couch in his apartment, head in his hand. "If you get this, please reach out to me somehow. I just want to keep talking to you." Another pause. The last pause. "All right . . . bye, Mel."

I kept the phone to my ear long after the voice mail ended,

like if I pulled it away, it might be like it had never happened. There was such a sharp sense of longing forming in the pit of my stomach I could barely breathe normally. It was sharper than any pang of hunger, any cry for food. I felt my sense of directionlessness swallowed up in the longing.

I had known all along why I had felt off course, but I was hoping it would pass with time. I still hadn't learned that these sorts of things never quietly passed but fought and grew until their urgency could no longer be ignored. No maybes, no more second-guessing. My pilgrimage required a detour to Billings, Montana. I got to my feet, ignoring the shaking in my legs.

I walked out of the rest stop with a sense of purpose, only to pull out my map and realize I still had at least a week to go before I would reach Billings. I immediately panicked—cold sweat and all—my default setting when I lost patience.

I was so wound up on old feelings and adrenaline I had no idea how I was going to last another minute without seeing Alex, let alone a week. In a week's time, I might have lost my nerve.

It only took me to the end of the parking lot to convince myself that by the time I arrived, Alex would have forgotten all about me, making our reunion even more awkward than expected.

I tried to take a deep breath, tried to remind myself that patience was one of the things I had set out to learn while on the road. My pep talk failed miserably, so I just kept walking at a slightly faster pace. It was the only thing I could do.

"Take, Lord, and receive all my liberty." I recited the prayer of Saint Ignatius Loyola as I found my way back to the trail. Reciting the words forced my breathing to slow, my mind to relax. "My understanding, and my entire will, all I have and call my own."

I reached my daily caloric intake through now-horrifyingly stale muesli and almonds without argument. I had places to reach and things to do once I arrived, and the only way that was going to happen was if I ate enough. I probably would have been shocked at how simply I was able to trick myself into allowing proper daily calorie consumption if my brain hadn't been fully occupied obsessing over other matters.

Each day hiking through the beige hills felt longer, every night endless. The sky was constantly overcast, robbing every day of a sunrise and sunset to look forward to and turning the shimmering Yellowstone River into a flat brown that matched the rest of the landscape. The world had been drained of color, which made my approaching destination all the more fluorescent in my imagination.

I would occupy my time by singing every song I knew, reciting every prayer, talking to myself, making up patron saints, telling increasingly absurd stories. Anything to keep myself from thinking about what was so agonizingly far ahead.

This strategy worked fine until one night when I could not find sleep beneath the starless sky due to my endless progression of thoughts. I was so tired, but of course, sleep didn't come. So I listened to the crickets sing and harmonize with the faint rush of water from the river.

"Why do they sound like that?" Claire had asked me through tears during the first father-daughter camping trip she was old enough to join. She had never heard anything like the sound of thousands of crickets trying to talk over each other. "Are they hurt, Melanie? Are they screaming?"

We were on the way back to our campsite after the final before-bed trip to the outhouse. The night was cooling rapidly, and the light from our flashlights bounced off the trees, making it feel like they were closing in to swallow us whole. I wrapped her tiny hand tightly in mine.

"Don't worry about them," I told her as I marched us back to camp. "They're singing. It might not sound like much to us, but to them, it's the most beautiful song in the world."

In the tent not two hours later, I shook my dad awake, tears streaming down my face.

"What is it, kiddo?" he asked me, instantly alert.

"Dad, it's the mountains," I whispered. "The Porcupine Mountains are going to turn into volcanoes any second and bury us all in lava. Like Pompeii. I learned all about it in school."

He was somehow able to calm my hysteria and talk me into going back to sleep. The next morning, he woke me earlier than Claire so we could sit by a morning fire and watch the sun rise over the ridges, pointing out the differences between these glorified hills and volcanoes. I was still a bit skeptical, which only made him laugh.

"Mel, nothing is ever as it seems to you, is it?" he said, wrapping me in a bear hug. "That heart of yours, it turns hills into volcanoes and crickets into a symphony. You better make sure to keep your head, young lady. Because that heart of yours is a blessing and a curse."

On this sleepless night, his words clicked into place for the first time.

This mad dash back to Alex, I was rushing headlong into another fantasy I had woven for myself. He was my knight, his shining armor the only thing of value in my bleak world. Morally flawless, just, and true, Alex would guide me back to a life of meaning like my North Star. And all it took from him was one forty-seven-second-long voice mail.

I sat up, shocked by how wholly wrong that was. Shocked by how fully I believed it. As soon as he walked out our door for the last time, every one of his transgressions had been forgotten. I chose to remember nothing but the good things, polishing them with each recalled memory until he had become this untouchable, unimaginably good blessing I had let slip out of my life.

I got to my feet, shoved my few possessions back into my backpack, and walked on. I trudged down the wide dirt path, illuminated ever so faintly by a full moon behind the clouds, as I tried to sort this out.

I reached back through the years, past the sparkling, rosy memories. Past every longing glance, every soft-spoken word, every gesture of love. I needed to see everything laid bare, digging down past the places that it hurt to the place where it constantly ached, the place I never gave much thought to exploring. I needed to seek the facts, not my interpretation of them.

I searched my past for the days that held all the big moments together. We weren't always out trying to save the world or in each other's arms. There was a lot of incredibly normal existing we did in between.

I remembered when things started to fall into a rhythm. Classes were over, real life had begun. We would wake up, go to work, eat dinner, and fall into a silence in front of the TV that became less and less comfortable over time. We used to talk constantly, never running out of words for each other. But our lives had so slowly drifted in different directions, and we were no longer a unit, more like cohabitants.

"I think I'm a little lost," I had confessed to Alex not long after my internship ended—my voice shaking and tight with tears. "I don't know what's wrong exactly, but lately it feels like a huge piece of me is somehow missing."

He was shrugging on his jacket, about to head out for some big important event. They were all big and important by that point. The sigh he let slip was one of barely contained impatience. His mouth was a thin, tight line as he walked me over to the couch and sat me down.

"Have you reached out to those contacts I sent you last week?"

"Yes, but—"

"Just because you haven't heard back yet doesn't mean they don't plan to respond. You have to be patient, Mel. How about that internship fair you went to last Monday? Have you followed up on those leads?"

"I have. I just don't know—"

"And those edits I made to your résumé—you reviewed them, right? You've been using the updated version? Your cover letter template also needed some tweaks."

"I've done all that. That's been done for weeks."

"Okay," he said, letting loose that same impatient sigh again. "Have you contacted your advisor yet this month?"

"Not yet."

He practically sprang up from the couch then, trying his best not to sprint toward the door. "There you go! There's something for you to do. Actionable steps." As he slipped his phone and keys into his jacket pocket, he added, "If you put the right kind of effort into it, you'll get results. It's as simple as that, Mel."

And I felt it then. I felt it as clearly as if I was back on that couch, watching the door close on his way out. That acute sense of not being worth enough.

He bought me self-help books after that, I remembered. He would ask me every night how much I had read, if I found anything that helped. I would lie, saying everything he wanted to hear. Those books didn't help, but I couldn't stand to disappoint him further. He would send me daily emails of job openings, and I would apply to every single one. When I never heard back, he lectured me on what I should have included in my résumé, how I should have worded my cover letter. He would send me information on professional events going on around town. At the beginning, I went to every single one of them and Alex even came with me to a few. But then he became too busy, and I became too exhausted. Too tired of ending the night in frustrated tears.

So I would tell him I went, even though I usually camped out in the library instead.

He had told me so many times that he admired me. He swore he was blown away by my relentless work ethic, my unique ways of seeing the world, my ability to handle anything with a creative solution.

But those compliments stopped with the increase in radio silence from prospective job openings. He'd find me on my worst days sunk deep into self-pity and depression, and he'd tell me to stop indulging those emotions. He'd tell me to focus on completing the steps needed to get my life back on track. I wanted to scream, "I'm doing everything I can!" But I was too tired. Besides, he wouldn't have believed me.

For a while I tried to make him my missing piece. I focused all my otherwise wasted time and energy on his success and waited for the feeling of fulfillment to come. And sometimes it would, when he shook the hand of an important member of society or when he strode into a packed room with confidence, ready to deliver a speech. But the gaping hole returned every time I looked in the mirror and saw the failure staring back at me.

I might have clung on to him forever like that. I could live with being another do-gooder-turned-waitress if I could still hold on to that uniqueness that was Alex. Being with someone so unequivocally good, someone so uncompromising in his morals and ethics and relentless pursuit for perfection. I might have fed off his specialness and his success until there was nothing left for the rest of the world. I probably would have, if he hadn't sat down heavily on the couch one night, head in his hands, and said he couldn't keep doing this anymore.

"This" referred to trying to be perfect in all areas of his life. He said he felt like things were going so well for him professionally. "Beyond perfect," I believe was the phrase. But he was wearing himself thin trying to be everything I needed.

"You used to be so independent," he said, not without sympathy. "Now it's like you need me for everything."

He said he had tried so hard to get me back to my old self but hadn't seen any results. I promised in that moment I would try to be better, but I knew it was over. He officially saw me as not good enough, and I couldn't keep being the thing holding him back.

The leaving was a slow, civil process. He didn't storm out in a fit of rage. I didn't passionately beg him to stay. He simply broke the silence in front of the TV one night and said he had accepted a job in Montana. He told me he would be leaving in two weeks. He did not ask me if I would come with him, and neither did I.

I had stopped at the top of a hill without realizing it. I looked up in time to see bats swooping overhead in and out of the dim moonlight.

"So where does that leave me?" I asked no one. Because no one, not the bats, not the river, not even God, had the patience to listen to my trivial problems. "What am I supposed to say to him? That it wasn't his job to fix me? That he should have sacrificed everything for a relationship that was no longer worth saving? Should I just show up and say, 'See? This is how hopeless I am without you!'"

I breathed, waiting for a response that would never come. I had never felt lonely on the road until this moment. I wished Claire was here. Or Amy. Or even my grandma. Just someone to touch, to bring me back from drowning. Any one of those people would take me by the shoulders, look me in the eyes, and tell me to calm the heck down.

So I did as I was told. "Obviously I know what I need to say," I admitted to the people who weren't there. "I need to apologize, not because of the reason you all think." I held up my hands to stop their silent disapproval. "I'm not looking to put back together what once was. Not anymore. That version of us died out long ago, and I can see that now. I'm going to apologize because he deserves an apology. And I know all my apologies to all of you have lost a bit of their meaning, but that doesn't mean they shouldn't have been said."

I trudged on—emphasis on the trudging. There was no point in trying to sleep tonight.

The night air was warm, and even though I was completely exposed to the elements, the way the night wrapped around me left me feeling safe and hidden. Overdue apologies were at the forefront of my mind, and maybe God couldn't make out my sunburned face in this dim light. He might not be able to see how much I feared His rejection. I bent my head low, just in case, and whispered an apology to the One I first disappointed.

"I'm sorry I let You down," I whispered to the night air. "I'm sorry I couldn't live up to what You expected me to be. I'm not asking You to accept me like this, but I need You to know I wish every day I didn't waste so much of the time You gave me on empty things, especially when You gave me so much to begin with." My mouth twisted in shame, thinking of how far I'd fallen. "But I'm making things right, so if You ever trust me enough again to call me to great things, I will not disappoint."

It was too much to ask for forgiveness, I knew. I hadn't shown enough change to earn forgiveness of that magnitude. But facing my past in Billings was the next step closer to earning it. To have that forgiveness from the One who created the stars and the sunsets . . . To have the slate wiped clean and my failings far, far behind me.

The thought kept me moving all night long.

24

HIGH SUMMER

"Sure, honey, I don't see why not."

Mary of Jim and Mary's RV Park stood on the landing of her massive RV, staring down at me with her hands on her hips. I had just asked her if I could spend the night at one of her camping sites, even though I didn't have a reservation or an RV.

"It's a pretty average Friday night by the looks of it," said Mary, peering out into the sea of trailers and RVs. "But I'm certain there are a few unclaimed spots out there."

"Thank you so much," I said with a smile. "I really appreciate it."

I was more than appreciative. This woman had just saved me from either a night on a park bench or walking up to Alex's door. Now that I was just outside of Billings, the thought of seeing him made my stomach curl into knots. I wanted to show up at his door asking for nothing and offering everything I had to give—my long overdue apology. But I needed a night to collect myself and form some semblance of a plan.

I fumbled with my backpack. "So how much do I owe you for a night?"

She waved her hand dismissively. "Don't you worry about that. Your plot of dirt is on the house. Just don't be hooking up any generators and blowing up our electric bill."

"Ma'am, you really don't have to."

"I insist. I was overdue for a good deed, anyway. Besides, looks like you could use a spot of kindness. Been traveling a long way?"

I grinned. "Yeah, a pretty long way."

She nodded. "And looks like you need some meat on those bones, huh? How about I get you something to eat before you head out to your spot?"

She clamored back into her RV before I had the chance to protest. Although I doubt my protests would have done any good. She was a figure of matronly perfection. Tight gray curls, a soft, huggable middle, and a floral-print dress. She looked like the type who kept meticulous photo albums of each grandkid and would serve you seconds at dinner whether you wanted them or not.

She stepped out a few minutes later holding three plastic Tupperware containers of food. The Tupperware was too foggy to make out the contents, but even I wasn't heartless enough to refuse food from this ridiculously kind woman, regardless of the mysterious contents.

"Wow." I laughed, and she handed over the containers. She even included a plastic cutlery set and a pack of napkins. "This is really too much. I can't thank you enough for your kindness. Honestly, people like you are the only reason I'm still standing."

She beamed then. It was the definition of heartwarming.

"I've got a daughter that's about the same age as you. She went out east for college a few years back. Loved the coast so much that she decided to stay. I know she's grown and can take care of herself. But as a mother, it will always be my job to worry." Her smile changed, softened by longing. "I send her care packages every few weeks, and she's real good about calling. But it's not the same as having her here where I can see for myself that she's all right. So you're somebody's daughter and I'm somebody's mother, and that's good enough reason for me to look out for you."

I stood there, wanting to look her in the eye and tell her that those words meant more to me than she could imagine. That even though the moment just happened, I knew I would remember it for the rest of my life.

But I lacked the courage. Or simply didn't want another stranger to see me cry.

I cleared my throat awkwardly and couldn't bring myself to look up from the Tupperware. "Your daughter's a lucky lady," I managed to utter.

She tsked and did nothing more to acknowledge the compliment. "You probably want some rest. Site eleven is all yours. It's got a few nice pine trees and access to the river. You come straight here if you need anything. And there better not be a scrap of food left in any of those containers. I want you eating all of it, you hear?"

I nodded obediently. "Yes, ma'am."

Her smile was pure sunshine. "Good. You take care now, honey."

I knew she was watching me as I walked away, making sure I reached my destination safely.

It took me approximately two minutes to "set up camp."

The tarp and sleeping bag I spread out under the pine trees took up a very small corner of the massive space. There was no need for a tent on a perfect night like this. There was a fallen log near the river that would do nicely as a seat for the evening. I planted myself on the log and carefully loosened the lid of the first container of food.

The smell of herbed chicken and roasted broccoli brought me instantly back to my own mother's kitchen. Back to a time when things were so much simpler. When I would do my homework at the kitchen counter while my mom hummed and prepared dinner. When all I needed in the entire world was my mom.

I missed her so much then. More than ever before. I missed the way she would wake me up in the mornings with a song. The way she would make my favorite meal when I had a bad day without even having to ask. The way she would tuck my hair behind my ears, telling me I should let people see more of my beautiful face. But that mother was long gone and had been for what felt like a lifetime. I guess I missed the mother who could only love me well when I was more hers than my own self.

I had found so many substitute mothers on my way here, every one of them giving me something I wanted so badly from my own. And I could feel my heart break when I realized they were each more dear to me than my own mother. Because important as those memories of her were to me, they were also so far into my past that their edges had begun to blur.

Those substitute mothers, they had all accepted me in a way my mother never had. And although I would never discredit all my mother did to raise me, I knew she no longer had to be the most important woman in my life. Whether intentionally or not, she had continued to tear me down for far too long. But that wasn't the way it had to be. I could surround myself with women who wanted to build me up, who focused on my strengths instead of obsessed over my weaknesses. *This could be a way to move forward*, I thought. And it was a beautiful thought.

I took my first bite of chicken without hesitation.

It tasted nothing like my mother's.

This chicken tasted too good not to have been cooked with plenty of oil, same with the broccoli. But I continued to eat, imagining all my favorite women around me, eating and laughing. They would all get along without any trouble, even Jackie. Their voices helped to drown out the voice of self-destruction that always shouted at the top of its lungs during mealtime. So when I opened the next container and saw what appeared to be homemade mac and cheese, my first instinct was to look around for a place to stash it, but that lasted only a moment.

I stared down at the pasta shells smothered in golden cheese. I thought back to my endless meals of almonds and muesli and nearly gagged. If I never saw another almond, it would be too soon.

In this instance, Amy would probably have said something about how I must like being miserable, since I was contemplating throwing out the only real food I'd had in weeks. "I'm sick of your complaining," I could almost hear her groan. "Just eat the freaking mac and cheese already."

I imagined Kat putting an arm around my shoulder. "You're strong, Mel. You're strong and you're going to be okay."

Leslie would have to hold back from force-feeding me.

She'd take my hands with solemn urgency and say something along the lines of, "Honey, you've got to do this. You know you've got to. If you don't do this now, you'll be sliding further in the wrong direction. We're all here, rooting for you."

Jackie would not-so-kindly remind me that having an eating disorder didn't make me special. It just showed that I was another victim of capitalist culture. And oddly, that would help.

Linnie would be near hysterics and Mary would try to calm her down, only to then turn to me and demand to know what kind of game I thought I was playing. "Don't you know there are people who care about you? Eat that mac and cheese. We want you safe and healthy and happy, that's all. Macaroni won't fix everything, but it's a start."

"It's a start," I muttered to no one after my conversation with no one. I took a bite. A courageous, emboldened, confident bite. That forkful was followed by another and another. And I felt like I had done something so extraordinarily ordinary. I felt reconnected to the human experience. I guess mac and cheese can do that to a person.

The last container was packed with still-warm, homemade applesauce. I had to stop halfway through though. Something was off. It took me a long moment to realize what it was . . .

I was full.

I was actually full, and I had completely forgotten the feeling. I laughed loudly and unrestrained because that's sometimes the only thing a situation calls for. Good grief, I was a mess. But maybe slightly less of one than before.

As people around me began to emerge from their campers to start their nighttime festivities around fires and lanterns buzzing with moths and mosquitoes, I tucked in for the night.

For the first time in a long time, I felt that warm familiar pull of a night of deep sleep pulling me under. I didn't fight it.

I woke the next morning with the early gray dawn. All the campers were quiet; only the river spoke.

There was a chill to the air, so I stayed tucked in my sleeping bag as I finished off the rest of the applesauce from the night before. I felt sick, but I knew it had nothing to do with the food and everything to do with my plans for the rest of the day.

I packed up quietly and stopped by Mary's trailer to drop off the empty Tupperware, along with a few flowers I found by the river as a token of my thanks. Outside her trailer hung a whiteboard with the RV park activities from the previous day still scrawled across in big looping letters. August 14. That made today the fifteenth. August 15 would be the day I would finally see Alex again. I released a breath, long and slow. Then with a familiar huff of exertion, I hoisted my backpack onto my shoulders and set off down the empty tree-lined road that led to the outskirts of Billings.

As the sun rose and I caught glimpses of the downtown buildings through breaks in the tree line, I couldn't help but think about what a perfect place this was for Alex. Open skies, a wild river, and a rugged landscape of hills and forests. I could see him relaxing in this environment, the gigantic expanse of sky reminding him of the grand scheme of things.

It was a city big enough to chase his polished dreams, but surrounded by enough jagged rimrocks and wild, sweeping bluffs to remind him that beauty and magnificence don't always come as perfection. This place would do his soul good.

I passed signs advertising Custer's Last Stand, the Yellowstone County Museum, the Yellowstone Wildlife Sanctuary, and countless opportunities for guided historical hikes, horseback riding lessons, and fishing trips. I wondered what it would be like to live in a place like this with Alex by my side. A place of wide, open spaces and slower paces where we couldn't hide from who we were but could take the time to explore what we could once again be for one another.

It wasn't that I wanted him back. Not now, at least. I was far too much of a work in progress for that to happen. No, getting back together wasn't why I was here, and I honestly believed that.

But it was like Amy said when she talked about her dreams. The thought of us living our lives with other people by our sides simply didn't seem right. I might not have been heading to his door to get him back, but that didn't mean I didn't believe with every part of me that we would end up together one day. I knew ever since I realized that Tuesdays and Thursdays had become the best days of my week because of seeing him in philosophy class. We were both so precariously designed, and he was my perfect fit. And I knew without a shadow of a doubt that a part of him still believed that about me.

The anxiety of what I was about to do returned the closer I got to civilization. People were milling about, ready to greet the morning with their fair-trade coffee and farmer's market purchases, as if today was like any other.

I began to wonder if I should have just called like a normal person. Even texted. But no, I had to turn this into yet another grand gesture, convincing myself that this sort of conversation was too monumental to have over phone lines.

Maybe I had a point, maybe I didn't. But the fact was that I didn't walk all the way here to watch other people live their lives. I came here to say something I needed to get off my chest so I could breathe normally again. I needed to close this door, even if only for a bit, so I could refocus on what brought me all this way in the first place.

And I needed to stop wasting my time agonizing over all the what-ifs concerning Alex Martinez and just do it already.

Out of all the nonsensical things I convinced myself to do on a daily basis, this might be the one thing with any actual meaning. With the wind and the rising sun at my back, I picked up my pace and headed toward my destination.

25

How many knocks is appropriate for an unshowered ex-girlfriend to execute on the door of the guy she's still hopelessly in love with?

There wasn't a doorbell in sight, so I stood dumbfounded in front of what I now knew to be Alex's apartment. It was a surprisingly normal door—gray with a black handle. I guess I had been expecting something more monumental.

Additionally, how *hard* does one knock in this situation? Does one knock in a pattern? I couldn't believe I came all this way for this ugly gray door to be my downfall.

"Knock. Just freaking knock," I told myself in the harshest whisper possible. But I wasn't sure I could stop my hand from shaking long enough. I raised my fist, determined to give it the old college try, when the door swung open.

He was slightly bent over, reaching for the newspaper that, in my panic, I hadn't realized I was standing on. He froze when he saw a pair of muddy hiking boots on his front stoop, and I remained frozen with my fist in the air. Slowly, he looked up.

His eyes met mine, and every reason I wanted to run all the

way here from Fargo came crashing back. I had to restrain myself from throwing my arms around him. I knew what it would feel like. It would feel exactly like belonging. But I also knew where my place was, and it wasn't in his arms.

The silence between us stretched past the point of comfort. And the look on his face told me he was too stunned to say anything anytime soon.

"Here, let me help you out," I said, apparently determined to break the silence as awkwardly as possible. "'Oh, hi, Mel. Long time, no see. You look . . . different. Have you lost weight?' Then I say, 'Why, yes, Alex. I have lost weight. And hiked all the way here from home. One of the perks of an eating and exercise disorder combo. No, I didn't come all this way to see you. You're great and all, but come on. I'm not that desperate. Well, maybe I am, but you've got nothing to do with it. Anyway, I figured we had some things to discuss before I continued onward.'" I gestured toward the open door. "May I come in?"

He was still staring at me. Then all of a sudden, something in his face broke. I only caught a glimpse of it before he pulled me to him, but I was certain of what I had seen: heart-wrenching pain.

I could feel that pain in the way he held me. He wrapped his arms around me in a way that suggested he didn't want to break me, but he also never wanted to let me go. My throat burned as I buried my dirt-streaked face in his soft, clean T-shirt. Returning to him was like the feeling of opening the door to a darkened, drafty home after a long trip. That feeling that slowly burns in the heart as the lights are switched on and the house once again fills with life and laughter and luggage. It was that comforting, sinking feeling of settling back into the place where I belonged.

"I'm so sorry, Alex." I couldn't bring my voice above a cracked whisper without breaking. "I'm so sorry I fell so short of what you needed me to be."

He pulled away from me then, placing a hand on either side of my face. "I thought I'd lost you," was all he managed to say before his words were choked back by sobs.

I knew then what he meant, and it was enough to make the tears unstoppable. They blinded me as Alex half carried me inside, all my strength gone. We both fell onto the couch, him refusing to let go of me. I cried into his shirt until my tears turned the streaks of dirt from my face into mud, until I could feel his own tears on my face.

I began to calm after a period of time that I would never be able to measure. Our breathing matched one another's, and as I looked up at him, he brushed a strand of hair away from my face. I waited for the horror of him touching my unwashed, greasy, thinning hair to make itself known in his expression, but it never came. His hand lingered on my face.

"I let you down," he said. "I knew it the minute I walked out of your apartment for the last time. And I could have turned around. But I couldn't bring myself to admit my failure." He smiled halfheartedly. "You know how I struggle with pride."

"I've seen you lose board games, so yes," I said in an attempt to lighten the mood. But I didn't come here to lighten the mood. "You didn't let me down, Alex. You tried everything you could to fix me, and it didn't work because of me, not because of you."

He shook his head. "That's exactly what I mean though. I let you down because I thought you *had* to be fixed. And you didn't. Well, not in the way I was trying to fix you. Do you know what I mean?"

I pushed back from him slightly and fell into his solemn expression. "No, I don't. I did need to be fixed. I still do. That's why I started this trip in the first place. Don't make excuses for me. That's not you. We always expected the best from each other. That's why we were our best selves with each other, because we never expected anything less."

I scooted farther back from him and moved to the end of the couch. Suddenly, I was acutely aware of my dirty, baggy clothes. The bruises and scars I had gathered all along the way here. I pulled my knees to my chest, assuming a new defensive posture.

"I mean, that's why I started this whole thing anyway," I said. "That's one of the reasons why I'm out here. I'm getting back to my best self. The self you fell in love with. The self that God can use for all the great things we would never shut up about doing, you know?"

He made a move to reach out and touch me but brought his hand slowly back to his lap when I involuntarily flinched.

"Mel, I fell in love with *you*. All of you. I've seen your good days and your bad days and loved you for both of them, just like you loved all of me, the good and the bad. And we both know I had bad days."

It was true. On days like that he would retreat so far into himself I couldn't pull him back out. All I could do was wait with open arms on the other side.

Alex was shaking his head. "When I started to really devote my time to work, success became so clearly defined, so close I felt like I only had to push through that extra mile to grab it. I was blind to everything else except this one idea of how I wanted my life to turn out." He rubbed his hands over his eyes. Releasing a heavy breath, he stared out the window across from us. "I never stopped to think why I wanted my life to turn out that way. I figured since so many of my mentors saw it as the goal, it had to be right. Don't you remember how distant I was in our last few months together?"

I looked out the window too. "We couldn't relate to each other anymore."

"Because of my tunnel vision. I've had a lot of time to think this over, Mel. I was convinced there was only one way to help you, and it was to get you on the same path." He was watching me now. I could feel his gaze, could almost feel him willing me to understand. Too scared to meet his eye, I kept looking out the window. "And when things didn't work out for you the way I wanted, I thought we were both failures. So I pushed away from you, because I couldn't associate with failure."

I didn't flinch this time. I had known that was true. I fully believed it myself.

"But you know what?" he added. "Then I moved here and did exactly what I wanted to do. I worked all the time, barely slept. And since I never gave myself the time to stop and think about my life, I assumed I was fulfilled. Then the campaign I was working on ended and the reality of my life came crashing down on me. And I was so completely miserable."

He said it in a way that made my heart ache. I turned away from the hypnotic flutter of the few tree branches visible outside and pressed my hands into fists to stop them from reaching out and taking his.

"Without you, I was like a machine who completed task

after task with no real passion, no greater goal. I always had the drive for success, but you were the one who gave the word a whole variety of meaning in my life. You would show me that every time you looked at the world creatively, every time you pointed out all the beautiful moments I would have otherwise missed."

He reached out again to touch me, and this time I did not pull away. He held my hand—mine cold, his warm.

"And when I missed you . . . well, the pain was physical, that's how badly I missed you. And it wasn't your drive for success that I missed. It wasn't your accomplishments. It was the way you would wrap your arms around me. The way you would look up at me from the pages of your book, like you were checking to make sure I was still there. The way you would make me laugh about everything, forcing me to take myself less seriously." His eyes were shining with tears. When his words came out in a choked whisper, my own eyes clouded over. "And now you're here, sitting next to me. And I can see all the pain you've endured, and I knew it was there, but I was too much of a coward to help you through it. You look so strong, Mel. You really do. And I know you are. But I'm also so afraid you're going to shatter into a million pieces."

I came back to him then. On my knees, I swung my leg over his so I could take his face in my hands, look into his eyes, and whisper, "I'm broken, but I'm not going to shatter. I promise you."

Then I kissed him. It was that last kiss we never had wrapped into the first kiss after a long goodbye.

I broke the kiss when his hands began to roam my waist. I watched his face, which showed an expression nothing short of heartbreak. He touched the zipper of my jacket and gave me a measured look. I nodded numbly.

He unzipped the jacket and slowly removed it from my shoulders. The tank top I wore beneath was worn and frayed. It had once been blue, but now looked more gray. He looked at me, and I didn't recoil. I didn't think about my arms or my belly, because the look he was giving me was one of such intense fear that I couldn't think of anything other than trying to make it better.

"I'm eating better these days, I promise," I said, failing once more to get my voice above a whisper.

He didn't say anything, and I knew then why I let him see me. Since the day I met him, I felt he had been the only person who ever really saw me. So despite all my hours standing in front of a mirror, memorizing my measurements, obsessing over my waistline, I knew that I was only now finally seeing myself as I really was, through Alex's eyes. And I wasn't fat, I wasn't ugly, I wasn't undesirable, I wasn't worthless.

But I was in danger. And I was not well.

Instantly, the way he used to look at me filled my mind. Back when I was so deliriously happy to be with him I didn't have time to weigh myself five times a day or count every single calorie. He would look at me in a way that made me know without a shadow of a doubt that I filled him with joy to the point of overflowing. Now all the sight of me filled him with was pain.

The sadness that swept over me was crushing. I think it would have dragged me to the floor and left me there to die if it hadn't been so quickly swallowed up by anger. I abruptly and awkwardly got to my feet, changing the expression on Alex's face to one of surprise.

I couldn't have him look at me like that, with all that fear. And it wasn't his fault. This was my burden to bear, my life to fix. I could never feel welcome here until I had earned that look of joy back.

"I have to go," I said, trying not to meet his eyes. I glanced at the movie posters from college he had taped crookedly to the white walls. He never was one for decorating. "I have to keep walking."

"But . . ." Alex rose and tried to come to me, but I busied myself by zipping up my jacket with shaking hands. "You just got here. Can't you stay a little longer? Can't we talk?"

I did look at him then. I stared. Then I flung my arms out in a wild gesture. "What more is there to say? You've seen me. You've seen what I've let myself become. It's still present tense for me, and until we can talk about this as something that already happened, there's nothing more to say. I've heard it all before. I've tried believing all the words. Those aren't going to help, Alex, I promise you. But the way you looked at me . . ." I picked up my backpack, hoping to hide the grimace on my face. "I never want you to have to look at me that way again. That look will help me more than any words ever could."

"Mel, I didn't mean to upset you—"

"No, stop." I closed the space between us and took his hands in mine. "It's not your fault. I don't want you thinking that, okay?"

He searched my eyes, willing me to say more. But there was nothing more I needed to say to him. Not now. His fear burned into my heart, igniting a fire that had only been a spark. My feet itched to move. My body hummed with new energy. I could see the path to recovery, and it was taking every ounce of restraint not to sprint down it.

Because he and I shared pieces of the same soul, he said nothing more. Nor did he try to stop me, try to tell me not to go, try to offer any advice, try to tell me that this whole thing was just a cry for help. He said none of those things because he knew this was something I needed to do.

I was at the door. He hadn't followed me, but I could feel his eyes on me. I turned around.

"I'll always love you. You know that, right?"

He nodded. "And you know that I'll be here waiting, right?"

I took in the sight of him for a long time. I imagined what that moment would be like. The moment I would return to him, triumphant and glowing. I would run straight into his arms like I had done a thousand times after countless bad days and good days and letdowns and failures and heartbreaks and celebrations and joys and victories. And I would know that I was back home, back where I belonged. Where the two of us could finally stop running and rest in each other's arms.

But until that moment, I had to continue onward. Onward and upward. There was too much on the line now—too much pain in his expression—for me to fall again.

"I do." I said it like a promise. Then I opened the door and walked out of his home. And I did not look back.

26

I think it was my newly acquired blinding determination to reach my goal that caused me not to see the root.

Things had been going great, better than great, for a couple of weeks. Thanks to a stop at a grocery store on my way out of Billings, I had a pack full of food that wasn't almonds and muesli. Every time I considered cutting down my calorie count for the day, all I had to do was think of that look on Alex's face and the thought would vanish. I knew this method wasn't exactly a remedy to all my problems, but I would use it as long as it worked.

Not for one second did I tire of the remaining miles through the Big Sky State. The windswept plains made the days feel effortless, and the nights were a production all their own, complete with cricket symphonies and showers of stars. I felt connected to the land in ways a person can feel only after spending night after night sleeping on its soil.

Just like my dad had said, I began to see parts of myself in my surroundings. The great emptiness of dawn, beautiful and vast and waiting to be filled with light. The shifting prairie grasses that swayed with the slightest wind, but grew roots that were deep and strong. Even the winding path that sometimes was too faint to follow with confidence or required me to crawl or climb to continue forward, but always ended up leading me a little closer to my destination. I felt these complexities in my own soul. And in those brief glimpses of clarity and connection, my whole being glowed in the knowledge of being loved.

The pang of loss I felt when crossing the Idaho state border was quickly replaced by a sense of wonder. It wasn't long until my views of the horizon became obscured by hardy pines, emerald hills, and even far-off mountain peaks. I followed the trail into the heart of the Nez Perce-Clearwater National Forests, where ancient wild places were carved by rivers, and the land remained unchanged by human hands.

The soles of my boots were so thin, they were practically see-through. But considering what they had been through these past couple of months, the pebbles and sticks underfoot didn't faze them in the slightest. Every part of me bore the marks of my endeavor. Scratches crisscrossed my arms, bruises climbed up my shins, and there was never an inch of me not covered in sweat and dirt. But I wore it all as a badge of honor. At least I had something to show for my journey, not like the months of running in place in that basement apartment.

It may have been the aura of fortitude surrounding me at all times or the growing sense of possibility at every turn, but I found myself daydreaming about my future more often.

For years, I dared to dream about my future in only the vaguest of details. Reality never matched daydreams, and when in reality I ultimately didn't reach the expectations

I had set for myself, I gained nothing but crushing disappointment.

But now when I daydreamed, people appeared. People I knew and loved. I saw myself by Alex's side in that little house in Billings. I saw a new job market, and I saw the first day of the start of my career. I saw myself working tirelessly for a greater purpose and the success that came with it. I saw Alex's arms around me, and I saw Claire coming to visit, and me showing her around my new hometown with a sense of pride.

I couldn't actually see what I looked like in any of these daydreams. The healthy version of me Alex longed to have back was hard to make out, but there was plenty else to daydream about.

I was right in the middle of imagining the dog Alex and I would ultimately adopt together when my shoe came into contact with the root.

I had fallen more times than I could remember up to this point. I had roots, rocks, holes, and yes, even my own feet to blame for that. It was always followed with my body hitting the ground hard, the impact knocking the wind out of me. But I would always stand back up, dust myself off, and carry on with no other damage than a few scrapes and bruises.

Not this time.

My reaction skills were poor to begin with, so there was absolutely no chance of stopping myself from falling face-first off the trail and down the ravine. The impact was shocking, but I had no time to process it because I was still tumbling toward my certain doom, swinging my arms around wildly in a desperate attempt to grasp any sort of lifeline.

The lifeline took the form of a thick root that shredded

my palms as I held on to it for dear life. The world took its time to slow to its normal pace around me. The sound of loose dirt tumbling the remaining thirty feet down the ravine shuddered into silence, leaving only the thundering sound of my heartbeat and my ragged breathing to echo through the still woods.

For about three seconds, I thought I had been miraculously spared. It took only one shock of pain to make me think otherwise. When that shock was followed by several more, I quickly began to clamber back up to the trail before my adrenaline completely subsided.

The ravine wasn't that steep, which was more of a relief once I realized the pain in my right arm rendered it nearly useless. But I refused to look at it until I had used my remaining good arm to drag myself back to relative safety.

I crawled over to the nearest tree, struggled out of the grasp of my backpack, and tried to take a few deep breaths as I leaned against rough bark. Looking down the trail, I saw the root.

If looks could kill, I would have withered the entire tree with the one I gave that knot of pure evil barely sticking up from the ground. Then, because I had the maturity of a five-year-old, I screamed every terrible word at the unfazed root. It actually helped me feel better for about two whole seconds.

I tried to build up the nerve to look at my arm. I knew it was bad, but if I kept avoiding looking at it, I could hold on to the hope that maybe it wasn't *that* bad.

Sweat poured down my face. I wiped it off with a shaky hand, and it came back bright red. Past my hand I saw what I was pretty sure was my thigh, but there was something sticking out of it that shouldn't have been there.

Not a bone, thank God, I determined upon closer inspection. But it was a very sharp, very splintered piece of wood. Trailing farther down my battered leg, my eyes rested on a jagged, wickedly deep slice across my shin. Through the gushing blood and dirt, something white gleamed. When I realized it was bone, the vomiting started.

"Okay," I tried to tell myself when the contents of my stomach had been thoroughly emptied onto a pile of pine needles next to me. "Okay, we need to figure this out."

I'm not sure who I was talking to. Maybe the voice in my head who told me starvation would solve all my problems. It seemed logical to think she was somehow involved.

I braced myself and peeked at my arm. It was too covered in blood to even fully convince myself it was still an arm. I looked closer, which made my vision blur for a long moment. Recovering, I assured myself that at least there wasn't any bone poking through.

"All right, arm is still attached." I had to stay out of my own head. Talking things out would get me through this. "Step two, let's see if walking is an option."

I scooted over to a low-hanging branch. Shaking with both shock and pain, I gripped the branch with a torn-up palm, gritted my teeth, and pulled myself to my feet. I may have sworn loudly several more times in the process, but if you swear in the middle of the forest when no one else is around, did it even happen?

Gently, slowly, I put weight on my ripped-up leg. The breathtaking pain wasn't exactly ideal, but it also wasn't completely unmanageable. I could walk, not far and not long and it would not be pretty, but I could walk.

I lowered myself back to the ground, screaming through

gritted teeth. I waited for my heart to stop pounding and blinked up at the soft beams of sunlight reaching down through the branches of the trees. In the midst of everything, I had the audacity to look up to heaven and send a silent prayer of gratitude that I could still exercise.

"Okay," I said, panting. "You can walk, that's great. That's so good. Now, step three. Time to see what we can do about the blood that's escaping at an alarming rate, okay?"

"Okay," I whispered back to myself. I unzipped the outermost pocket of my backpack with still-shaking hands. The first aid kit Linnie had insisted on all the way back in Wisconsin felt so terribly small and light in my hands now. I had only rummaged through it once or twice for a Band-Aid.

Band-Aids weren't going to cut it this time.

I could hear my mother's voice in my head, "*This was just the Good Lord's way of reminding you that He's the invincible one, not you. You needed to be knocked down a few pegs, and this was His way of getting your attention.*"

"That's not the reason!" I shouted. "I am well aware of how far I am from invincibility, Mom! It's not your job to assign meaning to everything in my life!" Screaming really did help alleviate the pain, so I screamed a few more things at my mom who wasn't there, took ten deep breaths, and returned to the first aid box.

Bandages, gauze, sterile wipes, tweezers, something that looked like it could be fashioned into a sling. Everything was there, but it was the quantity that worried me. The gash on my shin alone looked like it would take most of the supplies, and I didn't even know what the wound on my head or arm needed. Water would help. I had half a bottle in my bag, which wasn't nearly enough to clean this bloodbath. I had been anticipating crossing a stream in the next half mile or so, but I would need to stop at least some of the bleeding before attempting to move forward.

I wiped more blood from my eyes. Since I was still conscious, I figured it would be best to focus on the shin first. My legs were the most important thing to save, anyway.

It could also have been the lack of blood or the head wound that caused me to think this was the best decision.

I opened a sterile wipe with my teeth and stared at my leg. I wasn't great with blood, but I also wasn't in a position where that mattered much. I wiped the gash the best I could, not bothering to hold back my screams of agony as I did so. I was nearly halfway done cleaning it out when I reached back into the first aid kit for another sterile wipe and found none. So instead, I pulled out a gauze wrap and a rolled-up bandage, only to discover a moment later that I was unable to wrap the bandage around my leg one-handed. And this, I decided, was my breaking point.

"So what is this, a test?" I shouted at the sky. "Or was my mom right? Are You reminding me that I'm a fragile human in need of Your help? Well, guess what? I ALREADY KNEW THAT! You didn't have to throw me off a cliff to get Your point across. I'm not down here trying to deny Your power or my vulnerability. I thought You knew this! I thought You knew *everything*!"

Movement to my left made me stop my ranting against God. A boy who looked to be about six or seven stared at me, mouth open and eyes full of terror and fascination. I stared back at him. I almost thought to assure him that I was fine, just so he'd stop looking at me with that horrified expression, but then I realized the chances of him believing me were slim to none.

"I heard you screaming," he finally said, his voice a small and terrified whisper. "You look really bad."

I tried to smile, but it was useless. "I took an unplanned detour off the side of the hill. Do you think you could help me?"

He nodded, quick and certain.

"Thanks. Thank you so much. Are your parents around? Can they help too?"

"My sister's back at our campsite," he said, pointing behind him. "I was out getting firewood. Where's *your* mom?"

"My mom?"

"Yeah, I heard you yelling at her."

Nice, Mel. Real nice. "Well, my mom's not actually here. I was just pretending she was. It's a little lonely out here all by myself."

"You sounded like you were really mad at her."

I sighed. "Yeah, well, I guess I'm mad at everything right now."

"My sister can help you, I think."

I looked up at him, "Could you take me to her? Could you show me the way to your campsite?"

He nodded gravely. I nodded back.

I scooted over to the branch again and pulled myself to my feet, gritting my teeth so tightly my jaw ached.

"Can you hand me that stick over there?" I asked the boy. "The big one . . . Yup, that's the one." He brought the stick to me, holding it out at arms-length like whatever I had was contagious. I certainly couldn't blame him. I thanked him and leaned heavily on it, testing its weight. It would do nicely.

I peered down at my open backpack and the sprawling contents of the first aid kit. The boy packed the unused supplies back into the kit, tucked it into the backpack, zipped everything up, and hefted the bag, which was nearly the size of him, onto his own shoulders without a word.

I watched him in surprise. When he looked up with a new determination in his eyes, I finally worked up a genuine smile.

"I'm Mel. What's your name?"

"David."

"David, you're my hero."

He blushed, and I swear he stood up straighter, even under the weight of my enormous bag. I knew I would be just fine trusting this kid with my life.

"I'll get you to my sister. We'll take the trail because it's a lot safer. I usually walk through the woods because I know the way and I'm a good climber. Plus, that's where all the sticks are. But you'll be safer if we take the trail."

"Sounds good, David. Lead on."

He started down the trail. Every few seconds he would attempt to casually peer over his shoulder in my direction. The going was painfully slow. Literally. As a distraction, I tried to strike up a conversation.

"So, are you and your sister camping out here?" I asked through gasps.

"We live out here," David answered, keeping his eyes on the trail. He stopped suddenly. Turning around, he walked right toward me purposefully. "We're getting to a really rocky part. I'm going to help you so you don't fall again."

He was too short for me to lean on, so he took my good arm and held on tight as we maneuvered over rock after rock. Truthfully, it was more of a hindrance than a help, but

I would rather fall down a hundred ravines than admit that to the serious-faced boy by my side. When we were past the rocks, he let go of my arm but stayed close.

"How old are you, David?"

"Seven."

"And you live out here, huh? In a house?"

He shook his head. "It's a trailer. That way we can take our house with us when we go on adventures."

"That's very practical," I said. "So your sister's good at fixing stuff?"

He waved a hand in the air. "She fixes all kinds of things."

"Like what kind of things?"

He tried to shrug his tiny shoulders, but my pack weighed him down. "Like regular things. Like sinks and walls and toilets and stuff." He held out his forearm for me to see a swipe of a scar. "She can fix arms too, like this."

"That looks like it hurt," I said.

"Not really. I didn't even cry."

"Wow." I allowed a moment of silence so he knew I appreciated and acknowledged his bravery. "Do you think she could fix me?"

"Yes," he answered without hesitation. "She fixes everything."

"Well, that's a relief," I said, hoping this seven-year-old's faith in his sister was justified. "So, what do you do out here when you're not busy being a hero?"

"Lots of stuff."

"Like what kind of stuff?"

"Like climbing trees and exploring and reading books and playing pretend."

"I love to play pretend," I told him. He eyed me suspiciously. "Really," I went on. "I do it all the time. I think my favorite person to pretend to be is a girl from long ago who came from nothing but is brave and strong and goes on all sorts of adventures saving people and stealing money from the rich to give to the poor. I would live in the woods and take care of myself. I would hardly let anyone get close enough to know me, but the few who do I love dearly. To the rest of the world, I'm the stuff of legends."

I glanced over at him. He looked a bit taken aback. "I didn't think grown-ups played pretend."

I laughed. "Playing pretend is one of our favorite things to do."

"I like to pretend I'm a werewolf," he admitted quietly. "I try to do brave and nice things until the moon is full, then I howl and go crazy."

"I've never tried to be a werewolf," I mused. "It sounds like it could get a little scary."

"My sister is sometimes scared, but I think she's only pretending."

"Is your sister as brave as you?"

He thought about this for a moment. "Yes," he said, then added, "Almost. She's scared of spiders, so I have to squash them for her."

"I guess that does mean that you're braver. Even just by a little bit."

I asked him more questions about being a werewolf to fill the spaces between the pain. Besides, it wasn't every day I met a kid who's half werewolf. His answers were elaborate, so much so that for the rest of the walk I didn't need to ask any more questions to keep him talking.

At a certain point, he stopped abruptly and pointed.

"That's my house. I'm gonna go get my sister." And he ran off before I could say anything to the contrary.

I wiped my forehead again and hobbled after him into a clearing where a vintage chrome trailer was parked under a cluster of tall pines next to a quiet stream. Between the trees, two hammocks hung limply. A set of chairs that looked like they belonged to a patio set from the seventies were situated around a blackened campfire pit. There was a pop-up shelter with mesh walls next to the camper. Inside I could see a folding table and a camp stove. My eye caught something cherry red. A rusty old Ford pickup was parked at the far end of the clearing.

Despite the gear, the place did not feel like a campsite. It could have been because of the colorful prayer flags that hung across the trailer, the vegetable garden growing next to the pop-up shelter, or how moss grew around the wheels of the trailer. Whatever the reason, it all felt much more permanent. David wasn't kidding when he said he lived out here.

Granted, I didn't know where "here" was, exactly. I figured I was still in the Nez Perce–Clearwater National Forest, but I couldn't be sure.

In fact, I was starting to struggle with remembering where I was currently. The trees were all beginning to blur together while the rest of the world spun ever so slightly. I leaned against a nearby trunk and took several deep and shaky breaths, determined not to pass out in front of another stranger.

The door to the trailer opened right before David reached it. A woman who looked young enough to make my twenty-four years feel ancient stepped out. She had a long braid of thick black hair running down her back, and even with her loose-fitting clothes, I could tell she was naturally thinner than me. But the pain swallowed up any bothers I could have given.

So that was the cure to an eating disorder. Be in such immense physical pain that your brain literally can't process anything else.

David pointed in my direction and seemed to get out only a few words before his sister started sprinting toward me. I wondered if she ever ran the 400 in track, because her speed and form were incredible. David followed her with much less grace and speed.

She had my good arm slung over her shoulder before I even realized she had reached me. My walking stick forgotten, I leaned on her for balance. I tried to say something but speaking no longer seemed to be an option. Instead, I focused on breathing as she slowly led me to the trailer, talking to me in words I could no longer understand.

I felt my surroundings change, felt myself being lowered onto something soft. And with the weight finally off my screwed-up leg, I could think again. I was on a bed in the trailer, and I was horrified to think of what kind of stains I would leave on the quilt beneath me.

David's sister was murmuring instructions to him. He ran off, and she turned to face me. She looked surprised to see me staring back at her.

"I thought for sure you would be unconscious by now," she said, kneeling down next to me. "Do you want us to take you to a hospital? The closest one is about four hours away."

I shook my head and the room spun. "No insurance," I started, barely able to form the words. "Don't want to put you out. Bandages, that's all I need. Extra bandages.

She raised her eyebrows at me. "You need more than a few bandages. And we're going to take care of you. But first I needed to make sure you preferred our treatment to a hospital's."

"I don't have anything to repay you with," I said, gasping slightly as I adjusted myself on the bed. The edges of the room were growing fuzzier, my thoughts bouncing between muddled nonsense and abject panic. David's sister put a hand gently on my arm. I tried to focus on her face. Her soft brown eyes were flecked with gold, although that could have just been the stars dancing in my vision.

"We're here on this earth to help each other. We are all worthy of receiving help, we should all be called to give it without reward."

I let out a sharp breath. "Well, I'm not going to argue with that. Hopefully I can pay you back in some way though."

She shook her head. "Pay it forward, don't pay it back."

I gritted my teeth so hard I was sure they would crack. "Okay."

David came back carrying what appeared to be a tackle box stacked on top of a pile of clean towels.

"The water's getting hot," he told his sister.

She gave his shoulder a quick squeeze. "Good work. Keep an eye on that for me, will you? When it's hot enough, bring it in here."

David disappeared again. His hurried footsteps shook the whole trailer.

"I'm Mel, by the way," I said by way of introduction as I bled all over her quilt.

She slid a few towels underneath me so gently I barely had to grit my teeth. She handed me one as well.

"Are you able to apply as much pressure as you can stand to your arm?" I bit my lip and nodded. She handed me the towel. Her eyes crinkled at the edges when she smiled. "I'm Crystal."

"David said you two live out here?" I asked. She touched my arm slightly and I winced. Without reaction, she moved on to my leg. Her hands were cool as she traced the area around the giant splinter sticking out of my thigh, and she didn't even flinch when she shifted her focus to my shin. She flipped open the tackle box with the grim determination of a surgeon. A large part of me wanted to ask her if she had any idea what she was doing, but I quickly shut that down.

"We do. We've been out here for about four years now. Since my dad passed away." She glanced up at me, fixing me with a steady, serious gaze. "This is going to hurt."

My response came as a muffled scream. She had pulled the dagger of wood out of my thigh and quickly moved on to mopping up the river of blood.

"Doesn't seem to have left too many splinters behind," she said cheerfully, picking at them gently with a pair of tweezers. I thrashed slightly when she poured something burning into the gash. I could barely breathe from all the screaming I was holding back. The fuzziness around my vision was growing, and black spots danced around the room like tiny flies.

"Feel free to scream, Mel. It's all part of the healing process."

"How'd you end up out here?" I half screamed. I flung my forearms over my eyes, trying to block out at least the sight of pain. The gesture caused my wrist to scream in agony, but I barely had the energy left to care.

I knew I was asking far too much of this stranger to not only fix me but to distract me from the pain while she did so. But she talked as I heard David approach with a sloshing bucket of water. I felt her touch through the warm rag that wiped away the blood and dust from my forehead.

"Our mom died shortly after David was born," Crystal said. The rag moved over the gash in my shin, and I roared. It helped like screaming at the root did, except I kept it PG-rated this time.

"When our dad died, we didn't have any other relatives to look after us. I was ready to set out on my own anyway, so we took the family camper and headed out here.

"Our dad was a hunter, our mom an ultramarathoner. They taught us a lot about survival and living off the land. We were well prepared. Although there was still certainly a learning curve."

I felt something soft slip into my good hand. I squeezed David's hand even though it burned my torn-apart palm. Still, I did not open my eyes.

"But why here?" I gasped. My shin was suddenly on fire. I screamed again.

"We always went camping around here, so we ventured farther in until we found a place no one would mind us using. And for two years, no one has. Brace yourself, Mel. This is really going to hurt."

The fire in my shin turned into an inferno. With knives and needles and hacksaws. And despite my best efforts, my hand slipped from David's, and I lost consciousness.

27

MID-SEPTEMBER (PROBABLY)

Grandma,

The mail doesn't exactly reach where I'm staying right now, so I'm not sure when I'll actually be able to send this letter. Whenever I do get around to sending it, though, you can rest assured that I'm safe and well on my merry way. However, currently my plans have been slightly derailed. Also I'm going slightly crazy.

You know how you always tell me that I have to stop being so clumsy because one of these days I'm going to trip over my own feet and break my neck? Well, it was a root instead of my own feet and it was my arm instead of my neck, but you get the idea. I tried to carry on as soon as this superhuman brother and sister duo living out in the woods patched me up (true story, believe it or not), but I got about half a mile before I nearly keeled over. David, the seven-year-old brother, had to drag me back to camp on a sled. Not my *proudest moment. Definitely an eyeroll-worthy moment on your part.*

So, for the past few days I've spent my time trying to move as little as possible. I'd like to tell you I've been a real trouper, that I've been a courteous and grateful guest in the home of the people who saved my life, but that wouldn't exactly be true. I haven't exercised for days and it's excruciating. I wish I was exaggerating. I wish I could tell you I haven't cried tears of frustration over this, haven't snapped at the woman who stitched me up, haven't wanted to tear off my skin because I swear I can feel myself getting fatter and fatter . . . And I guess I'm telling you all of this because it occurred to me lately that you're the only one who knows this side of me.

You were the only one who stayed to listen when I tried to rationalize my disordered habits, the only one who heard me try and explain what it was like to look in the mirror with a sense of inescapable dread and horror. You talked to the doctors, you sat by my side. You drove me home and made me dinner after almost every single hospital visit. You weren't a saint about it—I swear I've never seen someone glare and scoff as much as you do—but you were also very much a saint about it. Just by being there. And you know what? Never once did you laugh me off. You never once trivialized what I was going through.

And I was no saint either, I know that. I guess the fact that I'm now burdening a stranger with my issues has made me aware of how I treated you. And how much I wish you were here. I know you couldn't talk me through this, and

I wouldn't expect you to, but I could do with some familiar comfort right now. And maybe an eye roll or two.

Love,
Mel

"Thanks for the pen," I said, handing the Spider-Man pen back to David. "And the paper. That was really nice of you to share with me."

He put the pen in his pocket, and I tucked my grandma's letter into mine.

"Wanna see my soccer moves?" he asked, already running to get his soccer ball.

I was sitting outside of the trailer in one of the camp chairs. It was a perfect day in the forest. A gentle breeze rustled the pines, sunlight made the stream sparkle and our skin warm, and I'd like to believe I was trying my best not to be grumpy.

It had been four days since I had done much more than limp the thirty yards to the outhouse and back. I tried to eat as little as possible, but Crystal watched me like a hawk.

Because of the slight fracture in my forearm, I couldn't even clap every time David performed one of his uncoordinated tricks with his soccer ball. Each clap would have been an extra half calorie I didn't have to worry about. I knew I would be well enough to start walking in a few days, but how much time would it take for me to get back to where I had been physically?

I told Crystal I just needed to walk for a few hours a day. I tried to convince her that it would be good for me, strengthening my injured body and all that. Unfortunately, this girl was far from an idiot. She allowed me three laps around the trailer a day and said I could add on once I was no longer dragging my injured leg behind me and my face wasn't a white sheet of pain at the end of each lap. And since she literally stitched me up and mopped up my blood, I could protest for only so long. I hated her for it, and I hated myself for hating her.

She came outside then, watching David with a smile as she made her way over to me. She sat down in the chair to my right and breathed in deep.

"Beautiful day, isn't it?"

I attempted to cross my arms and failed. "It really is."

"How are you feeling today?"

"Fine."

She leaned back contentedly. "That cut on your head is looking better. I think it will only end up being a faint scar if we keep tending to it."

I slumped in my chair, my heart pounding in my chest. I could run. I could start running right now. I doubted Crystal would stop me. I had learned by now that Crystal took a hands-off approach to most things. Well, besides playing nurse. She had a bedside manner that was the perfect mix of kindness, concern, and resolve. It was beyond annoying.

"Chicken soup is on the stove for dinner tonight. I also have bread rising."

I nodded distractedly, trying to think of how I could avoid eating the bread and drink only the broth.

I was brought back to reality when something was placed in my lap. A pair of jeans.

"Um . . ."

She held out a small metal box, waiting for me to take it. I accepted it hesitantly.

"I think it will help if you have something to keep your hands busy. It would be wonderful if you could mend David's jeans for me. They are his best pair, and if he keeps climbing trees at this rate, they will be more holes than jeans."

I stared at the pants for a moment, then opened the box. I threaded the needle a little awkwardly with my arm in a homemade cast. It wasn't walking twenty miles a day, but it was better than nothing.

"You already know how to mend clothes?" Crystal asked, settling herself deeper into the old camp chair, causing it to squeak slightly in protest.

I nodded. "My mom taught my sister and me. New clothing wasn't a purchase she thought fit into the life of the humble woman."

Crystal pulled a spool of thread and another needle from her pocket. "It sounds like you have some resentment stored up toward her."

I glanced at her. "Did David tell you about what he heard me yelling in the woods or are you also a psychic?"

She smiled slyly. "David told me."

"Ah. Well, yes. It's not really much of a secret. Anyone who knows us knows we don't exactly get along." I turned the jeans inside out and began to stitch. "It's the classic situation of the daughter not measuring up to the mother's standards. At least she taught me to sew though." I hesitated, but eventually asked, "What about your mother? What was she like?"

I could see she was conjuring up an image of her mother, a wistful expression on her face. "She was everything I one day hope to be. She had this way of making everyone laugh, no matter what the situation. She took pain and suffering in stride, always finding joy and inner peace in even the darkest of times."

Crystal held the now-threaded needle between her thumb and forefinger, absentmindedly twisting the string. "The day she died she had sent me a text asking me to look up what national day it was because she felt like we should have something to celebrate when we all got home that evening." She paused to take one long, slow breath. "It was national ice cream cone day. But I don't think she had the chance to read my response before she died." Crystal offered me a forlorn smile. "I was so lucky to know her. Even if the time was cut short. The only thing that breaks my heart is that David never got the chance to know her like I did."

I didn't reply at first. I let the memory of her mother come to rest around us.

"I'm not trying to say that you're a replacement for your mother," I said, "but by the looks of it, you're doing an amazing job raising David."

She flushed with color, and I wondered how long it had been since anyone had paid her a compliment, since anyone had given her the credit she deserved.

"There's always this voice in the back of my mind asking me if I'm doing the right thing, raising him out here. Most of the time, like on days like this when the sky is blue and the day is perfect for playing and exploring, I can answer the voice with confidence. But sometimes . . . I don't know."

"You're not missing anything in civilization, trust me." I grunted. Crystal laughed. "But seriously, anyone can see he's a happy, healthy kid. Smart too. You're doing survival the best way you know how, and both of you seem to be thriving. Try not to give that little voice too much power. It can overrun your life if you're not careful."

"That's good advice," she said quietly. "Thank you for saying that."

I gave her a half smile and moved on to another rip in the jeans. Crystal returned to her own mending—a scratchy-looking purple sweater.

"If it's not too personal a question to answer," I said a moment later, "why did you choose to live out here?"

"Well," she said, her eyebrows furrowed in thought, "I didn't give it much consideration at the time. But looking back, I suppose it's because I had the chance to reshape my life, and the life I craved was a simple one. I didn't want David to grow up aware of the world's complications. I wanted to give him a chance to discover how beautiful and life-giving the universe is meant to be. And I also wanted to rediscover that for myself, to be honest."

"When did life become so complicated?" I muttered empathetically.

She sighed. "I'm not sure, but I've learned it doesn't have to be."

"What were your complications?" I asked.

"Hmm?"

"You know, the things in your life that left things twisted. What were they?"

She laughed without humor. "Now *that* is a personal question."

I quickly backtracked. "You're right, I'm sorry—"

She held up her hand that wasn't holding her needle. "I like personal questions. It's what I miss most out here, getting to know people. People getting to know me. We have a few people who visit us out here, but for the most part, visitors are sparse." I felt her glance at me, and she returned to the topic at hand.

"My dad made life complicated. He was a drinker and a cheater, but my mom continued to stay with him through all of that. He would shape up for a few months, then come crashing down. His moods were impossible to predict, but only we knew that. To the outside world, he was spotless. He had a good job where he worked long hours, the perfect family who always supported him, the white picket fence . . . No one ever suspected the demons. They never showed their faces to anyone but me and my mother.

"I couldn't understand how someone could be so many conflicting things at once. I couldn't understand how my mom could continue to love someone like that. Why someone as wonderful as her would stay with someone like him. I couldn't understand how he kept finding new ways to break my heart. Those were the sort of complications I wanted to leave behind."

"I'm so sorry," was all I could offer because what else do you say when the worst thing your dad ever did to you was not have your back in an argument or not show up to a cross-country meet because he was too busy helping the homeless? Sighing, I turned to her, my pride a little wounded. "Also, I'm sorry for the things I can actually control. I'm sorry I've been acting like a grounded teenager."

She gave me a look with more sympathy than I deserved. "We all process things in our own way."

I shook my head. "That doesn't make it okay. I've got . . . issues. And again, that doesn't make it acceptable. I'm trying to work through some things. And apparently it's not going well."

She said nothing for a while, only watched David kick the soccer ball through fallen pine needles. With her eyes still on him, she finally spoke. "After my dad died, I struggled. I packed up whatever I could carry right after the funeral and took David out here. I was convinced our old house was cursed. For the first few months, I could barely bring myself to leave the trailer. I was paralyzed by anxiety, convinced that any decision I made would be the wrong one. I was certain that my first wrong decision would take David away from me as well. I would start obsessing over everything I did, every choice I made. I was consumed with the thought that I wasn't good enough, that I wasn't capable of giving David everything he needed.

"Then one day I was out in these woods at dawn. There was something about the multitude of trees swaying above me and the way the sun stretched out over everything in sight . . . At least, that's what I credit it to. It could have simply been time for my heart to unclench. Anyway, I looked around me at this vast forest, trying to comprehend how small I was compared to it, compared to the entire world, and I was enlightened with a truth that has brought me endless peace."

I focused on her, my mending paused. I waited impatiently as she worked out how to share the meaning of life with me.

"All my anxieties, they were centered around one thing, the thing I had subconsciously built my universe around—me. Everything was '*I'm* not good enough.' '*I'm* going to mess things up.' It was never 'What does David need?' 'How can I live my life so David can see me as a good example?' 'How can I help Earth grow and flourish?' When I opened up my heart to the needs of the world, I had no time or sympathy left to wallow in self-pity. We are not meant to obsess over ourselves because it will not take much time for us to realize what flawed creatures we are. The more we focus on ourselves, the more we obsess over all those flaws. We lose sleep over them, revolve our whole lives around fixing them because at that point, we are all we see. We become blinded by ourselves. Do you know what I mean?"

I nodded, my throat dry.

"We so limit our potential to help the world around us if we can't see past ourselves." She looked up sharply, startling me. "I'm not discrediting the value of self-care and the recognition, acceptance, and healing process that is necessary to overcome difficulties. Please don't think that's my intention. All I can say from my own journey is that true healing can happen only when life becomes outwardly focused instead of inwardly. When our world is once again expanded past ourselves to cover an expanse of wonders and possibilities greater than we could ever find in a spiral of self-doubt. When we take the second to see the sunrise over a world that doesn't only belong to the individual, true healing can begin."

The world spun slowly underneath us as I tried to process this, knowing all too well how deep in the spiral I was. I felt the soft pine needles underneath my feet and the compact dirt beneath them. The dirt that held the roots to the trees, the trees that covered acres of wild forest, a forest one could spend a whole lifetime exploring and still not know its every mystery. This *creation* I was intertwined with but had so thoroughly separated myself from.

"Buddhism?" I finally asked.

"Hmm?" Crystal replied, fully engrossed in her mending.

"The way you talked about all that . . . It sounded like Buddhism. Are you Buddhist?"

She smirked. "A little of this, a little of that. I take from religions what brings me comfort and keeps me persevering and try to leave behind anything humans have twisted into fear and hate. I'm still figuring things out, but I've come a long way. I believe it's nearly impossible to live in a place like this and not become a spiritual person."

I nodded. "What about a higher power? Do you believe in something like that?"

She gazed out past David and into the trees. She made a sweeping gesture with her arm. "Look at what surrounds us." She inclined her head in David's direction. "Look at who I get to experience it with. How could I not believe in a higher power?" She shrugged one shoulder. "I just haven't figured out exactly what it looks like yet."

"Speaking as someone who grew up never doubting the existence of a very specific God, I can agree with you there," I said, sighing. "The more I grow, the more I see . . . I'm not sure how the God I grew up believing in fits into all of it. I don't doubt His existence, just His characteristics."

She glanced at me. "Look at the ones who taught you about God. They tend to create Him in their own image. When you strip away all of that influence, what are you left with? Where does your truth of God come from?"

I stared at her, once again shocked to silence. "You're how old, again?"

"Twenty."

"I would say you're the wisest twenty-year-old I've ever met, but you might be the wisest person I've ever met, period."

She grinned. “People always said I was mature for my age.”

“No kidding,” I muttered.

We spent the next hour or so mending and talking while David moved on from soccer to building a stick fort.

“Dinner soon?” Crystal asked me when the sun started to sink close to the tree line.

I took a deep breath and managed a genuine smile at the mystical twenty-year-old.

“That sounds great,” I replied, looking past her at the trees, the forest, the sky, all of creation.

28

The days that made up the next couple of weeks followed a familiar pattern. Wake up on the small dusty couch in the trailer and remind myself where I was. Once that was figured out, I moved on to panicking since being there meant I was forced to spend my day without adequate exercise.

I would talk myself down, thinking of the sunlight splashed across the faded carpet, listening to the raspy whispers of the trees that surrounded us. David and Crystal would usually already be up and about, being quiet and careful not to wake me. Crystal was usually at the camp stove making breakfast while David was out doing whatever a seven-year-old with limited supervision does in the wilderness.

I would lie there and wait for the pain to return. Each day would bring a more tolerable reunion, and there was something to be said for taking the time to notice the healing in one's own body.

I would get to my feet with a groan, a little less dramatic with each passing day. After waving good morning to Crystal, I would set off into the woods.

These nature walks just sort of happened one morning

when I couldn't stand the thought of being stuck in the ten-foot radius of the trailer any longer and I realized Crystal wasn't keeping me as prisoner. The going was slow and painful. And it was *hard*. The reality that I had lost so much fitness in such a short span of time made me hyperventilate, which wasn't ideal since I was already close to doing so thanks to the physical exertion of the hike.

One morning I leaned back against a tree, letting tears of frustration fall freely. I closed my eyes.

I was a failure. *I must weigh at least three hundred pounds by this point*, I thought, not daring to even touch my stomach.

I'd start over. I could start dropping the weight again as soon as I got better. I'd work ten times harder than I had before and get back in shape ten times quicker. I would do it, even though the thought of going through all that again made me more exhausted than I had ever felt in my life.

The sound of birdsong caused me to open my eyes. All around me, life continued onward. The trees grew, the sun rose and fell, the leaves decomposed, the squirrels gathered food. My life was over, meaningless. But all around me, life held meaning just waiting to be grasped.

I remembered Crystal's words about looking past my individual self, looking out into the world and what I could offer to creation. I remembered what it had felt like in the wilderness to shift my focus from myself and instead pay attention to God's Spirit. A calm settled over me, dispelling the pure panic.

So long story short, my daily routine during my time at the trailer included a trek out to the great big expanse of nowhere so I could feel the world expand beyond myself. So

I could remember and re-remember and keep remembering. Because healing was at least fifty percent just relearning the lessons I'd learned and recalling the breakthroughs I'd already had. Crystal never said a word about it, but breakfast was always waiting for me when I returned.

"Didn't you have any mountains in Michigan?" David asked one day as the two of us walked—well, I limped—through the woods.

I shook my head. "We have something called the Porcupine Mountains, but nothing like the mountains out West."

"But weren't there any closer mountains? Like the Tetons?"

This kid had to stop reading so many *National Geographics* and give TV a try one of these days.

"Yeah, there were closer ones. But it wouldn't have been the same."

"Why not?"

I thought about this for a moment. "Well, do you have a place in these woods that's really special to you? More than any other?"

He thought about this for about half a second, then nodded. "Does the ridge south of home count?"

"Of course. It can be anywhere. What makes that place so special?"

He shrugged. "I don't know. I just like it best."

I let him think on that for a moment. That would have been a satisfactory answer for any normal seven-year-old, but this kid wasn't normal.

"Crystal used to take me up there for picnics when I was little," he said eventually. "We'd watch the birds, and we'd always name them. Now when I go, I like when I can watch the sunrise from there. It feels like it's warming my heart with the sky."

He put a hand over his chest solemnly. I fought the urge to be weird and hug him.

"That does sound special. But there are lots of other ridges in the world. Even in this forest. Do you think any of those would feel the same? That they would be as special as that southern ridge?"

He was quiet for a long moment, then looked at me pointedly. "No, I don't think so. That means it's the same with your mountain?"

"Exactly. Even though I've never actually been there, a piece of it feels like a part of me. I have to go find that part. And I can't find it on any other mountain."

"Okay," he said.

"Okay?"

"Okay, I understand now."

He took me to the southern ridge the next afternoon, climbing over fallen trees and scrambling up hills to reach it. After I caught my breath and could look around at the deep green blanket of forest and the sun-drenched ridges without seeing spots, I told him truthfully that it was beautiful. He beamed with pride.

One day on our walk, he stopped in his tracks and stared at me in surprise. "You're not limping anymore."

That night, following our daily routine of gathering around the campfire to read until nothing but the stars offered light, Crystal put down her book and considered me.

"Mel, David and I want you to stay as long as you'd like. We'd love to have you as a member of our family even, if that's something that you want. But something tells me you would be unable to accept, since you have other paths you need to follow. And I think the time has come when you can continue down those paths."

David looked at me. "She's saying we don't want you to go, but we know you need to."

I gave David a smile that I hoped expressed my thanks, but probably just looked sad. "I can't even begin to . . ." It was pointless trying to put my gratitude into words. They had already heard it too many times to count. I tried again.

"You two have become like family to me. I know we have our own lives to live, lives that most likely won't cross again." I gave my full attention to David then. "But I'm always going to carry a piece of you both. No matter where life takes me. And I'll hold those pieces close whenever I need to be brave, whenever I need to feel a little less alone."

David nodded solemnly. My hero.

The three of us rose with the sun the next morning. Crystal stuffed my bag with carrots straight from her garden, dirt and all.

"Be careful with that arm, Mel," she warned. "It still has healing left to do."

"I will," I promised.

I hugged them both, hard. "If I ever find myself lost in the Idaho wilderness again, I'll be sure to stop by."

How was it that I kept running into the best of humanity all across this big, wild country? Sure, there had been the stares from strangers, some gawking, some that made the back of my neck tingle with a sharp prickle of anxiety. There had been the people who crossed the street, clutched their handbags, and held their children close as I passed, though to be fair I might have done the same in their situation, considering how bad I typically smelled. And of course there had been the occasional unkind and uncreative thing yelled at me from a passing car, sometimes accompanied by an empty can or fast-food bag.

But all those slights paled in comparison to the unofficial trail angels who had saved me time and time again during this journey. Two of said angels who I now reluctantly released from my embrace.

I waved my goodbyes, then paused. I aimed a questioning glance at Crystal and she grinned. "Go north. You'll run into the trail in no time. The nearest town is about seven miles down the trail."

I laughed and offered her one last smile. "Don't know what I'd do without you, Crystal."

"You'll be okay, Mel. I know it."

I felt their absence almost immediately. I knew I would, but I was surprised by how sharply it stung. I wasn't afraid of falling again, even though I watched roots with laser-like focus now. The forest didn't scare me, nor the jagged ravine I walked along that dangerously plummeted to certain death.

Despite the new scars on my legs and head and the twinge I would forever feel in my forearm, I was not afraid of falling again. But for the first time out here, I was afraid of being truly and wholly alone.

I couldn't continue to carry this burden of self-hatred and harm and expect any different outcome from my life. I could either live worshiping a version of myself I could never become, or forget myself and open my life to others. It *seemed* like a simple choice, but then again so did choosing between eating to avoid death or starving to fit into a specific pair of jeans.

Crystal joined my group of influential women. I talked out loud to all of them as I made my way down the trail, hoping they could be my sounding board and knowing they wouldn't judge me for my convoluted thoughts.

Eventually I found myself on the outskirts of the town Crystal had mentioned. I was panting, covered in sweat, and exhausted. The hike had been much slower and more difficult than I had been anticipating, but instead of collapsing into a puddle of despair, I focused on my burning muscles. I wiped the sweat off my forehead. I slowed my breathing to a raspy rhythm.

My body had worked hard, and oh, how I had missed that feeling. I had a ways to go to get back to the shape I had been in, but my body would take me there. And I would relish every sore muscle along the way. This was not the plight of one who wished to be punished but one who wished to marvel at the strength that had been gifted to her own being.

I strolled down the main street, feeling buoyed by my physical exhaustion. It was an objectively beautiful day. The sun had traveled from one side of the cloudless sky to the other during my time in the woods, and there was an almost imperceptible hint of chill in the air, so slight it felt like an afterthought on my skin. But the message was clear, the season was beginning to change.

Also, nearly everyone I saw wore flannel—as sure a sign of an approaching fall season as I've ever seen. It felt like the whole small town was out enjoying this weather. They sat out on their porches, strolled the sidewalks, and enjoyed meals on patios outside restaurants made to look like log cabins.

It was slightly overwhelming to be reminded of the fact that all these people were living their lives while I had been tucked away in the woods for the past few weeks. The outside world had nearly ceased to exist. Now that I was confronted with it again, I realized reintroducing myself would require an adjustment period. It would not be easy for Crystal and David if they ever decided to come out of the woods.

I found the local grocery store and was taken aback by how bright the lights were, how I could see my reflection in the polished floor. The packages shone like neon lights from the shelves, too many options to process. I touched a package of off-brand potato chips gently, then watched as fellow patrons went about filling their carts like it was the most normal thing in the world. Because it *was* the most normal thing in the world. Geez, one would think I had just landed from another planet, not that I spent a couple of weeks with relatively normal people in a relatively normal trailer out in the woods not ten miles away.

I headed to the bathroom before tackling any shopping. As much as I loved living with Crystal and David, the damp and dark outhouse got old real fast.

There was something about peeing in peace in quiet while sitting on a shiny white toilet seat that made me feel like royalty. But when I looked down to see a smear of bright red blood on the toilet paper, my heart stopped.

I was so shocked that at first it was like I was fifteen again and I had no idea this wasn't a sure sign of imminent death. My mom thought a woman's "monthlies" was never an appropriate topic of conversation.

I sat there, stunned. It had been half a year since I had my period. Months of knowing I was doing something wrong but continuing to do it anyway. Not getting my period had become a sick sort of pride for me. As long as I didn't get my period, that meant I was undereating and therefore underweight.

But now . . . Now it meant I was getting better. But of course, there was also this relatively large part of me that wasn't sure I wanted to get better.

I could see this as a failure, the final tipping point that it would take to go back to starvation and never reemerge.

Something was welling up in my heart. Something huge and beautiful and undeniable. I blamed half of this feeling on the increased hormones, but the other half was very real. My body was no longer broken. And this, this meant I no longer had to be alone. My future could be altered, it could point toward growth instead of decline.

This was a moment. An important one. One that I felt I would point to in years to come. I could move forward and welcome this new season, or I could stagnate. So I thought about my future. About the family I envisioned, the husband by my side, the kids we would create.

I would not stagnate. No, I would not stagnate. I would go boldly forward.

But first, I would go boldly to the feminine hygiene aisle.

29

HOT SPRINGS
5 MILES

The sign was weathered and the letters faded, but I could still make out the beacon of hope.

It had been raining off and on for the past week. Nothing like what I experienced in North Dakota, but enough to chill me to the bone and bring on more than one flashback.

A sympathetic hiker told me about the hot springs when we crossed paths the day before. I had asked him for directions on a particularly confusing part of the trail, and he eagerly offered them to me. He pointed out the hot springs as a must-do detour.

"It's a few miles out of the way, but it looks like you could use some R&R," he said as kindly as one could possibly say something like that.

I was just grateful for the directions and that he didn't end up murdering me. Thru-hikes, I had learned, have the ability to greatly lower a person's standards.

I had crossed into Washington State earlier that week. Turns out the pine trees and ravines in Idaho look awfully similar to those in Washington, so I didn't realize it until two days later when I left what remained of the Lewis and Clark Historic Trail to restock supplies. The abundance of Washington license plates and even more flannel gave it away fairly quickly.

The Evergreen State, read the license plates. The outline of Mount Rainier loomed behind the jumble of letters and numbers, causing my heart to leap in my chest every time I saw one.

"Hello, Washington!" I yelled to the nearly full grocery store parking lot, something Michigan Mel would have never dreamed of doing but something Washington Mel embraced wholeheartedly.

"Hello!" someone yelled back.

I was filled with happiness to such a ludicrous level that I ended up adding a package of Peanut M&M's to the conveyor belt at the last moment. The cashier scanned them and added them to the rest of my groceries with an alarming lack of fanfare.

"Sir," I wanted to say, "you probably didn't notice, but those were *Peanut M&M's* I bought. I just thought you should be aware this is a very, very big deal. A very special occasion. I'm by no means the type of person who purchases Peanut M&M's on a regular basis, so this is a very important moment for me."

Thankfully, I kept my mouth shut.

It took me another full day to talk myself into actually opening the pack of M&M's. I came to an agreement with myself that I would eat one in the morning and one at night until they ran out. I was nearly convinced that it was my twice-daily M&M ration that had gotten me through the misty rain so far.

But M&M's don't last forever, even if only two are eaten a day. I was running low on candy-coated chocolate and energy, so I was hoping a trip to these random hot springs a stranger recommended would be my saving grace to get me through the last leg of whatever I was still doing out here.

I didn't want to admit I was losing faith in my pilgrimage, but that was exactly what was happening. Every day I woke up a little closer to the national park, and all of a sudden, it had become too real. This was no longer just an idea in my head or an idyllic painting on a postcard. This was right in front of me (give or take a few hundred miles), and there was a very real chance it wouldn't live up to my romanticized expectations.

But what if it did? What was I expecting to happen as a result? I had strategically avoided thinking about this question up to this point, but that was no longer an option. Was I hoping the heavens would open up and I would be showered with enlightenment at the sight of the mountain, never again doomed to struggle with food or fitness? Was I hoping to find some sort of cave and live out my days next to this giant piece of rock that I was convinced would save me? Would I take one look at the mountain and with a shrug of my shoulders wonder what the big deal was? Was I hoping that someone would come up and offer me a plan for my life on a silver platter like what happened to my dad?

I was at a total loss. Alex always said I had a tendency to think things through about seventy-seven percent of the way. It was a little annoying sometimes having someone in my life who knew me that well.

But I still had time to put off confronting the answers to these questions for at least a little longer. I finally waved goodbye to the Lewis and Clark Historic Trail at Sacajawea Historical State Park. Kids ran on the grassy lawn outside of the Sacajawea Museum and boats puttered along the Columbia River. It felt like a good omen for what lay ahead.

I no longer had a set trail to follow, but that didn't bother me. Like most of my journey, the rivers would be my guide. I followed the Columbia River to the Yakima River, banked by quiet, overgrown footpaths, residential streets, and bike paths constantly veiled in mist. It was in a particularly otherworldly patch of moody forest that I ran into the hiker.

I followed the densely wooded path toward the supposed hot springs, wondering more than once if this was all just a very elaborate way for that friendly hiker to murder me.

But then, like a desert oasis, it appeared. Small waterfalls of crystal-clear water cascaded down one natural pool into the next. Steam rose from each pool, up into the air and vanished beneath the towering branches of the black cedars.

All of that was great and all, but what really caused me to stop and stare were the bodies relaxing in each of the pools.

The *naked* bodies.

"Oh, heck no," I muttered, already turning around. But turning around meant walking five miles back the other way only to keep walking and walking through the rain and mud and . . .

I glanced back at the hot springs. The water looked unbelievably toasty. Rain had soaked through my jacket days ago and mercilessly refused to dry. I hadn't planned my wardrobe for fall, not expecting the delays in Fargo and Idaho. I would have to stop at a Goodwill soon and find a thicker jacket and pants.

In the meantime, my sleeping bag was now barely warm enough to stop me from shivering all night, even with all my clothes piled on top of me. It had been days since I had actually felt warm. I was desperate for these hot springs.

I let out a shaky breath and walked tentatively up the path leading to the hot springs. Maybe I could be the weirdo who kept her clothes on? I didn't have a bathing suit though, so at the very minimum I would have to strip down to my underwear. Something I wasn't even comfortable doing in broad daylight *without* an audience.

There wasn't much of a crowd and few people even glanced in my direction as I approached. Murmured conversations could barely be heard over the rushing water, but for the most part people were silent and pensive. Those people made me nervous. With little distraction, they could easily look in my direction at any time to see every single one of my flaws.

Management of the hot springs took the form of a singular rusted sign that listed the rules:

Visitors of Pineridge Hot Springs

1. Shower before entering hot springs
2. Remove clothing before entering hot springs
3. Hot springs close at dusk
4. Pregnant women should use at their own risk

There were plenty more rules on the list, but I read all I needed to. This was going to be my own personal hell in a place I figured came pretty close to looking like heaven. Should be interesting.

I found a water spigot that appeared to be the "shower" the rules referred to. It was secluded from the rest of the springs, so I hastily stripped off my clothes and stood under the freezing water for approximately five seconds. Any longer, and I was certain hypothermia would have set in.

The feeling of nothing on my skin but the gentlest of breezes was one of the oddest things I had ever experienced. I was in my natural state in the natural world. Well, besides my still-bandaged arm, my backpack, and the pile of clothes I was clutching to my chest for dear life.

I walked back up to the hot springs, still desperately covering every part of me that I could.

I can't do this. I can't do this. I can't do this. That sole thought was running on a frantic loop in my head. But I kept walking, telling myself I would only draw more attention if I turned and sprinted back to the safety of the trees.

I found an empty pool and stood there for a moment, shaking slightly. I realized I was definitely making myself more of a target for ridicule by standing here and clutching all my worldly possessions to my naked body instead of just taking the plunge.

So trying desperately to not appear panicked and hoping I gave off an air of having done this sort of thing a million times before, I threw my clothes and backpack near the edge of the basin and slipped into the water.

I let out an involuntary sigh, my heart still pounding. The water acted like a balm for my aching, shivering body. It would have been even more soothing if my body wasn't rigid with the fear of someone looking on in judgment.

But when I glanced around, no one met my gaze. They were all in their own headspace, completely immersed in this magical realm we were each lucky enough to find ourselves in. So I forced myself to relax, taking deep breaths to loosen my muscles and dispel the countless anxieties racing through my head.

A feeling passed in a fleeting moment, and I did what I could to hold on to it. For the first time in a long, long time, this body I was in didn't feel like a source of punishment. As my sore muscles were soothed by the water, I wasn't disappointed in my body, but almost proud of it for carrying me to this place.

Maybe, I thought, *maybe this vessel that carries around my tattered and weary soul was made for more than suffering.*

Maybe it was also designed for pleasure and satisfaction and joy.

I took a sweeping glance at those around me—humans of all shapes and sizes. All sinking into the comfort of their own bodies, enjoying being *themselves*. I wondered what it would be like to enjoy being in my own body. If my first instinct wasn't to cringe and turn away when I looked in the mirror. I could one day be a person who laid in bed with a book on a winter night instead of doing exactly one thousand jumping jacks before bed.

Maybe I could bring myself to enjoy a morning on a sunlit porch, eating breakfast with someone I loved instead of heading out for the first of multiple runs that day.

Maybe even be the person who joins her friends for ice cream so we could laugh and catch up on one another's lives instead of making excuses why I couldn't go.

Or on my next birthday, what if I blew out the candles and wished for something other than an easy way to get out of eating a slice of cake?

I once again observed the people who surrounded me. There was a man humming a Beatles' song who was sunk so deep in his hot spring, his massive beard skimmed the surface of the steaming water. Across the way, a young couple soaked in silence, their eyes rapturously fixed on the canopy of trees above them. Over to my left was a woman with a shaved head and tattoos covering every inch of her skin still exposed above the water. Her whole body arched in laughter at something her equally tatted friend said. To my left, an older woman rested her elbows on the edge of the pool and kicked her feet playfully in the water. All beautiful and free, not one of them like the other.

Around me, a cathedral was erected. Pillars of tree trunks, walls of swaying branches, and a domed ceiling as vast as the sky. Birds sang hymns, laughter echoed like a prayer, and the water we were immersed in became something of a holy sacrament.

Welcome, the cedars whispered. *Welcome to this wild church.*

30

EARLYISH OCTOBER

Dear Claire,

I hope I'll one day be able to get this letter to you. I don't plan to send it in the mail because I'm close to broke and international shipping costs are outrageous. But maybe one day you and Mom and Dad will come back for Christmas like you've been saying you will, and I can give it to you then. Or maybe you'll stay over there forever, saving the world. Either way, I'll have to get this letter to you eventually, because it contains information that's vital for you to know.

I've been on the road for a while now and while I've learned shockingly little that will be of any use to me in the real world, I have learned ways to make living with myself a whole lot more bearable.

I can only assume you hear the same voice in your head

that I do before making any decision and after every mistake. I have to assume that, because Mom's voice isn't one you can get out of your head easily. And for better or worse, we can't seem to shake the expectations she has ground into us.

You know how Mom always made sure we kept ourselves on the line that separated the "underweight" and "normal" section of the BMI chart? Remember how she would insist on going with us every time we bought clothes so we wouldn't buy anything "unflattering to our figure"? Remember how we women had to stick to our portioned-out meals at dinner but Dad could always eat as much as he wanted? Or how we would have to run laps around the house if we had a big dessert the night before?

I'm here to tell you—THAT ISN'T NORMAL. And I'm well aware that there are plenty of other toxic things Mom has done that aren't normal, but this is the one subject I can speak most confidently on. I know there are many things to blame, most of all myself, but believing in these "values" is a reason why I nearly ruined my life and caused myself so much unnecessary pain. I want more than anything to spare you from the same fate. And honestly, I think you might be the only person in the world who knows that the dramatic tone of this letter is totally warranted.

Lately, I've been trying something new. Every time I see someone, I try to notice something other than their weight. Whenever I go to measure my thighs or my waist or think about counting my ribs, I try to pull back and think of *something I want to do with my life instead. When I begin to worry about my weight or if I've eaten too much or if my calorie count is off, I listen to a song on my playlist that brings me to another place. If I find myself hesitating before I can bring myself to eat something, I try to think of all the little things I want to experience again. I try to see eating as a source of joy, not shame. It doesn't always work, but my track record is getting better every day.*

I have had a lot of time to think lately, and the other day something came to mind that I haven't been able to shake. You know how one of the most common imageries of heaven in the Bible is a feast? What if that was part of the reason God made us so we need to eat? So we would be able to experience ahead of time what it's like to be taken care of and fed? What if what we do here, eating together, enjoying food, what if it's the physical way we prepare for what we will be given in heaven? Just something that's been helping me through the past few days.

Claire, I know that we won't have the same struggles (and I'm so thankful for that). You are stronger than me in so many ways, smarter too. So this truth that how we look doesn't translate to what we are worth might not be the groundbreaking news that it was to me. But in case you ever need to hear it, I will shout it from the rooftops.

Love you forever,
Mel

I looked up from the newspaper I was pretending to read when the door to the Panera opened. Ten minutes before closing was an odd time for a person to come in. To be fair, it was also an odd time for a person to be pretending to read a newspaper while an annoyed employee cleaned around their table.

I was here on a mission though. One way or another, I was going to obtain the bagels they threw away at the end of each day.

A thru-hiker I met a while back told me about Panera's bagel policy. If you're in the store around closing time, chances are they will walk around and hand out the leftover bagels and pastries they were planning on tossing anyway. At the time, I thought this was beneath me. That was about a month ago when I thought my body and bank account were invincible. I had since then been proven wrong on both accounts, which was why I found myself in a Panera nine minutes before close.

I watched the visitor stroll toward the register with far too much confidence for someone ordering this close to the end of teenagers' shifts. But to my surprise, the girl sweeping behind the counter stopped what she was doing, smiled at the woman, and greeted her by name.

"Hey, Sandra, I'll be right back with your stuff."

"No rush, Alyssa," Sandra said with a wave of her hand. And she really seemed to mean it. Everything about her was approachable. She had on comfortable sneakers, a pair of jeans, and a faded sweatshirt. Her hair was gathered in a messy bun, and she leaned against the display case like she had done this a thousand times before. She looked to be in her fifties, and something about the way her mouth seemed to rest in a smile made me instantly take a liking to her.

Until Alyssa handed her all my bagels.

I watched in dismay as my means of survival for the next week was handed off in what seemed like slow motion. There were so many bagels, Sandra had to heft the bag over her shoulder like she was Santa who brought the gift of carbs.

She thanked Alyssa and headed back out to the parking lot, slightly bent under the weight of the bagels.

I immediately knew what this meant. This meant I had an excuse not to eat. Sure, I had a little money left, emphasis on "little." Plus, the small reserve I had decided to keep in my bank account in case I got to Mount Rainier and didn't feel like walking the two thousand miles back. But I had told myself that was only for emergencies or truly desperate situations. An excuse not to eat for an entire week did not count as either of those things in my book. It was a welcomed opportunity.

I had been getting better, but my improvement was so fragile that I knew a slight hiccup in my plan was all it would take for it to shatter.

I will not stagnate.

I stood up quickly, clumsily put on my backpack, and ran out the door.

"Wait!" I yelled to the bagel woman named Sandra. She was half hidden by the bed of her truck, rearranging items to make room for the giant bag on the ground next to her. She glanced over her shoulder at me, eyebrows raised, confusion written on her face.

"Please," I said, not really sure of how to continue. "I

don't know if you're throwing a bagel party or feeding, like, three thousand ducks with those bagels, but I could really use a few of those. I don't want to be too dramatic about it, but a few bagels from that bag might save my soul."

She had straightened and was examining me curiously. I cleared my throat.

"Again, not to be too dramatic."

Her face broke into an amused grin. "I think I can help you out. At least with the bagels. They're for those in need anyway, and you seem to fit the bill."

My face burned. I had guessed the bagels would be used to feed thousands of ducks before I guessed that they might be food for the hungry. I would be sure to check detective off the list of my possible careers.

"Oh, no. I'm sorry, I didn't know they were for— I'm good. Really. I can guarantee the people you're taking these to need them more than me."

Sandra studied me for a long moment. Her expression seemed to say, *Your appearance says otherwise . . .*

"Okay, how about this," she said, holding her hands out as if her words were an offering. "We drop these bagels off at the shelter and you come back to my place for dinner. I had planned to have my kids over tonight, but they ended up not being able to make it so I have a ton of extra food. You'd be helping me out, honestly."

This wasn't part of the plan, and the sick part of my brain knew it. Instantly, it tried to revolt. *What would she be making for dinner? What if it's fattening? Mel, what if it's* fried? *Look at her and be honest, does she look like someone we can trust to make us a healthy meal?*

"That would be really great, thank you," I answered. I said

it loudly, trying to drown out that voice in my head. Sandra raised her eyebrows slightly. Probably wondering what sort of lunatic she just invited into her home.

But her easy, natural smile reappeared instantly. "All right, then, let's get going."

Sandra, I quickly found out, was a talker. She started chatting the moment we got in the truck and didn't stop until we arrived at the shelter. And she paused then only because volunteers came out to meet her and she had to talk to them instead.

She would ask me a question, like what my name was, and I would respond. This launched her into a whole monologue about the name Melanie and how she knew someone named Melanie back in college and how they never really got along, but she always aspired to be friends with her because she had a car and Sandra didn't . . .

After ten minutes of chatting about a Melanie I didn't know, Sandra asked me what I was doing with the backpack. I told her I was heading to Mount Rainier National Park.

"Oh, Mount Rainier!" she gushed. "Have you ever seen a more beautiful place? I mean, it's stunning. Makes you feel small, you know? You can see the mountain from town on a clear day, but it's not the same, of course. You really have to be in the park to experience it. What with the wildflowers and the glaciers and the rivers . . . So many different ecosystems!

Sandra tapped out a rhythmless tune on the steering wheel, waiting for a light to change. "I remember when I went a few years back and I hiked around with a few friends. I think it was Mary, Olivia, and Sarah. Sarah and her husband had just divorced so we all said, 'Screw it, we need a trip to clear our heads.' We needed a change of scenery, some different air, you know? But we were all too broke for plane tickets—ha! So we figured Rainier would be a good destination. Although, is it really a destination if it's in the same state and you can sometimes see it from your front porch? I don't know. But Olivia used to camp there as a kid, and she raved about it. Said there's no place else like it on earth. I don't know if that's true either, but it's certainly something to see . . ."

My goodness, she was a lot. The story continued with Olivia, or maybe Mary, wanting to stop at a diner, which led to a long description of Olivia's (or Mary's) love interest, who worked at the local bakery. That somehow turned into a tangent about bad taxidermy used as restaurant decorations. She chatted ceaselessly in the easygoing manner I had noticed when she first walked into the Panera. Like life was grand and everything was worthy of a story. I was drawn to her exuberance. Something about it was both soothing and remarkable. I wanted to *be* her, I realized. With her arms open to others and new experiences, how she made and kept friends effortlessly, how she talked nonstop with a confident and carefree nature I could only dream of possessing. I wanted her approach to life and all its normalcies. But in the meantime, I just sat back and listened as she drove down the winding road through the gathering darkness, trying and failing to catch a glimpse of the mountain out of my window.

"I take it you do this sort of thing a lot?" I asked after Sandra distracted herself from her own story by excitedly pointing out a deer disappearing into the woods on the side of the road. "The bagels, I mean."

"Every chance I get," she said, returning her attention back to the road. "I started working remotely a few years ago, and it only took me about forty-eight hours to go completely stir-crazy." She hooted with laughter. "I'd head over to Panera a few nights a week so I could eat and work with other people. And I have a mad craving for their Fuji Apple Chicken Salad about once a week, anyway, so it worked out! It was such a relief to be around others again, to hear conversations other than the ones I had with myself!"

She laughed again, shaking her head. "I'd work until they closed, near desperate not to have to go back to my place, and I started to notice that after handing out a few of the baked goods to the last few customers, they would just throw the rest in the dumpster in the back! Well, that didn't fly with me. Not at all. My grandparents lived through the Depression and taught my mother everything they believed about conservation and 'waste not, want not.' Then my mother taught the same thing to me. That's how it goes, isn't it? We always had to clean our plates. Always, without exception. 'You never know when you'll get your next meal, Sandra,' my mother would say, even though she served dinner at six o'clock sharp literally every day of my childhood without fail. Still does. I know better than to call between six and six thirty, I'll tell you that much!

"Anyway, that kind of upbringing doesn't just go away. It sticks with you for probably your whole life, like it or not. So the first night I noticed what was going on with the bagels, I marched out back, jumped in the dumpster, and fished out the bag myself. I know it sounds gross because they were in a dumpster, but they were in a big plastic bag. Besides, I saw a documentary once on dumpster diving. You wouldn't believe the kinds of food restaurants and grocery stores throw away. Completely edible, tasty food. Even some really expensive stuff that has barely reached the expiration date or has a small little defect. The people in this documentary ate like kings, I'm not even kidding. I can't even begin to tell you how many problems it would solve if we did something else with all that food than throw it in a dumpster. Seriously, these bagels were perfect. Not even stale yet . . ."

At this point, we were pulling into a driveway that belonged to a one-story brick home with grass that needed cutting and a garden that looked like it was once well tended but was now overgrown with unruly weeds of all shapes and sizes.

As the garage door opened, there was still no sign of Sandra reaching the point of her story anytime soon. I wondered how she even found the time to breathe between sentences. She continued on unceasingly as she eased the truck into the garage. Once out of the truck, I followed her up a few steps to a door with a handmade sign that read BLESS THIS MESS.

We walked into a dark house. I tripped over what I assumed was a pair of shoes right before Sandra flipped a switch.

" . . . so I told them, I can either keep digging around in your dumpster every night or you can hand them over to me— Oh, my place is a complete mess. I like to think of it as part of its charm. Anyway, the cashier just stared at me like I had started speaking Portuguese . . ."

I let Sandra talk, adding an occasional "uh-huh" or "interesting" as she moved toward the kitchen and I took in the house. Growing up with my mother's close-knit, catty church friends, I had been to dozens of spotless, sparkling houses where the host would nearly fall over herself apologizing for the mess.

This was not one of those houses.

"Mess" was a bit of an understatement. There weren't piles of laundry, there were mountains of it. Stacks of magazines reached halfway to the ceiling, and bookshelves sagged under the weight of too many heavy, ancient-looking hardcovers. Boxes were stacked haphazardly, giving the layout of each room the appearance of a maze. The few items I could see sticking out of the boxes made little sense. Lamps, roller skates, fine china . . . I closed my mouth, not having realized it had been open while staring at the sea of stuff that surrounded me.

"Want anything to drink?" Sandra called from the kitchen. I walked into the room and stopped, confused.

The kitchen was spotless. Other than a toaster, a coffee maker, and a few spatulas and spoons arranged like a bouquet in an old ceramic jug near the stove, the vinyl counters were completely bare. Sandra opened the refrigerator door, which held a smattering of photos of smiling children and adults and a few wedding invitations. She emerged with a stack of Tupperware. I caught a glimpse of neat rows of identical containers lining her fridge before the door closed.

"Ah." Sandra interrupted her own story about her trip to Portugal when she caught the expression on my face. "You're wondering if you've willingly walked yourself straight into the lair of a psychopath, aren't you?"

I laughed normally. At least, that's what I tried to do. It came out more like a skittering yelp instead. Sandra laughed loudly. Not quite the laugh I'd imagine a serial killer to have, but I'd been wrong before . . .

"My kids said this would freak people out. Here, let me give the same introduction I give at all my meetings."

Sandra cleared her throat dramatically and gestured around the room, as if she was addressing a crowd of onlookers.

"Hello, my name is Sandra Blair. I'm forty-seven years old, divorced, with three kids. I love brunch, thrift store shopping, and taking trips with my girlfriends. Also, I am a hoarder." She looked at me, one eyebrow raised. "How was that? I've given some version of that speech many times, but that one usually gets the best response."

"Uh, yeah. It was good. Informative," I answered, like an idiot.

She waved her hand, indicating the kitchen. "Last month, my kids finally said enough is enough. They came over here with a few boxes of trash bags and a determination in their eyes that scared the heck out of me." She chuckled. "They meant business this time, I could tell. So I told them I could handle one room at a time. That was my limit. Any more would kill me, I was sure of it. Therapists tell me otherwise, but I know myself. I would have dropped dead right in the middle of the living room, and that's not something you want your kids to see." She laughed again, moving toward a cupboard to take out a couple of plates.

"Well, they could see I was just as serious as they were, so they agreed to my terms. They started with their old bedrooms, then moved on to the kitchen." She gave a low whistle and took a handful of silverware from a drawer. "You should have seen this place before. Steph, she's my oldest, she took a before and after picture. I don't think she sent it to me though. I think she thought I would see what it used to be like and miss it so much that I would fill the whole room again the first chance I got."

She chuckled and shook her head. "I kept telling her that's not how it works. At least not for me. But she stopped listening to me way back in the fifth grade. She was always my independent one. I'll tell you, it made her teenage years a complete nightmare. But it's got her far in life, there's no denying that. Anyway, I'll text her and see if she'll send me the pictures so I can show you. There wasn't enough room to move an inch in here before. I had to eat out all the time, which is something I used to do when I was around your age without gaining a pound. But it doesn't work the same way in your forties, I'll tell you that much!

Sandra rested a hand on her hip and leaned against the counter. A long sigh escaped her lips as she looked around the room. "It took them days to dig me out of here. They each took a whole week off of work to do that for me. So I know they're good kids, no matter how much they sass me—ha!"

She turned her gaze to the Tupperware she'd pulled from the fridge. "Do you like chicken? I'm on a bit of a health kick now that I can cook for myself again. I've got chicken, this brown rice and veggie thing . . . I found the recipe on Pinterest a few weeks ago, and oh my gosh, *so* good! You hardly know you're eating vegetables! It's one of the few things I've actually tried to make from Pinterest. I spend hours and hours on there, pinning things I swear I'm going to make one day, and I never go back to them! But maybe now I will since the rice and veggies were such a success. Oh,

I have watermelon too. It's practically just water, so it's the perfect diet food. Relatively cheap too. I was at Costco—actually it was Sam's Club. I switched to Sam's Club a few months back—"

"That all sounds great, thank you," I interrupted, then flinched at my rudeness.

Sandra was unfazed. "Oh, good. You're making this easy for me! I'll get this nuked in the microwave, and we can head to the backyard. It's a nice enough night out, and my other seating options are less than ideal. Steph and Daniel are planning on coming back in a few weeks to work on the living room. They are bringing reinforcements this time!"

"Is Daniel your son?" I asked, sneaking in a question as she punched in the numbers on the microwave.

"He sure is. He's a 'large and take charge' kind of guy. Him and Steph, when they get together on a project, nothing stops them. They must have got that fire from their dad. Daniel acts like he needs to protect me. I'm not an invalid! I can hold a job. I have friends! You'd think I was ready to ship off to a nursing home every time he talks about me. He's got a good heart though, just like his sister."

The microwave beeped. Sandra took a bite of rice, thought for a moment, then popped the plate back in the microwave. "I think it needs another minute," she said, punching in the numbers once again.

"What about your other kid?" I asked, remembering she mentioned having three children. I leaned my elbows on the countertop, ready to listen to another one of Sandra's over-the-top introductions. "Does he or she help out too?"

"No, no." She scooped rice and vegetables onto a second plate. "Jamie passed away ten years ago. He was always the quiet one, always my sweetest kid. I don't think he would have been able to stand the storm of his brother and sister as they sweep through this place," she said with a soft laugh.

I stood up straight, kicking myself for not being more perceptive. Honestly, these days it was hard to tell if I even had people skills anymore.

"I'm so sorry," I said. I realized now why everyone always felt the need to apologize when they heard of another's loss. It didn't make much sense to me before. What were they apologizing for? But when no other words are right and saying nothing isn't an option, we only have "I'm sorries" to offer.

Sandra took two glasses from a cabinet, placed them on the counter, and turned to smile at me. "Me too. My kids say it's the reason for all this." She waved a hand in the general direction of the living room. "Nine out of ten therapists agree. Just kidding, they all do. What would you like to drink? I've got water, Coke, some fancy juice that Steph swears by. She said it gives her the healthiest skin she's ever had in her life. Her skin did look good last time I saw her, although she was always blessed with good skin. Not like her brother. But really, ten dollars for that little container? I can't imagine it's worth it. I wouldn't mind glowing skin, of course. But at what cost?"

"Water is fine," I said quickly, my words tumbling over each other in my haste.

"Water it is! Why don't you take our plates and head out to the patio? I'll be right behind you with our drinks."

I pushed open the sliding glass door with my elbow and was greeted with air smelling of fresh-cut grass and rain. It made me realize how stale the air had been inside Sandra's home. I wondered if she ever opened her windows.

The night had settled, and the buzzing yellow porch light illuminated only about half of the yard. From what I could see, Sandra's kids had not been through this part of the property yet. I could make out at least two rotting play structures, the rusty skeleton of a trampoline, about a dozen bikes, baseball bats, a lawnmower or two, and an overwhelming amount of patio furniture that created their own bizarre, mismatched set. The furniture was arranged haphazardly, making it clear that there had been no use for extra seating for a long time. Deflated basketballs, volleyballs, kickballs, and soccer balls also littered the brown grass, like pumpkins forgotten in the harvest.

Sandra emerged with two glasses of water and placed them on a rickety wire table near my chair. She dragged a chair over for herself, one that looked like it once belonged at a dining room table before it was warped by rain and time. She sat down with a heavy sigh, and I handed her a plate.

We ate in silence for approximately two seconds before she started a one-sided conversation about the squirrel she'd named Satan who came and ate out of her bird feeder every day, despite all her elaborate measures to stop him. I wondered how Sandra managed to live alone in the quiet. Then I remembered her regular Panera outings. The sounds from the TV also came to mind, knowing without a doubt she had it on during all hours of the day.

I cut up my chicken slowly and mixed it with the rice and vegetables with care. I took a bite, then another. Sandra was right, Pinterest did not disappoint. I went through the routine I had been trying to follow the past few days. Letting the food fill me up, focusing on how it would fuel me and all I wanted to accomplish. *Fueling, not fattening. Strength over weakness.* I repeated it like a mantra, letting myself enjoy this meal as something life-giving. Giving no power to that voice inside—

"Are you okay? Is something wrong with the chicken?" Sandra's voice cut through my thoughts. She was looking at me with a raised eyebrow, and I realized I had completely zoned out.

"No, gosh no. The chicken is great. I'm just . . . I'm really grateful for this meal. For you inviting me over. Eating a protein bar alone in the woods gets old after a while."

She grinned. "Well, you have more the microwave to thank for your meal than me. And I think you're doing me more of a favor than I'm doing you. I love nothing more than having people over. Besides my kids, it's been a long, long time since anyone's stopped by. Sure, I see people. But it's always out somewhere or at their houses. And I'm not blaming them for not coming. I know being around all this is uncomfortable and depressing. Trust me, I wouldn't be here willingly if I would allow myself the choice. But I used to entertain all the time. All the neighborhood kids would be over at my house, all the dinner parties and Christmas gatherings would be held here. I loved playing hostess. And I was good at it too.

"But you can't host people if you can't fit them into your house." She took the tiniest of pauses, her thoughts overcoming her words for once. "Maybe someday I'll get back to that. I used to look at that version of myself like she was another person. Like she was buried with Jamie, never coming back. But lately, I don't know . . . I think she's still in there." She placed a hand over her heart. "And I think there's a chance I could get back to her one day."

Sandra leaned back in her chair, shaking her head and

smiling. "I've come a long way, Mel. Thank goodness you didn't run into me a few years ago. Well, that wouldn't have happened. I wasn't even leaving my house back then. See? That version of me couldn't even imagine this version of me as a possibility. If that's not hope, nothing is."

We were silent for a long five seconds. I looked down at my half-eaten dinner, then up at Sandra.

"I wish recovery was more pronounced," I said. "Like it could fit neatly into a story as a dramatic climax. The battle between good and evil and evil being defeated so thoroughly and completely that people talk about it for years to come. Why can't it ever be like that?"

Sandra's look was one of understanding. I instantly felt guilty.

"I don't mean to say my own personal struggles are anything compared to what you went through. I just . . . I don't know. I wish recovery had more triumphs, I guess. Not the everyday grind of making the same decisions over and over to be better, but more character-defining moments, more epic realizations, more startling epiphanies . . ." I trailed off, unsure of how else I could explain this feeling of mediocrity I was forever chained to.

"First of all," Sandra said, a serious expression on her face, "don't compare heartaches. I used to do it all the time, and all it led to was more of the same. You're in pain and just because others are experiencing different kinds of pain from different sources does not make your pain any less real, okay?"

"Okay," I said, a little taken aback by her serious tone.

"Good. Now, this other issue . . . That's a little harder to crack."

She stared up at the starless sky for a moment, then back at me. "Why is your story so important to you?"

I raised my eyebrows. I never thought to ask that question because I always thought of it as rhetorical. "Because doesn't it matter to everyone?"

"I'm talking about *you*, Mel. Why does your story matter so much to you?"

I didn't have to think long to have an answer. "Because it's the only thing of value that's mine."

"And why isn't your story valuable enough as it is? Why do you feel like you have to hike to this mountain to make your story more interesting?"

"My story is boring!" I answered, my voice already rising. "It has no purpose, no meaning! Every great story has a moral. Mine was existence and a slow decline. That's it. I have nothing inspiring to offer, nothing to pull others out of their own darkness. Not even anything that's dark enough to use as a cautionary tale. I've had no big moments, no grand achievements . . . even my rock bottoms lack drama. And if my story's worthless, what does that make me?"

My words lingered in the quiet night air like a heavy fog. Sandra pulled at the strings hanging from her sweatshirt and stared straight ahead into the blackness.

"I'm going to use the grieving mother card here and tell you my thoughts. No interruptions, got it?"

I had already figured out how hard it was to interrupt her even when I wanted to, so I nodded in agreement.

"Jamie didn't have much time for his story. It was only getting started when he died— Ah, I said no interruptions," she said, holding up a finger as I swallowed my unspoken words. "Keep your lips sealed, young lady. Anyway, to most of the world, he was your average boy with normal interests, average intelligence, and your run-of-the-mill adolescent male personality. He never won any awards, never got into any fights, never was picked first, never was picked last. Most of the time, he blended into the background.

"When he died, the people who didn't know him well grieved for the man he would never be able to become. They saw so much potential in his future, so many exciting chapters that would never be added to his story. Only the ones who truly knew and loved him grieved for the boy we had lost. Because it never mattered to us what he achieved or how far he fell. Personally, I loved him relentlessly the moment I knew he was a reality. His siblings loved him the moment they laid eyes on him and never stopped. We loved him *because* he was him. Nothing more, nothing less. He didn't one day earn our love by something he did or something we had to save him from. He had it, from the very beginning until long, long after the end.

"And you know what memories of him I keep the closest to me? The everyday ones. Which is weird, I know. It came as a surprise to me too. But I don't find myself thinking back to the big life moments like birthdays and graduations and sports games. I always find myself thinking back to nights I would stop in his doorway just to hear him breathing. Or reading books together in the hammock in this very backyard. Or eating breakfast together every morning. Just cereal and milk and sleepy conversation, if any conversation at all. But those quiet, normal, taken-for-granted moments are the ones I can never let go of."

She was crying now, and so was I. We were both quiet about it, letting the tears fall where they wished.

Sandra continued. "Mel, your story is worth more than gold whether you personally like it or not. It's priceless, because it's *you*. It's filled with moments that define you, full of the stuff that makes life worth it. Take it from a mother. You were loved and worth the world as soon as you existed."

I wished more than anything to have a mother like her. One who loved me like it wasn't conditional. Then maybe I could believe everything she said. But I said nothing, not wanting to add to this mother's heartbreak. I smiled gratefully and changed the subject. It took all of three seconds for Sandra to wipe her eyes and transition seamlessly into a story about her neighbor and his three-legged cat.

After hours of stories, Sandra invited me to spend what was left of the night in her home. I wasn't in a position to deny a roof over my head, especially since the temperature had only continued to drop and my thrift store fleece would fend off the cold for only so long.

The two bedrooms her kids had cleaned out were completely bare, no furniture to speak of. I rolled out my sleeping bag on the worn, faded pink carpet of what used to be Stephanie's room. I could still see outlines of furniture in the dust that settled on the floor. Sandra apologized profusely for the lack of bed, and I tried to no avail to reassure her that this arrangement was more than fine. Honestly, I was too filthy to sleep in a bed anyway.

After we had wished each other a good night and Sandra promised to take us out to breakfast the next morning at her favorite spot that she spent an additional fifteen minutes describing, the house went quiet. I settled into my sleeping bag, but for the first time in weeks, sleep didn't come.

I laid there, staring at the cracked ceiling for what felt like an eternity. It was a combination of Sandra's words and a full bladder that was keeping me up. Since I could fix only one of those issues, I wriggled out of my sleeping bag and went to find the bathroom.

I thought I had spotted it earlier when Sandra was leading me to my room, but all the identical doors were now closed. After knocking lightly, I turned the knob to what I believed to be the bathroom door. Something was blocking the entrance, so I gave the door an extra shove and flicked on the light switch. I found myself standing not in the bathroom but in what I was sure had once been Jamie's room.

Unlike the other bedrooms, this one was filled with every item, every memory it could hold. I doubted if Jamie's siblings would ever convince their mother to let them empty out this sacred place. Boxes, books, clothes, baseballs, and picture frames were stacked floor to ceiling. There was enough space to take three steps in and close the door. I was sure that any other movement would bring a cascade of odds and ends crashing to the floor.

I felt keenly aware that I should not be here. This was a heavy place. There was room enough for a mother to lock herself away in here with all the things her son used to be. Enough room to cry ceaselessly and enough padding so no one would hear her. I knew I was violating something unwritten, but I knelt down on the dusty, dirty patch of carpet and let the meaning of this place sink into me.

There was a battered card sticking out between a stack of boxes. I pulled it out carefully. It was a homemade birthday card with a roughly drawn puppy wearing a birthday hat on the front. Inside, the handwriting was faded. But I could still make out the looping letters.

My Jamie,

I can't believe you're thirteen years old today! It seems like just yesterday you couldn't sleep without a glass of apple juice and a chapter of Harry Potter. I am so incredibly proud of the young man you've become. Every day of being your mom is the best gift I could have ever asked for. Your kindness toward others, your curiosity of the world around you, your love of all creatures big and small make me prouder than I can say. I love you now and forever.

Mom

And that was when I sank low enough to be jealous of a kid who never got the chance to grow up.

I read and reread the letter, trying to imagine those words were for me. Trying to imagine the signature belonged to my own mother. I was tempted to tuck the card deep into my pocket, to carry it around until I could convince myself that every word was meant for me and no one else.

I pushed the card back between the boxes, my stomach twisting into knots.

That feeling I had wanted all my life, that feeling of worthiness, and Jamie's mom just handed it to him like it was no big deal.

That was fine. I didn't need those words from my parents. I knew after this "walking across the country" stunt, any chance I had of hearing those words went from slim to nonexistent. I could hope for those words and the kind of love that went along with them from others. I could build my own family, and maybe they would show me love without conditions.

But families get ripped apart, I thought while sitting in the room that held shadows of a past life. *They hurt or leave or shatter. And how would I even know how to love them properly?*

I could still go with the saint route. It wasn't too late. I could be loved by the people, seen as worthy in their eyes for my good works, my temperance, and my unquestioned devotion to God.

But most of the saints were hated by their own people. They were beaten and stoned and killed. Far from loved by the world, only to be respected by generations later.

There was God's love, which I was always told was unconditional. But I also learned all the things I needed to do to earn that love. My mother's voice filled my head.

You're disappointing God by wasting your time reading fiction instead of your Bible.

You're shameful to God if you skip another church service.

When you continue to sin even after you were warned it was a sin, how do you expect God to ever use you?

How could I expect God to use me? My joke of a college degree, my lack of any meaningful skills, my pointless job at Wendy's. What's useable material in all that mess?

There was just enough space in the room for me to lay down with my feet against the door. All those little moments Sandra loved so much with her son had been eradicated from my life. Who needed to sleep when you could work out at a twenty-four-hour gym? Why lie in a hammock reading when you could be running and burning calories? I couldn't even bring myself to run with anyone else, since I would spend the entire run comparing my physique to theirs. Then of course I would have to go on an extra run afterward, just to make sure I fit in more miles than they had.

Could I have been used? If I had ever had the strength to look beyond myself, could God have used me?

I had missed out on too many "could haves," all the extraordinarily ordinary ways God could have used me. All because I kept slipping into a soul-eating, all-consuming, life-ruining disorder based on, of all the things that matter in this life, how I look.

The pieces of me that used to be—the empathy, the hidden depths, the personality—they were still part of me. Buried deep below the surface and sinking deeper and deeper out of reach with every meal skipped, every mile of punishment run, every hateful thing I said to myself in the mirror. But they could be resurfaced, I knew. The excavation process had begun.

But why was God showing me a way out of the darkness?

What was that, grace? Mercy? Another thing I was indebted to Him for?

I blinked. The dim yellow light bulbs left black spots in my vision.

Yes, I realized. Yes.

Through all the noise of empty sermons and unforgiving parenting, this must have been the truth that left me tethered to belief in something greater. That there was someone who could forgive my ordinary failures and love me an extraordinary amount anyway, over and over again.

And if that was true, that would naturally lead to another truth: That before I was ever worth anything to the world, I was worth everything to God.

I stared at the light fixture until my eyes burned as much as my throat. The swell of belonging was heavy in a room of one so beloved, it could never be let go. This concept of a love stronger and grander than time and space and actions was too much to hold all at once. So I let it spill out around me and fill the room. Then I began picking up the pieces of this truth part of me had known all along but had never been broken enough to understand.

31

Dear Alex,

My love, I am almost there. After a good, long look at that mountain, I plan on running all the way back to Billings and straight into your arms.

Love,
Mel

The Styrofoam container was warm in my hands. The remains of my Healthy Start Omelette from the Sunrise Cafe would easily feed me the rest of the day. The almond butter and jelly sandwiches, Kind Bars, turkey jerky, and packets of dry roasted edamame seeds Sandra had packed into my bag while paying no mind to my protests would see me through the rest of the week. All the way to Mount Rainier.

I turned to the west, my boots scraping against the loose gravel of the Sunrise Café's parking lot. I could almost make out the mountain's peaks through the late-morning clouds.

On our drive to the restaurant this morning, Sandra had asked me, without much conviction, if seeing it from a distance was good enough. We both knew it wasn't. I didn't come all this way to see the mountain through the window of a truck.

"Are you sure you don't just want me to drive you?" Sandra asked for the thousandth time. She was standing by the open door of her truck, looking reluctant to climb in despite the chilly morning air. "I have more vacation days than I know what to do with. Besides, I've wanted to go back to Rainier ever since I left. We could make a weekend out of it!"

I sensed a long-winded description of said weekend coming, so I put a hand on her shoulder. "Sandra, camping with you sounds like it would be the best weekend of my life. But I've come all this way. I have to finish as I started. I think that's the hiker's code or something."

"I guarantee it's not." She sighed. "But I understand. I really do. Maybe I'll call up some girlfriends and see if they're free this weekend. Now that you got me all excited about camping, my Saturday of low-carb cauliflower-crust pizza and a *Game of Thrones* marathon seems lackluster."

I laughed. "The indoors have their perks every now and then, trust me."

"Oh, we know. My friend Karen has a trailer. One of those giant ones that you see driving and wonder how they can even make turns. That's the kind of camping we can commit to."

I grinned. I was going to miss this person I met less than twenty-four hours ago. "Next time I decide to cross thousands of miles, maybe I'll take one of those."

She gave me her easy smile. "Take care of yourself out there."

"I will."

She rummaged through her purse and pulled out a pen. She took my container and scrawled something along the top.

"Here's my cell. Give me a call whenever you want. I'd like to hear how it turns out."

I studied the numbers. Another beautiful new name to add to my contact list.

"I'd like to hear how it turns out for you as well," I said. We both knew I didn't mean the camping trip.

Sandra looked at me like we were the oldest of friends. "I think we're both going to heal, Mel. I just have a feeling."

I grinned. "It won't be pretty."

"No," she agreed. "But it'll be progress. And that's all that matters, right? Take care of yourself. I know I already said that, but it's a mom's job to say those sorts of things at least twice."

I hugged her as tightly as I could with my free arm. Her embrace was warm and comforting, I would store it away as another feeling of home so far from my own.

Sandra waved as I headed down the road. She kept waving until she was no more than a speck behind me.

"Are you coming through or are you going to stand there all day?" The annoyed park ranger stationed in the booth just past the Mount Rainier National Park sign clearly didn't understand the gravity of the moment. I waved him off.

"Shh. Don't spoil it," I said, closing my eyes once again to feel how even the air was different here. Sharper. Quieter.

I opened my eyes in time to see him gesturing around in dismay. “Spoil what? The trees? I hate to break it to you, but there are millions more just like them. Now come on, let’s move along. You’re freaking me out.”

I spread my arms out wide. “I made it.” Then I shouted, “I can’t believe I made it!”

“Good grief,” I heard him mutter through the breaks in my sobbing laughter. I dropped to my knees, sinking into the soft high grass on the side of the road. I took off my backpack and flopped out in the dappled sunlight. Nothing had ever felt better. “I can’t believe I made it,” I repeated, this time in a whisper. I closed my eyes again and let a peace I had never known wash over me.

I listened to the birds, the sound of the occasional car full of tourists stopping and starting. When what I guessed was the last car rolled past the booth, I heard the crunch of footsteps on gravel approaching. After they stopped, I opened my eyes to see an exasperated face underneath the brim of a khaki hat.

“My shift ends in ten minutes. I don’t get paid nearly enough to deal with all these concerned tourists asking why there’s a dead girl on the side of the road. So, please, don’t make my life any harder than it has to be. All I need you to do is hand over the fifteen dollars, then you can go scare people *in* the park.”

I blinked up at him. “I don’t have fifteen dollars.”

He groaned and rubbed his temples. “You have no money? Seriously?”

“Well, I *do* have fifteen dollars, but I need it. I looked up flight prices this morning for a one-way ticket out east, and I had just enough. Not even kidding. Like down to the dollar.

I've got about five percent battery left, but that should be enough to show you the scraps of what was once my bank account, and the cheapest flight I could find—"

"Just go." He sighed. "Forget about the fee if you promise not to come back."

I grinned and got to my feet. "Promise. Oh, wait . . ."

"*What?*"

"Can I have a park map?"

I waved my new map in a gesture of goodbye to my new park ranger friend as I hiked past his booth. He did not wave back.

As I walked, I studied the map while avoiding being hit by cars. By this point, I was an expert at staying alive while map reading. Almost immediately, I found what I was looking for.

The Wonderland Trail.

If there had ever been a more enticing name for a trail, I certainly didn't know it. Just seeing it written in tiny letters on the map made my heart skip. A person couldn't obsess over this place as much as I did and *not* know about the Wonderland Trail.

Approximately ninety-three miles, the trail encircled Mount Rainier, taking hikers past mighty glaciers, thundering waterfalls, lush meadows, crystal rivers, and ice-blue lakes. All with Mount Rainier as the backdrop. Once upon a time, I would have given in to the compulsory need to hike the entire loop, but the Mel of today was stronger. This Mel could find fulfillment in a few simple steps, maybe a mile or two, as long as there was a view of the mountain to go with it.

About two miles into the park, I came to the Ohanapecosh Campground. According to the map, I could access a trail from there that would eventually connect to Wonderland.

I hiked past smoking firepits, kids enraptured by a banana slug making its way across the footpath, couples quietly reading (or napping?), their hats pulled low. Some families were beginning to set up for dinner while the kids ran free, shrieking with laughter.

It wasn't the first time during the trip I had missed having someone by my side, but it was the most powerful. The longing to share the magic of this place with another felt like a pang of hunger, sharp and empty.

But I was not here to feel lonely. I was here to see a mountain.

So I continued on past the sea of neon tents, the smells of roasting hot dogs, and the twang of guitars. I continued on until there was once again dirt beneath my feet and the only smells belonged to the pines and the damp earth, the only noise to the birds and the cascading river, the only sight to the bursts of life growing all around me.

When the sun began to sink and the golden hour settled all around me, I was too stunned by the transformation to go any farther. I still hadn't seen any peaks, but I had a feeling that if I got off to an early enough start the next morning, tomorrow would be my day.

I made camp a little ways off the trail just in case any rangers walked by. Even my stale almond butter and jelly sandwich tasted better out here. The grasses and bushes littering the forest floor were a collage of autumn—fiery reds and sunlit golds. I watched emerald water spill over rocks that were smooth as glass. I had never seen anything like it, that emerald color. If I wasn't in a national park, I would have convinced myself it was artificial.

But there was nothing artificial about this place. Its beauty was uncompromising and overwhelming. The pines that stretched to what seemed like miles above me whispered as I rolled out my sleeping pad and chose a tree to string up my pack. I had been in bear country for long enough to know that keeping food safe was no joke. Unless you wanted to be food, that is.

I was so excited, so in awe, I wondered if I would be able to sleep. But as the sky turned from robin's-egg blue to purple to a velvety black brimming with stars, I drifted off.

There are no mistakes in this kingdom, in this cathedral, I thought as I struggled up another incline. The morning light was deep blue, but just light enough to see my breath and for me to avoid the many hazardous roots and rocks along the path. Every tree, every rock, every fern, every changing leaf added to the wonder of this place. My quads burned with exertion, and the sweat that trickled down my neck was cold against my skin. This place made me believe there were no mistakes, no wasted lives.

I forced myself to eat a Kind Bar during my next break even though my stomach was churning with nerves. One would think I was hiking to meet a long-lost love, not a mountain.

The sun was rising, and the day was slowly warming. The fall season was in full swing, and this whole place was probably mere weeks away from being buried in snow. The elevation change would keep temperatures down, but the hike and my excitement worked to keep me plenty toasty.

I was even tempted to take off my fleece, to finally be brave enough to show my arms to the empty trail and the world.

But I wasn't there yet. Progress had been made, but reminders like this showed me how much further I still had to go.

"One step at a time," I told myself as I started up yet another incline. And then the last few lines of Saint Patrick's prayer came to me as naturally as my next breath.

> Christ beneath me,
> Christ above me,
> Christ in me,
> I arise today,
> Through the mighty strength
> Of the Lord of Creation.

I almost didn't see it at first. I was so focused on the words of the prayer and not tripping over another root that if I hadn't glanced up to wipe sweat from my eyes, I would have just walked right on by.

There was a clearing to my right. One that showed a sky on fire with the brink of a sunrise dotted with cotton-candy-pink clouds. Beneath it, peaks buried in snow, a long-dormant volcano slumbered. Mount Rainier—the great peak of the Pacific Northwest in all its grandeur.

I remembered how to breathe a few moments later. The enormity of it could never have been captured in a photograph or painting, I now realized.

I had never doubted the existence of God and after taking in what now stood before me, I knew I never could. It was enormous, all-consuming, immovable.

As the tears that blurred my vision fell and my breath was once again snatched away by the monument of God's promise that stood before me, I was so far from starving. I was filled.

For the first time in longer than I cared to remember, I longed to stay full instead of hungry.

I was suddenly ravenous for the life I left behind. The one I could finally make right. I could fail again, I realized. Failure could happen, but abandonment would not.

My life might never be extraordinary, I admitted to the mountain. But if I offered God what I could, I guaranteed it would be one of purpose.

I sat down, my back against a tree, and watched the mountain wake to a new day. Maybe later I would walk farther down the trail for another vantage point. Maybe I would hike back down to Ohanapecosh and spend the night among the literal happy campers. Maybe I would just stay in this spot forever.

But I wouldn't stay. I had dreams to pick up and dust off. I had relationships to repair and grandmothers to call. I had meals to eat, friends to love, therapists to visit, and a boy waiting for me back in Billings.

My whole life stretched before me, waiting to be filled.

AUTHOR'S NOTE

While I can't say I share the same thru-hiking experience as Mel (I've driven from Grand Rapids to Mount Rainier, but Mel would be personally insulted by the comparison), we do share the same self-destructive thoughts. Like Mel and millions of others, I struggled with an eating disorder when I was younger. I'm still learning day by day that it's not the sort of thing you ever fully get over. Even when the healing lessons learned during recovery are repeated like mantras on a daily basis, they sometimes still don't stick. Healing is messy, lengthy, and anything but linear. And when bravery takes the form of eating that extra helping instead of running that extra mile, society doesn't really know what to do with that.

If you or someone you love is struggling with an eating disorder, I'm sorry to say this book doesn't hold the key to learning how to finally stop obsessing about weight and calories. It's also not a recommended treatment plan. (If you want to hike over two thousand miles, for goodness' sake, please spend more than an hour planning your trip.) But I do hope Mel's story holds the promise that you are not alone, and despite everything, hope remains.

The road to recovery can be so very lonely. When you've been empty for so long, it can sometimes feel like there is nothing big enough to fill you up again. And maybe that's true in a way. Recovery doesn't happen in one sudden burst of clarity and healing, but through the slow and steady pace of making microscopic decisions that help instead of hurt and surrounding yourself with those who make the journey feel a little less lonely. As well as finally walking, one step at a time (and maybe even a few steps backward) toward the One who created you and your flawed, beautiful, hungry, broken, glorious body.

ACKNOWLEDGMENTS

I have more thanks to give than anyone's attention span will allow for, so I'll try my darndest to keep this brief.

To my editors: Despite working in publishing for a few years, I wildly underestimated how tough your jobs are. Kelsey, thank you for your patience and grace while walking me through the editing process. To my editor by day, pen pal by night, and 24/7 friend, Robin—thank you for still talking to me even after witnessing how little I know about the finer points of English grammar.

To Andrea Doering and Dave Lewis: I can't thank you enough for your belief in this project and the hours of personal time you sacrificed to make this book a reality. You were the ones who looked at some of the roughest versions of my manuscript and still saw something there that shined.

To my mentor/best friend/surrogate sister, Kara Saur, for being the safe space where I could open up about my dreams for this book and for believing they could come true even when I didn't. Same goes for Caitlin Eyestone, who I think might have been more excited about this book release than I was, which is really saying something.

To George Lytle, for always asking how my writing is coming along, then really and truly listening to the answer. You always like to remind others of how amazing they are, so I'm here to mention that you're pretty amazing too.

To my dog, Wilson, for his listening skills and because he would never forgive me if I failed to mention him in the acknowledgments.

To my dad, who has read all of three books in his life, one of them being this one. I hope I never stop hearing your ideas about which famous people would best play the roles of Mel and Alex.

To Jackson, who loves me better than anyone.

And finally, to my mom: You were the one who walked alongside me the best you could during the worst of my eating disorder, holding my hand and guiding me through the darkness. You were all of Mel's trail angels wrapped into one superhuman. It's because of you and your unconditional love that I was ever able to find my way back to myself.

And thank you to all those out there walking alongside those of us struggling through eating disorders. Your task is neither easy nor simple, and the work is often ungratifying and frustratingly slow to progress. But you are heroes to us. You stubbornly fill us with light and love until we have the strength to accept it, and there is no greater gift.

Meet Autumn

Find Autumn online at

AutumnLytle.com

to sign up for her newsletter and keep up-to-date on book releases and events.

Follow Autumn on social media at

AutumnLytleAuthor

AutumnLytleWrites